JAKE ROGERS' PLANET

PHILIP WILDER

JAKE ROGERS' PLANET

PHILIP WILDER

ISBN 979-8-9864293-6-6 (eBook)

ISBN 979-8-9864293-4-2 (Paperback)

ISBN 979-8-9864293-5-9 (Hardcover)

ISBN 979-8-9864293-7-3 (Audiobook)

Library of Congress Cataloging-in-Publication Data

2024927517

Printed in the United States of America

25 26 27 28 29 LSC 5 4 3 2 1

This book is dedicated to those who long to follow God but are held back by fear. I pray Jake's story inspires you to step out in faith and follow the wonderful plan God has for you. God made you unique and has a path only you can walk. The world needs you to walk this path.

CONTENTS

ABOUT THE AUTHOR

Philip Wilder has been writing since the age of seven, has authored seven novels, two nonfiction books, and is both an ACFW Genesis Contest finalist and a Realm Makers Aurora Contest double finalist.

Philip is a twelve-year-old with nineteen years of experience. He believes that as God's children, being mature isn't about not acting like a child, it's about knowing *when* to act like a child. He loves playing with lightsabers, climbing trees, and taking his wife, seven-month-old son, and dog on adventures.

The wilderness has always drawn Philip. He achieved the rank of Eagle Scout and has dreamed of surviving out in the wilderness if his extreme extrovert side would ever allow it. He loves the outdoors, whether he's camping, hiking, snowboarding, or floating miles down a river on a handmade raft.

Philip has served in full-time ministry since 2015. He has lived in the Middle East for two years and traveled to more than thirty-five countries. His great passion is to help others enter into a loving relationship with Christ and journey with God on their own wild adventures. He's seen the great need of the lost around the world and wants to use his writing to help others step out and reach the lost by using their own God-given passions and talents.

Learn more about Philip Wilder and how you can find your own God-orchestrated adventure at www.PhilipWilder.com.

CHAPTER 1
THE PORTAL
AUGUST 10

My dad forgave me when I totaled his sleek 1966 Ford Thunderbird on my sixteenth birthday. He forgave me even though he and my brothers had spent seven years restoring it.

But he won't forgive me this time. From his perspective, I'm about to total my life with this decision, and he labored nearly eighteen years building it into what he wanted it to be.

"There it is," Dad says as we round a bend in the forested trail.

As we hike into the clearing, the trees slide out of view like giant curtains to expose the Grand Tetons. They tower over the smaller mountains. Their jagged peaks jut into the sky like crumbling skyscrapers of some long-forgotten civilization.

"The tallest one is called the Grand Teton." Dad stops in the afternoon sun and reaches for his water bottle in his backpack. "That's the one your brothers and I climbed."

I stop beside him. The daunting peak is sheer rock.

"Now that's an adventure I'll never forget." He laughs. "We almost had to turn around. Could've died too. A lightning storm swept in from nowhere, forcing us to shelter between the rocks. We were terrified, but I couldn't be prouder of how your brothers faced the danger. Especially when the mountain shook from the thunder. We—"

"Dad, you tell this every year at the Sandia Labs family picnic."

"I do?" He wipes the sweat from his forehead and gulps his water.

I pull out my water bottle. "Sometimes you talk about them for half an hour." *Without mentioning me once.*

And the odds of him ever bragging about me will be zero after I tell him what I'm going to do.

My heart pounds. Should I wait?

"Isn't this place beautiful, Jake?"

"Yup."

His green eyes lock on me.

I might've gotten his green eyes and brown hair, but that's it. My brothers all inherited his muscular build and tall frame. I look away.

Soft white clouds drift so far out of reach across the happy blue sky. A red-tailed hawk's call pierces the slow breeze. Its signature red tail tilts as the hawk dips to the right, gliding toward the Grand Tetons and disappearing behind the trees.

I'd love to explore every nook and cranny in those rocky peaks, except I hate the outdoors. Why does the outdoors make me panic when so much of it draws me in? I should find a mountain-exploring video game. That way I could explore without all the discomfort or pressure of being with my dad.

"Do you know why I like to come here for these entering-manhood trips?" He takes another drink, then screws the cap back on.

"Because it's tradition?"

"Well, yes, but I initially chose to bring Tyler here because of these mountains. The Grand Tetons can be seen a hundred miles away." Dad turns to me. "They stand out. And that's what I want for you. Your brothers have worked hard to get to where they are. They've taken risks and stood up for what's right. And now, people look to them. I want you to be a man who stands out like them."

I drop my gaze to the ground. He's wrong. I'm not one of the towering peaks. I'm one of the small hills at the base of the Grand Tetons that are forever trapped in their shadows.

"Now that you're starting your Servant Leadership Project, you're one step away from earning the Freedom Award and becoming a Freedom Ranger." He smiles at me. "Your decision to persevere through the Trail Life program has proven you're now a man."

I bite my tongue. If this "path of success" is so good, why do I feel weaker every time I step down it?

"Think of all the college scholarships you'll win with that on your résumé." Dad slides his water bottle back into its pocket.

College.

I'm never done.

My accomplishments are never enough. And what will come after college?

A shiny green beetle crawls onto my hiking boot. I let the complex creature enjoy the sun. It lifts its outer shell and flutters its wings. It can fly? What else hides under that shell?

"We should keep going if we want to reach the camp before sunset." Dad gives me a firm pat on the back and continues down the trail, which curves down to the right and toward the creek.

I don't follow.

The green beetle races off my shoe like an obedient dog trying to keep up with Dad's quick pace.

Don't try to walk his path! You'll only fail! I want to yell after it.

Just as I did.

Football, calculus, Trail Life, and now college. With each step, I always found one more rung on the endless achievement ladder with the baiting promise of my dad's approval at the top.

I need to stop climbing.

I take another drink of water. It doesn't wash away the growing nausea.

I sigh.

It's time.

"Dad?" I cringe in anticipation. "I'm not going to do my Servant Leadership Project."

"What?" He comes to an abrupt stop and turns back to me. "You're joking, right?" His frown weighs on me like the shoulder pads I wore to live up to his expectations.

My back dampens with sweat.

"Why?" He takes a step toward me. Gravel grinds under his boot. "Why quit when you're this close?"

I don't want to quit. I love Trail Life and I'd love to earn the Freedom Award. In fact, I first realized I needed to break free of his plan for me because of what Trail Life taught me about being unique and staying true to myself. Not becoming a Freedom Ranger feels like a personal badge of honor because it will prove I'm strong enough to face my dad's disapproval and start down my own path.

He'd never understand that, but I hope he'll understand my other reason.

I clench my fists. I've rehearsed this response a hundred times. "This is my senior year. I need to commit extra time with the officers in my birder club so it will continue after I graduate."

"Jake, that's on them. It's not your responsibility if they let it die."

"It *is* my responsibility. I'm the founder. Many say this club is the only place they can be themselves. I can't let it fall apart." I fidget with a strap on my backpack and focus on the beetle as it races down the path.

"Why can't you do both? You'll age out of Trail Life before the end of the year."

I let out a deep breath. "Because I don't want to—"

"Don't want to?" He scoffs.

I don't want to walk this path you've scripted for me! I want to scream, but there's no point. My mom could've helped him see things my way a few years ago. Now she's too busy.

"What kind of excuse is that?" He strides toward me, but the beetle doesn't stop or run away. "What if I stopped working just because I didn't want to? Where would you live? Whose food would you eat? Where would you get the money to buy your precious video games?" Dad's shadow falls over the beetle.

Crunch.

Dad walks on, eyes locked on me. He continues his tirade. His words sound distant. Behind him, the fractured beetle lies motionless.

Something so intricate, complex, and unique. Gone. Killed underfoot by a giant who never took the time to notice it.

My eyes sting. My jaw trembles. I focus on the trees as the ache in my chest grows. Why do I have to like odd things like track and bird-watching? Why did God have to set me up for failure by throwing me into this scrawny body?

Dad's rant ends. He stops two paces from me and lets out a huff. "Jake… I'm sorry." His voice is softer. "It was wrong of me to yell at you. I just don't want you to give up on something you've worked so hard for."

"But I don't want to be a Freedom Ranger."

He gives me a curious look. "You've worked toward this for years."

"No, Dad, *you've* worked toward this for years."

He throws up his hands. "What are you talking about?"

I shake my head and push past him on the trail. "I'm sorry I ruined your life," I whisper. I don't need his help to feel like a failure.

We hike for the next hour in silence. We set up camp in the tall pines just off the trail and eat a pad thai freeze-dried meal around our fire without a word. Neither of us comments on the beautiful sunset far off on the horizon as the sun dips between two smaller mountains. The air cools, and the shadows deepen around us. The evening birds grow quiet as they shelter against the invading night.

Dad stares at the crackling fire and rolls up the sleeves of his flannel shirt. "Jake, I love you and want to help set you up for a bright future."

I pull a stick out of the fire. A small flame flickers on the end. Its light is nothing compared to the campfire's, but the tiny flame dances without a care.

"When I came here with your brothers, I gave them each a compass like this." He pulls a compass out from under his shirt and lifts its string from around his neck. He holds it out for me to see.

It's a regular compass, except on the top is the Trinity Peaks Trail Life symbol with the Trailman Motto "Walk Worthy."

So *this* is that infamous moment my brothers talked about.

Tyler framed his compass, Anthony wears his around his neck, and Nathan hung his up on his car's rearview mirror. Their compasses are proof my dad is proud of who they've become.

"After I reached the rank of Eagle Scout, my dad gave me a compass. It was the last gift he gave me before he passed away." Dad sniffles as he stares through the fire. "Though I decided to put you four into Trail Life rather than Boy Scouts, I continued the tradition with your brothers. I gave them each a compass as a reward for becoming Freedom Rangers and for entering manhood. I brought it because I was certain you'd finish too. I'm torn now whether I should give it to you." His deep green eyes bore into me.

"Why does becoming a man have to be tied to earning the

Freedom Award?" The small flame on the end of my fire stick pops in and out of existence.

"I'm not saying it is. But if you quit now, you won't earn this compass."

"So I haven't earned the right to be a man?"

"No, Jake." Dad shakes his head. "Part of being a man is finishing what you start. You can't keep wandering through life leaving everything half done."

"*Everything,* Dad? What about winning my sophomore piano competition and lettering in track last spring? What about starting the bird-watching club at school? Do any of those accomplishments count?" The little flame on my fire stick flickers out. Smoke replaces it and swirls into the night sky.

"I'm proud of you for those, but you can't make a living watching birds or playing the piano." He keeps his voice gentle, but his grip on his knee tightens.

I give an exasperated sigh and throw my stick into the fire. "But I could make a living by becoming a Freedom Ranger?"

"No, but it prepares you for bigger jobs."

"And track and playing piano don't?" I search for my fire stick in the firepit, but it's gone, lost in the monotony of all the other burning sticks and logs. Even worse, adding my stick to the pit changed nothing.

"The Freedom Award goes much further toward winning you a job than playing the piano or starting a bird club."

I abandon our log bench and trudge to the tent. My backpack leans against the tent. The can of bear spray clipped to it reflects the fire.

"So you don't want to be an engineer like me, a pro-athlete like Tyler, a professor like Anthony, or a doctor like Nathan. You don't want to be a Freedom Ranger. You don't want to go to college."

I turn back to him. My heart thumps against my ribs. The

firelight exaggerates my father's massive biceps and forearms.

"What do you want to be, Jake?"

I plant my feet on the ground. "I don't know." I glance down and whisper, "I wish you could stop focusing on my future and just see me."

Suddenly my hair prickles under my clothes. My medium-length brown hair stands on end.

A bright pink light cuts across the ground in front of me like a flare. It grows into a line and arcs around me, separating me from my dad. I back away, but it moves clockwise and cuts me off while encircling me and our tent. The light rises three feet into the air like an unmoving flame.

"D-Dad?"

He's already on his feet. His mouth parts, but no words escape.

I dash for the final gap.

The light completes the circle, and the ground drops out from under me.

Light blinds me.

I'm falling.

CHAPTER 2
BIRDS

AUGUST 10

I land on a smooth surface and tumble down it. I squint in the bright light.

My hand latches on to a cool surface. My body jolts as my grip stops my fall.

Our tent rolls past me down a rocky slope. The tent stakes clatter somewhere downhill.

Above me rises a giant tripod. I'm gripping one of the three legs. The structure's base—which I tumbled down—is curved like a satellite dish.

It's all at an angle because it's built into the side of a… mountain?

I gasp and turn.

Mountains covered in snowfields surround me. I'm above the tree line. The warm sun beats down on me from a beautiful teal sky. Tall, crumbling skyscrapers jut out of the forested valley.

What in the world?

"Jake!" Dad's voice sounds warped and garbled like I'm underwater.

In the center of the tilted dish glows the pink circle that formed around me. I must've fallen through it…

Like a portal in a video game.

My dad stands upside down on the other side of the glowing circle like a reflection on a pond. The bright daylight here illuminates his face and the night-shrouded forest behind him. Deep lines etched on his forehead reveal his terror.

"Are you okay?"

I wedge my fingers into one of the small grooves cut into the satellite-dish base and pull myself up the slope toward him and the portal.

"Help me, Dad!"

"Don't worry, Jake. I'm coming." He rushes to the circle's edge.

Starting from the outer edge of the pink circle, the image of our campground begins to dissipate. Desperation and horror mix in Dad's eyes as his grip on the compass loosens. He dives toward me.

"Jake!" His warbled yell comes through a second before his image disappears. Only the compass passes through the portal before it closes.

The compass clatters down the sloped surface. I reach out, snatch it, and quickly hang it around my neck. All that remains of the portal is a glowing pink rim, but even that fades a few seconds later.

"No," I whisper.

I scramble up the angled surface using the lines etched into the metallic base. When I reach the spot where the pink circle shone seconds before, instead of passing through, my hand meets cold metal.

The glowing circle I fell through—that separated me from my dad—is gone.

"Dad!" A gust of wind smothers my words.

I hold out his compass. The only part of him that came through the portal with me. A reminder of my failure to be the man he wants me to be.

"Dad?" I whisper.

I am alone.

My hands shake. My dad is gone.

No. I'm the one who's gone.

A deep ache grows inside me as the terrible danger of my situation takes root. I grip the small grooves in the surface under me like they're the only things anchoring me to reality.

Everything I know is on the other side of this surface.

Another gust of wind blows past me, then stills as silence fills the massive world around me. The air is chilly, but it's warmer than the crisp night air of the Grand Tetons.

The snow-patched mountains stretch out into the distance. Between them, lush forests full of blue, green, and orange trees grow in the valleys. White clouds float overhead while others slide between peaks, rolling down their slopes like a slow-motion flood. It's beautiful and wild.

Is this place real? Am I dreaming?

The ruins down in the valley don't appear Greek or Roman. Vines grow up structures thirty stories tall. Plants and trees spill out of broken windows. Their dark silvery surfaces shine in the patchy sunlight.

My friend Sophie would love this view. She always stopped at beautiful spots during our cross-country or track practices to soak in sights like this of Albuquerque. She'd climb a boulder during one of our La Luz Trail runs and sit there until half the team passed us. I'd sit with her, watching her long blonde hair blow in the wind. The sinking sun would light her dazzling blue eyes.

I glance back at the dark metal where the pink circle was a moment before.

Was that a real portal? If it was, then this place is real and I have no clue how to get home. Portals are impossible, aren't they?

The strange grooves carved into the metal on the slanted

surface look like some kind of script, but it isn't any language I've seen before.

Please, God, let this all be a dream.

No, it can't be a dream. I was awake a minute ago.

Am I hallucinating?

According to my watch, it's a quarter past nine at night in Wyoming, but it's midmorning here.

I rub my eyes. It feels so real. Except it can't be.

Portals don't exist, yet I fell through something.

The sun peeks out from behind a cloud as the satellite dish hums to life under me. My hair stands on end like it did a second before the portal opened. The bright pink rim of the circle glows. It arcs around the whole circle but stops short of connecting on the top side.

Being in the center of the circle, if the portal opens, I'll fall back through to our camp.

I take a deep breath. "Please, Jesus."

I wait, but nothing happens.

The pink rim follows a narrow slit that separates the center's black metal from the lighter gray metal surrounding it on the satellite dish. The darker substance must open the portal, but why isn't it now?

I wedge my fingers into the chiseled-out etchings and climb a few more feet on the angled dish-like base. I reach the top of the pink rim where the pink lines fail to connect and complete the circle. A shadow starts where the glowing light ends.

The sun shines through a large pink lens in the top of the tripod. The shadow comes from the rim around the lens.

Not that I know anything about how to create a portal, but it seems as if the pink light through the crystal lens must perfectly line up with the black circle for the gateway to form.

The portal isn't opening because it's off a bit. The sun is too high in the sky, which means it's too late in the morning for sunlight through the lens to light up the center black circle and open the gateway.

I let out a defeated sigh and slide back down to the leg of the tripod at the bottom of the satellite dish base.

My chest tightens as the truth hits me.

This is real.

This isn't just a beautiful picture someone took or a cool scene in a video game. I'm actually here in this wilderness.

I'm a speck on this giant mountain range that stretches as far as I can see.

I pound my hand against the hard metal. How could I be so stupid? I should've acted quicker when the pink light first formed.

Instead, I stood there for the first second just like I did while playing safety on my freshman football team when the giant running back plowed through me to score the winning touchdown.

Why am I so weak?

The question on everyone's mind that day when I cost us the game rings in my head: *"That's the youngest Rogers boy?"*

So I quit just as Dad says I always do.

And now, somehow, I managed to fall through something that shouldn't exist. If my terrible luck continues, I'll end up dying in a unicorn stampede.

My hands shake as I stare at the foreign mountains surrounding me and the city ruins below. Where am I?

If it's morning here at 9:00 p.m., I must be on the opposite side of the planet... unless the portal transports through time too.

My mouth goes dry. *God, please no.*

What should I do? Where should I go?

The high alpine is starting to turn green between the receding snowfields. That could be an easy way to walk, but it would be cold and windy. Down in the valley, a forest of blue-, orange-, and green-leafed trees grows like a fluffy blanket. It would be warmer down there, but what vicious predators await me?

I've gone camping several times for Trail Life. I've even completed the Trail Skills badge, but I always had a trail. I always knew where I was going and how to get home.

A compass does nothing if I don't have a map or an end destination. The only way I know how to get home is to go through this solid metal dish.

It's like someone handed me a controller in the middle of a video game I've never seen before and left the room. I don't know the controls, I don't know the goal, and I definitely don't have the skill.

This isn't a game of make-believe in my backyard. I'll have no bed at night and I have no food.

How many miles am I from civilization? How far will I need to walk?

How do I know which way to walk?

Dad would know. This is a game he's familiar with. Not me.

"Jesus, please, I really need your help. I can't—"

Rau! Rau! The animal cry pierces through the wind. A bird flies over the crest of the mountain.

My jaw drops. It's huge! It's easily four or five times the size of an albatross, which is impossible; the albatross is the largest flying bird.

The monster bird has a long beak and is all gray with leathery wings.

Wait, aren't pterodactyls extinct?

I can't identify every bird on the planet, but certainly I'd know if a pterodactyl-like bird existed. Incredible! My fellow birders would freak right now.

Raaaauuuu! The bird's call hammers me like a clap of thunder. Its wings tilt as it turns… toward me. Its eyes lock on me as its large talons reach for me.

I gasp and jump to my feet.

"What are you doing, God?" I yell as I race downhill.

Farther down the slope, my tent rests against a large boulder. The tent can't help me, but the boulder…

I fight to keep my feet under me as I careen down the mountain.

Large rocks dislodge and tumble beside me like cross-country runners fighting to beat me to the finish line. I jump over a larger rock and fall another six feet before landing back on the steep slope.

Rau!

It sounds like it's right behind me, but I'll trip if I look.

Wind whistles off the massive bird's wings.

The moment I reach the boulder, I grab a bulge in the rock and use my momentum to swing myself behind it.

A shadow engulfs me, and a massive gust of wind crashes into the rock. I press myself against the boulder and pray.

Half a second later, the shadow passes, and the giant bird flies overhead.

"Ha! You missed me, you stupid—"

But it wasn't aiming for me. The green tent hangs in its talons.

As it flies away, Dad's red sleeping bag slips through the tent door and falls to the ground like a giant, slithering air worm.

The bird doesn't seem to care or notice as it carries our tent into the distance.

I sigh and stand to watch the massive creature flap its impossibly huge wings. Its wingspan must be thirty feet or more! How many times have I longed to see one of these legendary beasts alive?

The bird soars over a ridge, then glides down the valley, toward the city ruins.

What other animals dwell here? What other ancient ruins hide under the canopy in the forest below? If my friends Oliver and Matt were here, we'd explore this place like we did all the forests and caverns in *Minecraft*. We'd build an awesome fort at the top of one of these mountains and make a—

What am I doing? I can't treat this like some sort of fun exploration video game. If this is real, I'm in terrible danger. And, unless there's some big conspiracy, pterodactyls should be extinct. Something is off about this place.

Where am I?

The sides of my vision grow fuzzy.

How far am I from home? How do I get back?

My fingers and toes tingle. My chest contracts and expands so fast, all I manage is a million half breaths a second.

Where will I get food?

I barely sit before everything goes black.

N
E
S
W
(Magnectic North)
PORTAL MOUNTAIN
ALIEN RUINS

CHAPTER 3
TAKING ACTION

AUGUST 10

A gust of cold wind blasts my skinny body. I open my eyes and sit up. The air races down my shirt to chill my sweaty back.

I'm on a mountain? How did I get here? Trees grow far below, but all I get here are gray rocks.

Oh, right. I fainted.

I rub the side of my head as I recollect the past thirty minutes. Why am I the one living this nightmare? I'm probably the least capable of surviving outdoors, and fainting from fear definitely doesn't help my case.

What am I supposed to do? Do I stay and hope the portal opens again, or do I start walking and hope I find someone who speaks my language? If I'm lucky, someone may still live in the abandoned city.

It would be nice to know where I am, or *when* I am. But how do I figure that out? There's no sign with a giant red arrow pointing to a spot on a map saying "you are here."

My dad and brothers would love to be transported to an unknown land and have to find their way home. My mom would hate it, but maybe she'd like the peace and quiet away from her demanding nursing position and my grandparents' ever-increasing health problems.

Why would God let this happen to me? I know he must care about me. I felt him with me all those times I walked down the school hallway and faced my mocking peers. He rescued me many times from the football jocks by sending a teacher or the principal down the hallway when they were humiliating me. God comforted me when they called me "Fake Rogers" because I couldn't get a single tackle, unlike my legendary brothers who led my school through numerous winning football seasons.

God cared for me and helped me then. Where is he now?

"Show up whenever you want to fix this mess, God. I'm only in terrible danger and desperately need your help! But take all the time you need."

Except I don't have time. Once another pterodactyl swoops in I'm dead. I'd like to see one again, but I'd rather study it as it hunts something else.

I shake my head and force away the smile that somehow crept onto my face. What's wrong with me? I hate this place.

Without a tent as a decoy or someplace to shelter, I'll be toast if another bird shows up.

Shelter. That's my first priority. The birds can't find me if I'm hidden. Unfortunately, the only form of shelter is the trees far down the mountain.

My chest aches at the thought. I gaze back up at the portal tower. Now only the bottom of the pink circle is lit up by the sun. On the other side of the portal are my dad and the safety of my home. The farther I travel, the harder it will be to get back.

What if Dad finds a way to come through but can't find me because I wandered off? Besides, who knows what other predators are hiding in the forest or in those ruins?

"Dad, please come soon." I shiver in the wind.

But at least I now have a game plan. I know my next—

Rau!

Not again.

The pterodactyl call sounds distant, but I don't dare search for it. There's no point in staying near the portal if doing so means I die. I *have* to cross all that open ground to the trees.

My legs shake as I stand and force myself to take slow breaths.

I have to do this.

I find my backpack on the other side of the boulder where the tent had been. Thank God I left it by the tent or else it wouldn't have fallen through the portal with me. I swing the backpack onto my back and clip it in place.

Using several small rocks, I make an arrow on top of the boulder pointing downhill. If Dad does find a way through the portal, he'll know where to find me.

As I sprint for the trees, Dad's red sleeping bag catches my eye. If I'm already cold here during the day, there's no way I'm risking a night without a sleeping bag.

A night here by myself? Oh, man. I'm doomed if I have to—

No, focus. I can't worry about two things at once.

I sprint across the slope toward the sleeping bag but stop halfway to catch my breath. My lungs burn for air.

Right, the high altitude. I stagger on at a much slower pace.

I drop my pack to the ground as I reach the sleeping bag and quickly stuff it into my backpack before I turn downhill. Thankfully, the trees are downhill. It would take me all day if I had to climb up to them.

Rau! The call is much louder this time.

I double my pace, jumping as much as five feet downhill in each bound. Despite the weight of my pack, I feel lighter. Every landing isn't as jarring as I expect it to be.

Is gravity less here?

I break into the trees like the first runner across the finish line, but I don't stop. Once I'm deep in the trees, I plop down on a fallen log and unclip my pack with shaky hands. My chest rises and falls as I fight to catch my breath.

I scan the teal sky between the trees. The pterodactyl is gone. Did it see me?

Being in the trees protects me from the birds, but what about other beasts? On the exposed mountainside I could see anything coming from a long way off, but now a mountain lion could be hiding behind a tree fifteen feet away and I'd have no clue.

The breeze tugs at the top of the trees, but the air is still down here. Green and blue grasses grow between the trees. Fallen logs scatter the forest floor. Birds chatter from their unseen perches. Looking up, the sun illuminates the orange, green, and blue leaves like they're a beautiful stained glass window.

I inhale. I'm safe now that I'm in the trees. Well, *safer*.

Wait. I did it!

I escaped two pterodactyls!

Have my dad or brothers ever done that? Surviving a pterodactyl attack is way cooler than earning the Freedom Award. And I did it by myself. Next time I sit in the cafeteria for lunch, who knows how many people will want to sit by me to hear the story!

That is, if they believe me.

And... I have a greater chance of dying here than I do of getting home.

I'd rather be the weird kid in high school than the dead kid in some unknown mountain range.

So that's my goal then. I may still be lost, but I know what to do. Like a video game, I have two objectives: survive this unknown land and go home. I've already beat level one by surviving the two pterodactyls.

Perhaps I'm not as helpless in the outdoors as I thought.

So, what do I do next? Where do I go? There's no path to follow.

Is this my first time journeying through a forest without a trail?

I smirk. I'm not following some preplanned path Dad laid out for me. Nor is he here to tell me where to go or say I did something wrong. I get to make my own trail. I get to go wherever I want.

It's like *Minecraft* but in real life.

If only Matt and Oliver were here. We could explore this place like we used to pretend to do in our yards back in elementary school.

A spire from one of the buildings rises high enough to spot through the trees. How can I not explore the old city? It's also my best shot at getting answers.

A soft rustle sounds. Something moves through the grass to my right.

My breath catches.

A large animal stalks across the forest floor with its head low, like a tiger stalking its prey.

Right, I forgot I may die any second.

Welcome to level two, Jake.

CHAPTER 4
THE RABBIT THING
AUGUST 10

I quietly grab my backpack.

The creature glides through the forest without a sound. I catch glimpses of its orange coat between the foliage.

It's big.

Fortunately, I've been sitting on this log in silence. If I'd been walking, no doubt this beast would be tracking me.

The animal crosses to my right and toward a small clearing. In the middle of the blue and green grassy patch crouches a blue critter the size of a rabbit chewing on something.

The beast pauses for a moment, then slowly advances. Its orange pelt blends in perfectly with an orange patch of grass. It stops at the edge of the clearing and waits. The little guy has no idea.

I don't want it to die, but I can't risk alerting the beast to my presence by warning it.

The forest is deathly still. The rabbit-thing notices the change in forest activity and searches for the danger.

The beast charges forward, and the rabbit-thing chirps a frightened *kee! Kee!* It flips around and races for the nearest tree: a small one in the middle of the clearing.

The beast—which looks like a compact lion—gains on it

fast. Using its powerful hind legs, it launches over fifteen feet with every bound. It leaps one last time and is about to land on the defenseless animal, but the rabbit-thing jumps straight up. The beast twists and flounders midair to catch it, landing only a nasty scratch on the rabbit-thing's hind leg before it's out of reach. Gravity catches hold of the little guy, and it starts falling back toward the beast.

Except it doesn't.

The rabbit-thing spreads its legs to reveal a skinfold between its front and hind legs. It uses these skin wings to glide the few remaining feet and land safely in the nearest branch of the tree.

How in the world? Did I really just see that?

No way! I nearly laugh as the reality of what happened dawns on me.

But the little guy isn't in the clear. The beast jumps and grabs the branch with monkey-like hands. Its weight pulls the branch down. The rabbit-thing sits still as the beast reaches hand over hand to pull the branch lower.

Poor guy. It did its best.

The rabbit-thing's gaze locks on me as if pleading for me to save it.

My breathing stops.

I shouldn't. It would be stupid to risk my life for a random animal. But it needs help.

The plea in its eyes reminds me of Benny, the only person who joined my bird-watching club that first semester. I wanted to end it because everyone teased me about our tiny birder club. When I saw how much Benny needed the club, I knew I couldn't turn my back on him.

I carefully crawl off the log. I can't believe I'm doing this. But if I distract the beast without alerting it to my location, perhaps that will give the little guy enough time to escape.

It's a stupid idea, but I can't resist.

A jagged rock covered in blue moss sits beside the log. It fits in one hand. I aim and chuck it.

It flies farther than I anticipated and strikes the trunk with a loud *thomp!*

The beast's focus locks on the tree for a second, then spins to me.

I drop to the ground. The small pot in my bag clangs.

I wince.

Please, please, please, I mouth.

Slowly, I rise above the grasses. Both the rabbit-thing and the beast are staring at me. The beast stops pulling the branch. Its hairless, wrinkly face resembles that of a monkey, but not in a cute way. With one last glance at the rabbit-thing, it settles on me and lets the branch swing back upward.

The rabbit-thing barely keeps itself from getting catapulted out of the tree.

The monkey-lion takes a step toward me and stops.

I stand and stumble backward until I'm pressed against the log. My pulse pounds but I don't run. I can hardly move.

The monkey-lion angles its head to the side as it eyes all 112 pounds of my skinny body. It leaps toward me.

I need to run, but I can't. Even if I ran, there's no way I could…

The edges of my vision grow black. My chest heaves.

No! Focus, Jake!

With each bound, the monkey-lion picks up speed. It charges at me just like the running back who plowed through me to win the football game.

I hold my backpack between us like a shield, my hand gripping a smooth metal container on the exterior of my pack.

Wait.

I tear my gaze away from the charging beast.

My bear spray!

My vision snaps back into focus as new energy floods me.

My shaking fingers fumble with the clip as the monkey-lion charges.

I give up on the stupid clip and yank off the safety. The devilish substance spews out right as the monkey-lion leaps at me.

I dive to the side as the beast flies over me and through the cloud of bear spray. I jump back to my feet.

The monkey-lion howls and rolls in the green and blue grasses. It paws at its face. The creature barrels through the forest. It hits a tree and stumbles over a log before turning back to the clearing and rolling in the grass. Its screeches and pained howls fill the forest.

A shadow passes overhead, followed by a gust of wind as a pterodactyl swoops in. It plunges into the small clearing and hauls the monkey-lion into the sky. A few hundred feet in the air, the massive bird drops the monkey-lion. The beast twists and falls with much less grace than Dad's sleeping bag. It disappears beyond the trees with a disturbing *crack!*

Whoa. I give a short laugh. That was crazy! I shake my head as my smile grows. I protected myself against a monkey-lion!

Several more pterodactyls soar past, but they don't notice me.

Now that I see them without being in danger, it's clear from the two antennae protruding from their heads that these aren't actually pterodactyls. Oh well, it's still a fitting name.

In seconds, a very unfriendly pterodactyl potluck begins with horrifying screeches and *rau*'s.

That could've been me. I was an inch away from death. But I won.

Pterodactyls with antennae, monkey-lions, strange rabbit-things, portals. Where am I?

A soft *kee* sounds from behind me.

The blue rabbit-thing crouches in the tree. The leaves shake from its trembling. As I approach, it tenses.

"Don't worry, little guy. I won't hurt you."

It tries to jump and glide away, but one of its back paws slips. It falls awkwardly. I leap forward and catch it.

It doesn't jump out of my hands but stares up at me with wide, trusting eyes. It has the face of a rabbit, but small sheeplike horns curl on the sides of its head beside its catlike ears.

"It's okay, little… thing." It twitches as I touch its soft forehead, but its trembling subsides. Something warm trickles down my arm. A purple and blueish substance oozes out of its back thigh.

Blood.

I pull my hand back.

The critter looks up at me with pleading eyes just like my old dog, Pax, did as she died in my arms.

My throat tightens. Tears tease the corners of my eyes.

Kee!

The critter's call snaps me back to the moment.

I couldn't save Pax, but I can save this little guy.

"Don't worry, buddy. I'll help you." Thank God Dad and I put the first-aid kit in my backpack.

Once I wrap the rabbit-thing's leg with gauze to stop the bleeding, I set him down in my lap and sit back on the wide log. It can't bend its leg with the bandage, so it sticks out unnaturally. It should be fine, provided it manages to escape predators long enough for its leg to heal.

I rummage through my bag and pull out my four-inch knife. Bear spray is great, but I want every weapon readily accessible. Since I can't clip it to my pants and don't want to lose it, I stash it in a side pocket for quick retrieval.

The rabbit-thing's adorable round eyes follow me. What a beautiful creature. Its soft fur coat is striped like a tiger's, except his is blue with black stripes. Its nose and mouth are almost identical to a rabbit's, especially when it wiggles its black nose. It's about the size of a cat and has paws that resemble a cat's with retractable claws, but it doesn't try to claw or bite me. Why does it trust me so much?

I've saved plenty of baby animals from our dogs and tried to take care of them, but they never trusted me like this.

Why is everything here so different? How far from home am I?

A bird flies past me and lands on a tree to my right. Unlike all the other animals, it seems familiar. It appears to have feathers too. Its spotted pattern resembles a northern flicker, except its wings are a darker brown, and only its belly is red. It hops around on the trunk before hammering its beak into the wood like a regular woodpecker.

Okay, so not everything is different here.

The bird squawks, then darts from the tree with a siren-like call. Before it flies forty feet, a loud *boom* rocks me as the tree explodes right where it pecked.

I wince and shield my face with my hands. Small wooden fragments pepper me. A thin trail of smoke wafts skyward from the blackened wood.

The bird quickly redirects its momentum and dashes back to the tree's base. It hops between the wooden fragments and gulps down a few bugs. A sulfuric scent drifts toward me from the explosion.

"Where are we?" I say to the rabbit-thing. I've watched tons of nature documentaries. I read dozens of books about strange animals, but I've never heard anything about animals like these.

Between the blue and green forest vegetation, a strange tree catches my attention. It has multiple branches, but instead of leaves, one big orange sheet hangs over the tree like a giant umbrella leaf.

I've never heard of a tree like that either.

Now that I think about it, something beyond the plants and animals feels strange about this place. Maybe it's the earthy smell, or something in the clouds, or the general environment. It all feels... different.

Rocky, bare mountains rise as far as I can see. Each one has a slightly rounded peak. Large patches of snow hide in the crevasses of stunning rock formations. The sun appears as bright as normal, and the sky is a soft teal. All of that isn't so strange, but down here is a different story.

The tree colors form a patchwork of greens, blues, and bright oranges.

Orange makes sense in the fall, but blue?

And the sky. It isn't just blue; it has a soft green touch to it. I can breathe the air just fine, so it's not poisonous, but I've never heard of anywhere on earth having a light teal sky.

A yellow squirrel-sized creature dashes across a branch and glares at me. It caws and flicks its tail. With each caw and tail flick, its fur pulses with yellow light.

What in the world?

Did I go back in time? I know time travel is impossible, but I thought the same about teleportation. So, if teleportation is possible, why not a portal to the past?

No, this can't be the past. If anything, it would be the future since the portal opened from this end. But it can't be the future either since there are pterodactyl-like birds. Which means...

I set a hand on the log to steady myself as the thought occurs to me: I must be on another planet.

Alone.

There's no point in fighting it. No amount of breathing regulation or picturing myself in my warm bed can calm me in this nightmare.

I lie down on the log and hyperventilate. The corners of my vision go black. The darkness closes in around me.

CHAPTER 5
LOSERS
AUGUST 10

Kee! Kee!

I sit up and blink. Why am I in a forest? What's that noise? I hold my hand to my head as the dizziness subsides. My memory of this terrifying planet floods me.

My wristwatch reads 10:23 p.m., August 10.

I've only been here a little over an hour? It feels like days.

I'm so glad I kept my watch.

Matt, Oliver, and I first bought *Star Wars* watches back in elementary school to form our secret watch club. Though the club ended when we went to middle school, I liked the practicality of it. Plus, it made me feel unique: My brothers never had watches. This is now my third or fourth watch since that first one broke.

A creature *kee*s from somewhere above. A rustling sounds in the trees.

I startle and raise my hands to defend myself against another monkey-lion or pterodactyl, but it's another rabbit-like creature scurrying from branch to branch. I sigh.

It spots me and *kee*s a few times. My rabbit-thing calls back.

The other one leaps out of the tree and spreads its legs to

glide down to the ground beside its wounded friend. It smells my rabbit-thing, then inspects the bandage. When I step closer, it tenses, then relaxes and lets me pet it like my bandaged rabbit-thing.

"You guys are trusting little fellows, aren't you?" They're identical, except the new one doesn't have horns. Perhaps the horns identify the males? "Are you mates?"

They don't answer. The wounded rabbit-thing tries to move and sniff the other but squeals with pain and settles down.

I flinch as another rabbit-thing glides right over me.

I jump to my feet and scan the forest. If these little guys can surprise me without meaning to be stealthy, could another monkey-lion creep up on me too?

I search for orange fur. Every patch of orange leaves or grass makes my heart pound. The coast is clear, so I lower my guard... for now.

But my pulse still races. I'm never safe here. Even when everything appears fine, a predator may be stalking me, waiting for the right opportunity.

The newest rabbit-thing joins the other two, but this one has yellow fur with black spots. They sniff each other and let out soft *kees* as a few more glide in.

Soon, over a dozen of them stare at me and sniff their wounded friend. A few are blue with black stripes, but the majority have different colors and black patterns. Some have spots, others have speckles or patches, and some have no black at all. They all trust me and let me pet their silky pelts.

At least there's one nice thing about this place.

Wait. Shouldn't Dad be here by now? He normally responds pretty quickly. He—

I sit down as the realization hits.

Dad's not coming.

I've never had to worry about getting lost or stuck somewhere before because I knew I could call him. Even when I totaled the Thunderbird, he arrived on the scene within minutes.

A sick feeling settles in my stomach.

My safety net is gone.

Only I know the portal is powered by the sunlight through the pink crystal. It must line up with the black circle, but the sun is already too high in the sky.

But… tomorrow the portal will open again.

I can go home. I let out a relieved laugh.

High up on top of the mountain, the portal tower sticks out from the side of the peak. It's going to be one heck of a climb, but I can do this. I just need to be back at the portal early tomorrow morning when the sun is shining through the pink lens. All I need to do is be alert and attentive enough to survive one day and one night here and then climb to the top of the mountain.

I inhale. My dad can't save me. I have to make it back on my own.

My gut twists, but I feel strong at the same time.

I know what to do now, and only I can do it.

I'm not stuck here. I can beat this video game.

The sun blinks as something passes over us. A pterodactyl glides away from the potluck.

The rabbit-things give frightened *kees* and hop away. My wounded rabbit-thing *kees* after them, but they don't stop. As it tries to follow them, the bandage and wound make its hops clumsy. By the time they've all disappeared into the forest, it's only made it two feet.

My chest aches for the little guy. I reach down and stroke its neck. It rubs its soft cheek against my hand.

"I understand how you feel. I've had to watch my dad take my older brothers on adventures I was too afraid of or too weak to join."

I tried going snowboarding with them a few times at Santa Fe. They'd fly down the hill and wait fifteen minutes for me to inch down after them.

On my last snowboarding trip with them, I went to the bathroom moments before Nathan and Tyler walked in, not knowing I was in a stall.

"Do we have to take Jake every time?" Nathan said.

"Of course. He's our brother, and he's still learning. It's our duty to care for him even when it's hard and frustrating."

"He's been learning for a year. He's no better now than on his first day. We could snowboard three times as many runs if we didn't have to wait for him."

I never tried snowboarding again. As beautiful as the snowy mountains may be, going with them was far too much pressure to make the beauty worth it. Why burden them with my presence when I didn't have fun?

I scratch behind the rabbit-thing's ear. It presses its head into my fingers. "It's okay. We can be losers together. Maybe one day we'll both be cool enough to fit in, but until you are better, I'll protect you."

The promise feels empty coming out of my mouth. This little creature trusts me, yet it has no idea how incapable I am of protecting myself, let alone it.

Pax trusted me when I was on a planet I understood, and I still failed her.

Realistically, we are both dead. I doubt we'll survive the night. Even if we do survive and I make the journey up to the portal, a pterodactyl could pick me off like a cherry from the top of an ice-cream sundae.

I'm a level-two character trying to outrun a level-thirty pterodactyl. And unlike a video game, I only have one life.

But I did fight off the monkey-lion. What if there's a way to fight off pterodactyls?

My stomach groans from hunger.

Whatever I decide to do, first I need to go to the crumbling city to find food and prepare for the night. After that, I'll figure out how to protect myself from the pterodactyls. Then I need to reach the portal and go home. Those are my mission objectives for this video game.

The rabbit-thing makes another pathetic attempt at a hop. Instead, it flops in the grass and squeals in pain.

I grab the little guy and hold it until its trembling subsides. "It's okay, little buddy."

The rabbit-thing seems to believe my lie. At least I fooled it because I'm not fooling myself.

If my mom were here, she'd hug me and tell me everything is going to be okay, but she isn't. Nor has she been there for me since Grandpa's Alzheimer's progressed and Grandma lost her mobility from osteoporosis.

I'm all alone.

I've felt alone before, but I had friends in the bird club and I could always go home and escape the pain or my fear in one of my video games with Matt and Oliver. This time I can't quit and go home.

I have less than one day to equip my five-foot-five self with enough armor, weapons, and upgrades to face off and win against those flying predators.

And unlike in *Minecraft*, I can't just punch a tree to get usable planks and sticks to arrange into a *T* to make a pickax. I don't know how to make anything other than a spear by sharpening a stick with my pocketknife.

This is real life with real threats and no do-overs.

If only real life had cheat codes.

CHAPTER 6

BEETLE LUNCH
AUGUST 10

The rabbit-thing glares at me as I set him in the sling I made by tying my *Minecraft* pajama pants with one of my shirts.

"If you're going to stick around, then you'll need a name. What about Jerry?" No, Jerry sounds too normal for something with tiny ram-like horns. "Or Jinx?" What am I doing, naming a cat? I'll figure out a name later, but a *J* name seems fitting.

I head off toward the ruins. They are my best shot for food, shelter, weapons, and answers.

But what if some of the creatures that built the structures still live there? What if they aren't friendly?

I walk carefully through the low brush, stopping often to scan the forest floor and trees for any predators. Every second it feels like some unseen beast is waiting for me to walk closer.

I finger my bear spray as I walk onward.

For the hundredth time, I picture the bear bag Dad and I hung up away from our campsite. He made me search through every pocket in my backpack to make sure every scrap of food went into that bag.

I can't fault him. Why leave food in a pack and risk a

semi-common bear attack to be prepared for something impossible like falling through a portal?

Unfortunately, the impossible happened.

Dad never taught me how to hunt, trap, or forage for food, nor did I learn much of that in Trail Life, but I did watch several shows and read some books. As much as I hate the outdoors, it's still cool to see other people survive in the wild and read incredible stories like *Hatchet* or *Endurance*.

Dad never understood how stories like those could captivate me since I loathed hiking and camping with him. And honestly, I'm not sure either. Something in it calls to me. The adventure. The thrill. The unknown. If only real-life adventures weren't so dangerous and uncomfortable.

Their go-to meals in the TV shows were always beetles or worms, which they found from overturning a log. But there's no way I'm following that reckless path. Who knows how terrible that would taste, and it's not like I have my toothbrush to clean out the taste afterward.

Man, I'd kill for a green-chile cheeseburger right now.

"What do you eat around here, Jacquel?" I cringe. No, definitely not Jacquel. "Do you know of any good burger joints in those old ruins?"

I direct my trek toward the bottom of the valley, where science says I'll most likely hit a stream—this I did learn from my wilderness shows. The lush forest canopy that snakes through the flat valley is another good indicator that, according to science, I'll find water.

After walking quite a way down the mountain, I stumble across a green fruit a tad bit smaller than my fist hanging from a tree. I pick one and am about to eat it when Jingle—I cringe at the terrible name—*kees*.

"Do you want one?" There are plenty of other fruits in the tree, so I set him down and place it before him.

He stands on his hind feet and grabs it with his front

squirrel-like paws. After sniffing the fruit, he flinches and drops it.

"Okay? So you don't like it. But does that mean it's poisonous?"

Tons of birds are flying everywhere, but none of them come to this tree.

On one of our runs, Sophie warned me about fruit that birds don't eat. If birds don't eat it, people shouldn't either. She said the brighter the fruit, the more likely it's not poisonous because trees typically only grow bright fruit if they want animals to pick it and eat it, thus dispersing its seeds.

This fruit is green like the leaves, and the birds don't like it.

This stinks. Five hours ago I complained about eating my dad's terrible pad thai freeze-dried meal, and now my concern is whether or not a fruit will kill me? Next I'll be forced to choose between letting a monkey-lion or a pterodactyl tear my body apart.

My stomach rumbles, but I toss the fruit aside. I'd rather be weak on my journey home tomorrow than dead.

"I hope you're right, Gypsy, because my stomach hates you for making that call."

"Hmm. What about Gypsy? That kind of fits you. I know it doesn't start with a J, but it sounds like a J."

Gypsy stares back at me and blinks.

No, he's not a Gypsy. I scoot him back into the center of the sling and pick it up.

Looking up at the trees reminds me of Sophie. She'd always search for fruit trees during cross-country practice last fall. After picking a good apple, she'd give me a beautiful smile and toss it to me before finding another for herself. We'd find apples, peaches, and pears. I'm sure by now she would've found fifteen different edible fruit trees.

At the bottom of the valley, the ground flattens out. A

stream babbles no more than a hundred feet ahead in the dense vegetation.

As I push through a few small trees, a branch whaps me in the face. Several brown pods hang off it. I snap one off and break into it with my fingers. A brown-shelled beetle races out of the opening and onto my hand. I jump and flick the bug off. It lands on the forest floor and rights itself.

Strange. It carries a small plant shoot as it scuttles away.

I step closer and use a stick to pick it up. Bizarre. It's not carrying the sprouting plant; it's attached to it. Instead of eyes or an antenna, it has a little seedling growing out of its body like a head.

I let it scurry off as I go back to the bean pods. As I break into the next pod, another beetle races out. I jump again and fling it to the ground. I catch Jade—hmm, maybe—staring at me like I'm an idiot.

"It could be poisonous for all I know." But my excuse doesn't curb Jade's judgment.

Like the other beetle, a plant shoot grows out of its body instead of a head. I set the sling down and use a stick to bring it to Jade. He picks it up and bites into its shell. A pink goo oozes out.

No, he can't be a Jade; it sounds too much like Jake. Besides—even though I'm not certain if it's a he or she—it's a he in my mind, so I may as well give it a more boy-like name.

After he cracks it open, he licks out the pink juice. "Of course it's bugs you like. Let me guess, you eat worms too?"

Jip looks up at me for a moment before slurping up the rest of the beetle's insides.

"You could be a Jip. It's short but fun, kind of like you. Let's see if it sticks."

After Jip discards the beetle shell, I kneel and examine the dead creature. The shell seems more like a nutshell than it does a beetle's. It doesn't have any wings either.

I go back and search for the other beetle. It's in a patch of sunlight digging a hole. After it loosens up the dirt, it turns around and crawls backward into the small hole. It uses its legs to essentially bury itself until all I see is the small plant shoot. Once it's buried, it stops. If I hadn't watched it happen, I would've thought nothing of this tiny little plant shoot sticking out of the soil.

"Are you a beetle or a plant?" I leave it alone and go back to find another pod.

All I can think of is the beetle's nasty guts sliding down my throat with a leg or two still trying to escape. If I felt it kicking around in my stomach, I'd vomit.

I told myself I wouldn't eat a beetle or a grub, but is this really a beetle? It comes from pods in a tree and it plants itself. Doesn't that make it a fruit or a nut?

I open another pod and catch the beetle before it runs away. Its tiny legs brush my fingers. Goose bumps race across my body.

I grab the two lips of its turtle-like shell. Its legs grip onto my fingers and try to push away. I grit my teeth and pull the shell apart. It splits open, exposing a pink goo. The legs frantically try to escape.

"It's a fruit, not a beetle," I whisper over and over.

Jip stares at me like I'm a moron.

"Don't give me that look. I'm sure you didn't want to eat these nasty things the first time your parents made you try it."

He blinks.

"Seriously, though, show some respect. I saved your life, bandaged your wound, and now I'm carrying you to food and water. Didn't your mom ever teach you not to judge others before you know them? You have no idea what I've been through today."

Despite my convincing arguments, Jip still watches me with his big, round eyes as if I'm the weirdest person on the planet. Which would be true if I'm the only person here.

I turn my back to him; his judgment isn't helping.

I touch the pink goo and sniff it. Honestly, it doesn't smell too bad.

Should I scarf it down or give it a quick taste test? Sometimes rushing to eat something makes stomaching it easier, but if it's truly horrific, I'd have a whole mouthful to spit out.

I've taken enough risks today. This time I can pamper myself and start with a taste.

Pamper? Did I really just consider tasting a beetle's guts as pampering myself?

I lick a tiny smidgeon and immediately cringe.

It tastes tart and a little sweet. Like an unripe blueberry.

I try a bigger lick off my finger and turn back to Jip. "You know, I think I like it." I break off the beetle-fruit's legs so they don't touch my face as I lick out the inside. *It's a fruit, not a beetle.* I close my eyes and try to swallow.

With one beetle-fruit eaten, I quickly pluck off another pod and go through the whole process again. Despite what I know now, it will take far more than one beetle-fruit for me to get over the immediate repulsion of the disgusting little legs clawing at my hands and face.

Once I finish it, I drop the shell—I mean peel. Fruits have peels, not shells. Shells are for beetles. I pick another branch full of pods and head to the stream. The water burbles through the rocks, just as it does on Earth. Blue moss grows over the rocks on the edge of the stream. I set down my pack and pull out the water filter.

As I straddle both sides of the stream, Jip *kees* and thrashes about in the sling.

"Calm down, dude!" I push off the far side to stand near my pack. "Are you thirsty?" I pull him out of the sling and carry him to the water.

Kee!

Jip lashes out at me, his tiny claws cutting my forearm.

I drop him on the bank. "Ouch, Jip! What's your problem? Don't you drink water?"

As I watch the stream, the water moves a little too slow. The ripples seem exaggerated. My chest tightens. Is the water different here? What if the plants and animals drink a different fluid than water?

What if I can't drink the water here?

I force myself to exhale and breathe in again. So many what-ifs. How can I plan for or do anything when everything here is different?

I reach out and touch the liquid. It feels as cold as other mountain streams I've felt back on Earth. I lift my hand and watch the water drip down. The droplets are bigger than normal, and they fall to the ground slower than normal.

I step back and eye the stream. It looks and feels like water, but it behaves differently.

But why would it fall slower? Any liquid should fall at the same speed. My science teacher said something about that in class.

So, maybe the problem isn't the water but different gravity? Could it be? I did feel lighter running from the pterodactyl.

I cup my hands and carry a handful of water to Jip. I approach him cautiously, half expecting him to claw me again.

He glances at me, then the water in my hands. He leans forward and laps the water.

I roll my eyes. "Seriously? You got me all freaked out that something was wrong with this water."

After he drinks his fill, I take a step back and fold my arms. "You're a jerk."

Jip stares at me and licks the water off his lips.

I turn my back to the freeloader and start pumping the stream water through my water filter and into the first water bottle. I stop when it's half full and lift it to my mouth. It smells like nothing, which is probably a good thing. I try a little sip.

"Oh, thank God," I breathe out in relief, then guzzle the fresh mountain water.

I glare at Jip. "You nearly gave me a heart attack. I have enough to worry about. I don't need you adding any unnecessary fears."

When I finish, I sit on the bank and break open another beetle-fruit.

"Wait a second." I turn to Jip. "I've already found both food and water. Now I just need shelter, and I'll have completed my first objective."

I jump to my feet. "Take that, planet!" I yell at the mountain I descended. "Jake Rogers has food and water! You thought you'd get the best of me. Well, not today!"

As if in response, an animal screeches and hollers in the direction of the city ruins. Its frightened cries cut off abruptly. A moment later, a deep roar echoes through the mountains. A chill travels down my spine.

I swallow.

Just when I thought I was winning at this whole survival thing…

RABBIT THING "JIP"

CHAPTER 7

THE ANCIENT CITY
AUGUST 11

I press my back against a large, rusted metal wall. "Is this a good idea?"

Jip wakes and stares up at me from inside the sling. After nonverbally scolding me for waking him, he curls back up into a ball and closes his eyes.

The pterodactyl flew to these ruins, and this is where I heard that terrible bellow, but I've always longed to explore ruins. Besides, there's enough shelter to evade a pterodactyl, and I still have my bear spray.

The wall is hot from the afternoon sun. It's already this warm and muggy when the sun is barely reaching the highest point in the sky? How much does the temperature swing here? I wipe the endless sweat from my forehead and peek around the corner.

My jaw drops.

A metal street runs straight through the ruins as far as I can see. Small plants and tall trees grow out of the buildings and cracks in the street. Vines hang from the structures. Skybridges three to ten stories above the ground cross between the tall towers farther down the path. Several tall structures have fallen, leaving jagged rubble strewn across the alley. The ruins are small near me, but farther down, they rise higher, casting long shadows that shroud the street in darkness. It would take me a whole month to explore this big city.

Investigating these ruins would be more fun and less scary if Matt and Oliver were here.

Birdcalls echo from farther down the road. The air smells damp and carries traces of mold. Several green-shelled creatures the size of a dog mill about in the road. But there's no indication of intelligent life.

"What happened here?" I whisper.

As far as I know, nothing hunts me from the higher levels, so I step out from behind the corner with my bear spray in hand.

The giant beetles spot me and scurry off through a gap in a structure's wall where a panel broke off.

Creepy.

I step around a puddle that formed where a large chunk of the metallic road is missing. I again check any dark holes in the sides of the buildings for movement before continuing down the road.

"It's like I'm living in a zombie-apocalypse movie," I whisper to Jip.

In a side alley, a large mound of dirt sits in the middle of the street.

Wait, no. It's poop. It's all poop. It rises up to my waist.

I back away and check the streets for any predators.

"Have you seen a poop tower that big?" I try to help Jip peer out of the sling, but he doesn't care.

Any creature that drops a turd that big must be massive. There's no hair or bones in the poop tower. Hopefully this means it's an herbivore.

Rau!

I duck and slide to the side of the street. I can't see the pterodactyl, and it likely can't reach me here between the buildings, but that's one more thing to worry about.

"Actually, this is like living in a zombie-apocalypse movie that takes place in *Jurassic Park*."

Jip doesn't laugh.

"Tough crowd." I smirk.

It's time to get out of the street.

The doors are all large and triangular. They are six feet wide at the bottom and only two feet wide at the top. Lines decorate the door in cool geometric patterns. I approach the closest door on my left. It's ten feet tall. No human would need a door like this.

So these are alien ruins.

I feel lightheaded. I lean against the door and take several deep breaths. I knew this planet wasn't Earth based on the animals, but seeing such concrete evidence drives the fact home.

Despite the dread, something sparks within me. I'm the first human to see these ruins. What mysteries lie hidden in these crumbling buildings? If I find a cool alien trinket and bring it home with me tomorrow, I'd be famous!

If I don't die trying to get home.

I push against the door, but it doesn't budge. There's no knob or any place to push it into the wall. Are the lines a puzzle?

I press on several triangles and diamond shapes, but nothing happens.

Bummer. That would've been cool.

But why try breaking into one house or office—whatever it may be—when there are hundreds more with holes in the walls? It's not like anyone's been here to loot all the easy-to-access rooms.

I continue down the crumbling road checking for a building with a large opening. Slats of metal rise at every angle to show how much the ground has moved since these streets were last maintained.

A building down a street to my left is missing an entire

wall. I skirt around an older poop tower and navigate the uneven road. As I reach the opening, a small chunk of road shifts under my weight with a loud *screech!* The sound sends goose bumps down my spine.

Several large scaly birds launch out of the opening with fluttering wings. They honk at me as they fly into the sky.

Are they nesting in there? Probably not since they don't glance back as I step into the building. It feels like a cave. Bushes and grasses grow at the mouth of the opening, but farther in, the plant life ends. The walls are made of panels that curve inward as they meet the ceiling. Strange trinkets cover the walls and floor. In a mound of blue vines, something pink flashes.

I part the vines and pull out a pink orb a little smaller than my fist. Along with the transparent orb comes a five-inch metal rod. I wipe away some of the dirt. Brackets hold the orb to the metal pin, like a giant earring.

Weird. What does this go to?

I slide the trinket into my backpack and journey deeper into the building. I don't bother pulling out my headlamp. Instead, I test each step before I take it. Small critters dash away from me.

Everything is made of metal: the walls, floors, and the trinkets. Or maybe anything made with wood already decomposed? No windows though. Interesting.

What happened to this civilization? They must be advanced if they have the tech to create a portal. But why a portal to Earth?

Three rooms in, I come to a dead end. No doors, at least not that I can find. I turn back to the exit.

Sploosh.

My foot sinks ankle-deep into a puddle.

Gross. At least the cool water is refreshing as it seeps into my boot and soaks my sock.

The floor moves under me. I stagger to the side, but it moves again.

Water drips from the ceiling. Dirt slides through cracks and flits through the air before settling on the ground.

Did I do that?

I lift my foot out of the puddle.

The floor shakes again.

Poop towers! The whole building's going to fall on me!

I stagger toward the exit, using the walls for support as the floor continues rolling under me.

A cloud of dust falls between me and the opening. I charge through it, blinking away the particles.

My foot catches on a raised crack in the floor. I stumble the remaining distance until I fall to my hands and knees on the street outside.

The shaking continues. It's not just the building I was in? I race back to the main road and freeze.

One of the tallest buildings deep in the city tilts to the left.

A pterodactyl launches from the roof with a baby pterodactyl in its beak.

Dozens of smaller birds fly away from lower perches with distant squawks.

With deep creaks and groans, the structure falls. It collapses onto another building, buckling its supports. Both towers crumble in slow motion.

As they hit the ground, dust billows into the air. It rolls toward me like a slow shock wave.

The ground stills.

The whole valley grows silent as the dust cloud glides toward me. It slows. The crisp edges of the dust cloud turn soft until its progress halts a good half-mile down the alley from me.

One by one, the birds pick back up their chatter like nothing happened.

I'm not falling for it.

What in the world did I trigger by stepping in that puddle?

———

The leaves on the vines and bushes in the building tap against each other as a refreshing evening breeze flows through. I sit inside the same building I explored before on a metal box I found in one of the other rooms.

It was an earthquake that toppled the tower. I know because two more have hit since then. As much as I'd like to find shelter somewhere else, this building is my best bet. It has one exit, which my fire guards to keep any predators away. The smoke drifts into the sky as I roll the lighter in my hand.

Puffy clouds slide eastward over the mountains, or at least I'm calling it eastward since it's the opposite direction of the sunset. Directions are weird here.

Time is weird too. I appeared on this planet early in the morning according to here-time, but according to Mountain Time, it's now 1:46 p.m. on the eleventh.

The shadows darken as the last of the sun's pink rays fade from the clouds. The night quiets. It sounds both peaceful and ominous.

"It's about time, Jip. I thought the sun would never set."

Jip cocks his head before settling back down into his curled-up position on my dad's sleeping bag.

"Assuming the sun rose two hours before I arrived here, the day was about eighteen hours long. So either we're like Alaska—far from the equator—or the days here are much longer than on Earth."

I lay out my clothes beside a wall near the fire. It's much cooler now than in the middle of the day. It got so hot in the afternoon that I had to stop and rest in a building. I suppose that's what happens with longer days. But if I'm right, then that long and hot day means I'll also have a long and cold night.

My fire crackles. I hope I gathered enough wood to keep us warm in here. I don't know much about surviving in the wild, but I do know two things from Trail Life and from the book *Hatchet*. The first is how to build a fire and maintain it. The second is that animals are terrified of fires. But are animals on this planet scared of fire? If not, I'll be an easy midnight snack.

"Sorry, dude. I have to move you."

Jip glares at me without moving his head.

With my clothes laid out to create a makeshift sleeping pad, I move Jip to the side and lay out the sleeping bag on the clothes.

Every movement feels sluggish as hunger gnaws at my stomach. I'm weak and exhausted. What a perfect opportunity I am for a predator. At least I have this building to help protect me.

I crawl into the sleeping bag, and Jip hobbles in to join me. I don't know why he trusts me so much, but I don't trust him with those claws. Especially after he sliced me at the stream. "Okay, fine. But it's just because you are cute, and I can use the extra warmth."

He crawls in and nestles up right next to me. He slides perfectly into place between my arm and chest.

"Good night, little buddy."

He watches me for a moment, then lays his head on my arm and closes his eyes. He smells of dirt with an earthy scent that reminds me of Pax.

Oh… Pax.

My heart aches at the thought of her.

My dad and brothers loved our two golden retrievers and black lab, but Pax was my dog. She was a strange little Chihuahua and shih tzu mix that my mom found on the side of I-40 east of Albuquerque.

My mom and I loved her out of sympathy, but Dad hated her, probably because she was never fully potty trained and ruined our carpets.

Pax was my friend. I took her on walks when I was lonely, and she always slept in my bed. When my mom had to start caring for my grandparents and was too busy to have our deep conversations over a game of Scrabble, Pax was the only one I could truly talk to.

We don't know how old she was, but we had her for five years. She lost all her teeth and had stiff joints. Even with all these problems, she didn't die from old age.

A lump forms in my throat.

I push the memory away.

Jip is slightly bigger than Pax, but he trusts me as Pax did. This time, I'll keep Jip safe.

The ground shakes.

The sticks in my fire collapse into a pile, spitting out a puff of sparks into the air. Beyond the fire, the street and city is pitch black. Why are there so many earthquakes here? Or are they earthquakes? This is the fourth one today. Each quake feels like a giant creature moving in a cave underground.

I lock that terrifying thought out of mind.

Leaves tremble as the shaking continues. A branch falls somewhere in the darkness. Dust settles on me from small cracks in the ceiling. I blink and wipe my eyes.

Jip snores beside me. The shaking doesn't bother him, so that's a good sign. However, he can likely sleep through a hurricane.

Lucky.

My body aches with exhaustion. It's been thirty hours since I last slept. I close my eyes and try to imagine myself tucked into my bed back at home, where I'd be safe from this nightmare.

My stomach rumbles. Even after all those beetle-fruit, I'm

starving. A green-chile Lota Burger sounds like heaven right now.

I let out a slow sigh. "You're lucky, bud; if it had been my dad or brothers here instead of me, you'd already be in a stew."

Jip snores in response.

The shaking passes.

A green light darts out from deeper inside the building. Three more green lights zip overhead and out the opening with quick flaps. They dance together as they disappear down the street. Glowing green birds? That's cool! My bird-watching club would be so jealous.

Night angels—that feels like a good name for these creatures because they are a reminder that not everything about this planet is terrifying. This place is beautiful. The animals are incredible, particularly the birds. I just wish it wasn't so dangerous or millions of miles from Earth.

Scaling the mountain and fighting off the pterodactyls to go home tomorrow is already nearly impossible. But who knows what could go wrong here? For all I know, the entire mountain could be alive. A tree could swallow me. An insect could burrow into my skin and eat me from the inside out or turn me into a zombie. Anything could happen!

"God, please help me get home tomorrow."

CHAPTER 8
HOMEWARD BOUND

AUGUST 12

The mountain looms above me. Early sunlight bathes its rocky face. The warmth of the sun feels wonderful in contrast to the crisp, chilly air. Morning fog crawls through the base of the valley like a relentless army marching down the slope for battle. Only the tallest buildings rise above the growing lake of fog. The birds are still waking up. Hopefully, this is also the case with the pterodactyls.

A dozen pterodactyls must be sitting on their unseen nests, licking their beaks as they wait for me to journey beyond the safety of the trees.

I shake my head. This is going to be brutal if not impossible. Have I ever climbed a mountain this tall before? Let alone run up one?

I rub my eyes. My mind is fuzzy with exhaustion. The night lasted twelve hours, which means each day must be about thirty hours long. Despite the long night, I woke up every ten minutes from either a stick snapping or the shaking ground.

At least I survived the freezing night and didn't get eaten.

Ugh! I'm sick of this place. Why is not being dead the only good news I have?

"Jesus, I'll forgive you for letting me get transported here if you help me get home now."

Jesus has to answer my prayer this time. How can he not? If he loves me, he will make a way for me to get home. He's the God of the impossible, isn't he?

I adjust the strings on my drawstring day pack. In it, I carry only a water bottle, the pink orb trinket, and a change of warmer clothes so I won't freeze to death when I appear back in Wyoming at 1:00 a.m. If all goes according to plan, I'll prove I was here with the pink artifact. Maybe it will make me famous.

The rest of my gear rests under the tree with Jip. I need a light load so I can wield my new weapon and shield.

With my left hand, I pick up my full-body shield: a strong chunk of bark I found on the ground that's remarkably rectangular. I slip my arm through the two loops of paracord I made after cutting two holes in the shield.

In my right hand, I wield my spear: a sharpened stick.

I feel like I'm seven again pretending to be a knight with Oliver and Matt as we prepare to fight the dragon. Except I don't feel brave or heroic like I did back then. But I have to do this…

Ugh. As I lift the spear and shield, my raging hunger makes them feel stupidly heavy. Every step up this mountain so far has drained me. The only thing that gives me the strength to take each weary step is the hope that on the other side of the portal, Dad will have a nice, hot freeze-dried meal for me. For the first time, one of those terrible backpacking meals sounds delicious.

Kee!

I set down my shield and pat my new little buddy on the head. He closes his eyes with each pat. "Sorry, Jip. I have to leave you here."

He gazes up at me with those wide, trusting eyes.

"I wish I could take you, but this is your home. You know

this place. You have a better chance of surviving here than I do climbing this mountain. Even if you did come and we make it home, there's no way you'd go unnoticed. Sooner or later people would find out you're from a different planet. They'd turn you over to scientists who would put you in a cage and do all sorts of crazy tests on you."

This predicament reminds me of the time Sophie and I found an injured rabbit while running near the Rio Grande. We wanted to keep it, but we let it go because we didn't want to take it away from its home.

Jip rests his head on the nest I made for him out of my clothes, while his round eyes follow me. The way he looks at me reminds me of Pax whenever I gave her a bath. I was the only one Pax let bathe her. Every time, her eyes seemed to say, *I don't understand, and I don't like this, but I trust you.*

My heart aches. I pat Jip once more on the forehead and step back.

Kee!

I swallow. "Yes, I know I promised I'd take care of you. And I did. I kept you safe for a whole day and found food and water for you." I point at the top of the mountain. "That's my way home. I can't survive here, and you can't survive there. I have to go. If I stay to protect you, I'll die."

Jip blinks.

It would be foolish to stay, right? He's just an animal. Why sacrifice my life to save his?

But I promised I'd keep him safe.

I inhale and pull the small straps of my day pack over my shoulder before I turn and pick up my shield.

The warmth of the sun greets me once again as I step out from the last of the trees. From here on, it's all rocks and snow, which means I'll need to move fast if I want to make it without becoming pterodactyl breakfast. I squint against the bright sun. There aren't any pterodactyls in the sky, but that could change in a moment.

"Jesus, please protect Jip," I say with one last glance back at my furry friend. "And please, please bring me home."

I charge up the mountain. Weakened by hunger, my knees give out several times, but I press on. The shale shifts under me. A rock dislodges and slides downhill but stops well before threatening Jip. I use my spear as a hiking stick to catch myself and groan as I take another step.

In no time, I've covered a good hundred feet, but I'm panting like a husky on a hundred-degree day. My head pounds and my eyes don't focus.

After a quick break and another scan of the sky, I continue at a much slower pace.

The air is so thin it doesn't feel like I'm breathing anything in.

Five minutes later, I stop again. My left shoulder throbs from carrying the shield, which must weigh thirty pounds. As I switch my shield to my other hand, I sigh. Sweat beads on my forehead from my arduous climb. I wipe the sweat onto my shirt and continue scaling the endless mountain.

Soon, my right arm is killing me. I look at my watch. Fifteen minutes has passed. "Ugh!" Why do people do this for fun?

My arms feel like they're going to fall off. I'd give anything but my life to leave the stupid shield behind and save myself the pain. Unfortunately, dropping it would likely cost me my life.

I throw the shield to the ground and hurl every insult my parents ever let me use at it. If only pterodactyls led with their heads like a bear or monkey-lion instead of their talons, then I could use my bear spray on them.

Rocks crunch under me as I pace frantically. I'm a sitting duck up here. I need to keep moving. But how am I going to carry this shield?

Now that I see my shield on the ground, the two loops I cut for the handles resemble the drawstring in my day pack.

My spirit soars.

I reverse my day pack so it hangs on my chest. Then I feed my arms through the shield's loops and… oh, praise God!

The string cuts into my shoulders but having the weight straight on my back makes it feel half as heavy. And now I don't have to worry about the hot sun because it doubles as an umbrella.

I face the mountain once more and climb. I take slow and careful steps as I scale the endless rockslide at a pace my burning lungs can manage.

How much longer can I do this?

I spot something in the distance and squint. It's just a dot in the sky, but it's got to be big if it's visible this far away.

My heavy breathing transforms into quick, sporadic gulps.

I focus on the rocks. I can't faint. Not now. Not when I'm so close to getting home.

Home. My comfortable and warm bed without any predators. My Xbox and PC with hours of incredible adventures that don't threaten my life every step of the way. Our refrigerator full of meat and fruit that I don't have to kill and won't have to worry about poisoning me. What a dream!

It all feels so far away. Is it possible I may be back in a few minutes?

The rocks slide under me. I grip the jagged edge of a larger boulder to stabilize myself and keep pressing on.

This nightmare will be over once I reach the portal.

The wind picks up, but it's a natural breeze, not a pterodactyl-gust.

I glance back again. Now there are flapping wings on the dot. It's big.

Raaaaaauuuu!

My stomach lurches. Above me, another pterodactyl appears over the top of the mountain. It tucks its wings and drops toward me.

"Are you kidding me?"

There are no big rocks or bushes to hide behind, no dad to think up some heroic plan, no dream to wake up from.

"God, do you care about me?"

In seconds, I pull off my shield from my back and hold it over my head, but at the speed the pterodactyl's diving, the impact will crush me.

I lie down and hold the shield over me. The bark arcs over me like a protective coffin covering my entire body.

Terrible. Absolutely terrible. I'm using a piece of bark to protect me from a man-eating bird. I can't believe *this* is my plan.

Wind rushes through my small coffin as a shadow darkens the outside world. Wings flap and suddenly the shield yanks in my hands. It wrenches my arms, but I keep hold of it.

My back and feet leave the ground.

"No, no, no!"

The ground is just below me. I can let go and run, but then how would I protect myself?

In seconds, I'm thirty feet above the ground, dangling from the loops in my shield. The pterodactyl's lifting me higher, and the sides of my vision darken.

"Jesus, help me!"

Not only am I way above ground, but this pterodactyl could drop me any second… like an eagle.

That's right! These pterodactyls act like eagles. Eagles swoop their meal into the air and drop it, letting gravity do their dirty work. The pterodactyl did this with the monkey-lion yesterday.

I formed the birder club. How did I not recognize or plan for this?

As I imagine the impact, I feel my bones crunch.

And if I don't die from the fall, it'll slowly pick me apart as I try to crawl away on broken legs.

I shudder.

The sides of my vision grow darker. My fingers tingle.

"No, Jake, you can't faint! Not now. Absolutely not now."

If I fainted, I'd release my grip and I'd fall to—

"Stop it!"

I close my eyes. My bed. My warm bed. The soft pillow. The glow of the sun through my shades on a late Saturday morning. The sound of my video games. My sweaty grip on the controller.

Something smashes into my pterodactyl and jerks us to the left. Two pterodactyls fight above me.

The rope tears at my arm as we begin spinning. I drop my spear and grab the side of my shield.

As they grapple for me, we twist in every direction. First, the ground is under me, then it's above.

Aggressive *raus* fill the air. They jab their beaks at each other.

"Deep breaths, Jake, deep breaths," I say through clenched teeth. The darkness in the sides of my vision stops moving inward. "Jesus, I need you!"

The ground is closer each time it flashes into view.

A clawed foot grabs the corner of the shield. The attacking pterodactyl spreads its wings and pulls away, trying to take me with it. The bark breaks away instead.

The bird drops the piece of bark, which continues free-falling beside me. Then it reaches for me. I dodge, but its talon snags the leg of my nylon pants. It beats its giant wings and pulls away.

"Gahh!" I clench the shield as the pterodactyl pulls. The force threatens to tear my arm out of its socket. My grip weakens.

Rip!

The fabric of my pants gives way. The attacking pterodactyl pulls away with only a chunk of nylon in its claw.

Everything stabilizes for a moment as my pterodactyl

regains control. It turns our downward velocity into controlled forward momentum.

I'm still alive! For now…

We're no more than twenty feet above the ground, but we're flying at least fifty miles an hour. If I let go now, the rocks would shred me like a giant cheese grater. Is that a worse fate than if I let the pterodactyl carry me until he drops me from a much higher altitude? If we fly over a snowfield, then I could—

The ground disappears as we sail over a cliff.

My stomach drops.

My feet dangle hundreds of feet above the ground.

The thin line of a stream weaves through the trees far below.

I adjust my grip on the straps. The moment I find a better grip, an updraft rips us skyward.

Just behind us, the other pterodactyl closes in.

Will this ever end?

My pterodactyl flips around. It angles downward. My eyes tear up from the extreme wind. We are only fifty feet above the ground once more. The pterodactyl tilts left and around the ridge of a mountain.

Down below I spot the boulder the bird must be planning to drop me on. On the boulder are several small rocks forming an arrow. My arrow.

The portal tower!

It's only two hundred feet up the slope from the boulder. The pink rim of the portal glows, but the bottom isn't lit up. The sun isn't high enough yet.

I still have time. My way home is within reach.

Two more *raus* pierce the howling wind.

Right, but first I have to not die.

Two pterodactyls seemingly materialize before us and join the Jake Rogers dinner party. My pterodactyl quickly flips us back around, then ducks toward the ground to avoid the first bird. I glance back.

All three pterodactyls are gaining on us.

Outmaneuvering one bird is impressive, especially while carrying me, but there's no way it can dodge three. We are back over the side of the mountain with the portal. This time we're only twenty feet off the ground.

A green light flashes to my left. A split second later, a rattling thunderclap hits us.

A massive black plume launches from a peak across the valley. Another bolt of green lightning flashes. Dark specks erupt out of the mountain while the base of the plume glows red. A deep rumbling fills the air, like that of a massive rock giant grinding its teeth.

I blink away tears to get a better view of the incredible sight.

It's...

A volcano.

CHAPTER 9
JUST AN INCH
AUGUST 12

A shock wave hits us. The blow rolls the pterodactyl to the side. It lets out a terrified *rau* and releases its grip on the shield.

I gasp. My stomach rises into my throat as gravity takes hold of me.

The ground rushes up to destroy me, the shale ready to snap all my bones and shred me to pieces.

I flail in the empty air. I find nothing but the shield to cling to.

My momentum carries me directly toward the crest of a ridge. But if I clear the ridge, then…

I twist in the air to place my shield beneath me and sit on it like it's a sled.

Maybe, just maybe, I'll sur—

I hit the top of the ridge with a skull-rattling thud. My entire back and neck compresses before I bounce back into the air.

I fly another thirty feet down the slope.

The next impact forces a grunt out of me, and I again bounce into the air. I clench the two loops and keep the shield under me.

The third collision rattles my whole body. Ice crystals spray my face as I enter a snowfield. At the bottom of the snow patch rise jagged rocks. I dig my heels into the snow.

Snow flies everywhere. I clench my eyes shut.

My shield hits something, and I fly forward. The force rips me off the sled, breaking my grip and wrenching my arms. I reach forward to stop my fall. My hands and face meet gritty dirt.

Then everything stops.

For the first time in what feels like hours, I'm motionless.

I exhale and roll onto my back.

The ground rumbles and thunder blasts through the air.

I wipe the snow from my eyes and watch the billowing black clouds fill the sky.

A small burning sensation grows in my bloodied hands until it feels like I'm holding hot coals. My arms ache deep inside their sockets. My back and bottom throb from the three impacts. Something rolls down the side of my face. I wipe it with my finger and find melted snow and blood.

But I should be dead. My back should've broken from the fall and hitting the ground should've felt harder. Yet it all felt muted. As if I weighed less.

That's right! Gravity is less here.

Thank God! I'd be dead if it wasn't.

Something taps my shoulder. Nearby, more rocks clatter against the mountainside. Then another boom shakes the ground.

I bolt upright. The volcano!

A massive rock crashes into the mountainside, throwing up dust and debris. A strange burnt and dusty smell fills the air.

Only on a planet with weaker gravity could a volcano throw rocks that big this far.

I jump to my feet and dash to the side as another rock

barrels into the ground and shatters my shield into a thousand tiny fragments.

As I move, my body aches, but I don't feel any sharp pangs from broken bones.

Rau! Rau!

The four pterodactyls flee with frantic calls. Their antennae bounce in rhythm with their wings.

Down in the valley, hundreds of birds all flap vigorously in a desperate escape southward. A giant boulder crashes into one of the taller buildings. The structure teeters, then collapses.

A large beast bellows from somewhere in the valley.

Another shudder from the eruption knocks me off my feet.

As I stand and turn to run, I spot the teleportation structure and smile. I don't have to run; I'm going home.

Giant rocks pummel the mountain as I race toward the portal. Without skipping a step, I flip my day pack from my chest to my back.

Smaller rocks pepper the entire mountainside. All the while, the black plume of smoke and ash grows. The sky darkens. Bright lava flows over the top of the volcano. A rotten-egg smell invades my nose.

But what about Jip? He can't run from the volcano. I push the thought away. I can't fix every problem.

After a lot of stumbling and sliding on the loose rocks, I reach the structure. The dense smoke covers the sun and causes the glowing portal rim to vanish. Then it parts and the pink circle glows once more, but the center of the base doesn't light up. Again, the smoke covers the sun and the pink rim fades.

I dig my fingers into the narrow grooves etched across the base of the structure and climb the forty-five-degree surface into the dark center of the portal.

Another spray of small rocks stings my skin and clatters against the metallic frame with dozens of *tinks* and *thunks* like hail on the roof of a car. Then the billow of smoke passes, and the sun shines on me through the pink crystal. The rim lights up.

I close my eyes and soak in the sunlight. I can't believe it. I'm actually going home.

The hair on my arms stands on end.

But the hard substance under me doesn't open into a portal.

I check the rim, but it's complete. There aren't any gaps in—

I groan.

An inch.

One stupid inch!

The circle is complete except for a little gap on the left-most side of the rim. I climb over to it. Sure enough, the metal ring around the pink lens casts a shadow that covers a fraction of the circle.

Yesterday, the top of the circle was covered by the shadow because the sun was too high in the sky. A bit ago, the bottom wasn't lit up because the sun was still too low. But if the south side isn't lit up, then the problem isn't the time of day but the time of year.

I slam my hand against the metallic base and yell as the realization sinks in. When my lungs burn for air, I inhale and scream again.

The sun passed its peak in the summer and won't line up with the portal for another year, however long a year is here.

Until then, I'm trapped here.

"Are you kidding me, God?" My throat burns from screaming. "Why would you do this? I thought you cared about me?"

I slide down to the bottom leg of the tripod frame.

I hate this place. I hate the danger. I hate my pain.

I'll never survive this nightmare.

Billions of miles separate me from planet Earth and everyone I know. I'm all alone.

I'm dead.

Volcanic pebbles clatter against the portal structure, but I'm too weak to move. The only thing that drove me forward was the hope of returning home today. Now what? I'd be foolish to believe I might survive a year here. I almost died four times trying to live through a single day.

My future will never come. I'll never train the next birder club officers. I'll never prove myself to my dad or figure out what I want to be. I'll never get to tell Sophie I like her or ask her to homecoming.

A massive boulder from the exploding volcano careens toward me. It cuts a chunk out of the crest of the mountain and tumbles down the other side. The ground trembles with each impact.

My heart hammers in my chest and fingers and feet.

If this is how I'm going to die, then so be it. I fought a monkey-lion, ate beetles—whether they be fruit or not—and survived six pterodactyls. I might not have made it home, but I did my best, and somehow, I did a good job.

If I'm going to die, I'd rather it happen now than later. Dying now is better than enduring the fear of this terrible planet every second. Dying would be so easy.

But something within me doesn't sit well with that idea.

I know Dad would be disappointed if I gave up right now. He'd probably say something like, *Don't quit again, Jake.* But he's always been disappointed in me, so why press on for him?

I pull out the pink alien trinket from my day pack and chuck it down the slope. It's useless to me now that I'm stuck here.

I drop my head into my hands. What's the point in pressing on when there's no chance I'll survive?

How do you know you'll die?

The thought hits me out of nowhere. Did I think that? "God?" I whisper.

I clench my fists at the thought of God. How can he love me if he let me fall through the portal? This doesn't seem like something he'd do. He's the one who's supposed to save me from problems, not push me into them.

As mad as I am at God, if he protected me during impossible situations with the high school jocks, can't I trust him now as I did then?

"God, if this is all your doing, I'm done. Bring me home. I don't want to be here anymore."

Another blast bursts from the volcano. It starts as a perfect gray sphere and explodes outward. Soon the gray sphere vanishes into an invisible shock wave. The wave ripples through clouds without slowing or dissipating. In its wake, more massive rocks launch into the air.

Like a tsunami, the shock wave flattens the trees on the mountain across from me. Dust and small rocks fly toward me like an unstoppable flood.

I duck behind the support beam, cover my face, and do my best to plug my ears.

Boom!

The jarring blast shakes every part of my body.

It races along the rest of the ridge before it disappears down the other side to where I first started climbing up.

Jip.

I glance back at the volcano, small specks—which must be huge boulders—hurtle through the air toward me.

The image of Jip trying to run away from such a boulder only to be squished flashes in my mind.

I climb to my feet.

Whether I die today or tomorrow, I can at least give Jip a chance. I won't let him die as I did Pax.

The dark plume of smoke billows out of the volcano. "God, we aren't done with this conversation. I may try to survive today, but it's only for Jip. I'm still not okay with you stranding me here."

I jump out from behind my cover and race toward the crest. Rocks clatter around me, some strike my throbbing back, but I charge on. I reach the crest of the mountain and bound down the other side. Rocks tumble and roll downhill with every step.

More green lightning flashes behind me.

A rock the size of a car flies fifty feet to my left. The wind almost knocks me to the ground. When the boulder hits the side of the mountain, it leaves a crater, then bounces back into the air.

My knees buckle as the mountain ripples from the impact. I tumble a few times before I catch myself and slide to a stop. Streaks of white cover my arm where the mountain rocks scraped away my skin. Blood oozes out. It's nothing serious, but how much more of a beating can I take?

Meanwhile, the boulder soars another mile downhill before bouncing again. Finally, it crashes into the trees and rolls and rolls.

"Jip." I stagger.

The boulder flattens the unsuspecting trees, flinging mangled logs into the air like toothpicks.

At last the cannonball—which had once been a tiny speck in the distance—comes to a rest.

How in the world did I end up in this insane situation? Portals, pterodactyls, and now a volcano. It's like I found a glitch in a game and accidentally skipped from level four to sixty.

I jump back to my feet and continue my race downhill as rocks clatter around me.

With every step my back aches from my crash landing with the shield. Yesterday I ran down this slope to escape giant birds. Now I'm running from giant boulders. If my terrible luck continues, I'll be running from knifelike hail tomorrow.

I reach the first of the trees and scan for Jip. My feet skid on the dirt as I slow to a stop.

"Jip!" I yell.

I strain my ears against the distant rumbling.

Kee!

I sigh in relief. I follow his faint call to find him sheltering in the nest I made him. His eyes are wide. His whole body trembles. When he spots me, he *kee*s again and hobbles out of the nest only to stumble and fall to his side. His bandaged foot sticks out awkwardly.

Unlike all the other animals on this mountain, he can't flee the coming destruction. I'm his only hope.

Another large rock pummels the mountain a quarter mile to my left.

"We've got to get out of here, little guy!" I scoop him up and carry him back to the nest. My backpack and supplies lie next to the pile of clothes. I frown. "Looks like we're going to need this gear after all."

Jip gives me a confused stare.

"We're stranded here on this planet for the next year." I glance up at the billowing smoke. "If we survive that long."

I throw everything into my pack and swing it onto my back. Jip's eyes never leave me as I set him in the sling and pull the strap over my shoulder.

I rush downhill in the dark ambiance of the smoke-blackened sky.

I hate this.

CHAPTER 10
A BLACK AND BURNING LAND

AUGUST 12

I set Jip on the ground and collapse onto the large rock that sits on top of the ridge. It took me a good two hours to descend Portal Mountain and climb this mountain.

The sky is black. The sun resembles a bloody eye behind the thick smoke. Ashes fall like a nightmarish snowstorm. The ground still rumbles, but it doesn't shake nearly as much as my bloody hands.

Portal Mountain rises high above me to the north, and behind it to the right is the volcano. Smoke still billows from the top. It seems to be slowing down since it hasn't exploded for a little while, but I'm not falling for it.

That thing is a ticking time bomb. I learned the story of Pompeii, and I'm not going to end up like all the inhabitants in that long-ago-destroyed city.

Lava pours over the top of the death trap. The forest is on fire from all the lava, but the fire doesn't roll downhill like the molten rock. The whole side of the volcano is an inferno, silhouetting the tallest alien structures.

Both peaks are shrouded in ominous darkness from the smoke and falling ashes. Everything about it screams death to me, and that death holds my only way home.

I can't see the portal from here, and that scares me. If I lose track of the portal, then it doesn't matter if I survive an entire year.

I glance at my watch: 5:45 a.m. August 12.

I grunt, open the timer display, and hit start. Seeing the date and time only makes me mad. I don't care what time and day it is on Earth. None of that matters anymore. I'm trapped here, and the days are about thirty hours here instead of twenty-four. Besides, a year on this planet won't be exactly a year on Earth. It could be much more or much less. Either way, today isn't the twelfth, it's day two of who knows how many.

"I can't do this, Jip."

He looks up at me and blinks, then uses his front paw to scratch behind his ear.

"Why should I try? I'll never survive a whole year. And what's the point of living here if I'll be by myself?" I pull my knees to my chest and bury my face between them. How did my old life vanish in one instant? Thinking about the thirty trillion empty, space-filled miles separating me from my home makes me sick to my core.

All I want to do is sit and do nothing and waste away. If only I could wake up and find that this was all a dream.

Kee! Jip's large brown eyes dart from me to the flames on the other side of the valley. The fire's creeping toward us. Flames lick up around the city ruins to the northeast. I lift the sling and set Jip on my lap. He gazes up at me with a trusting expression as if to say, *I can't move, but you can. Please save me.*

Pax looked at me the same way as I watched her bleed out. She fought me a few times. She wanted to see the source of her pain, but I wouldn't let her. Instead, I kept her eyes fixed on me as I lied to her over and over saying, *"It's okay, girl. It's okay."* until the light faded from her eyes.

I wipe away my tears. I could've prevented her death. I

was the reason she ran into the street and got hit by the car. My best friend died because of my selfishness.

We held no funeral for her. Dad never thought of it, and Mom was too exhausted from helping my grandparents all day. So I cried over her alone.

Now she's gone, and I'll never make it up to her.

"Except now I have you."

Jip presses his head into my hand, and I rub his chin with my thumb.

"I couldn't save her, but I can save you."

He licks my palm, then watches the falling ash.

I stand with Jip in my arms. "I know we need to go, but it feels wrong." I turn back toward Portal Mountain and the death-volcano one more time before I face the way we need to go. "The farther we travel from the portal, the farther I am from home. What if we get lost and I can't find the portal when we come back?"

Kee! Jip's whole body jolts from his well-thought-out response.

"You're right, there's no point in knowing where the portal is if we die before it opens." With the monkey-lions, pterodactyls, the volcano, and other unknown beasts, it's too dangerous to stay. This treacherous land is level sixty in this horror game. At most, I'm now a level-four character. I need to find a land that matches my level. And hopefully, by some miracle I'll survive and level up enough to come back.

To the south, the mountains slowly turn into hills, and the hills flatten out into a plain. Who knows what's out there. "I'm already scared enough, but to add this—"

Kee!

I glare at the insensitive rabbit-like creature. "Look, if I'm going to save you, then you need to be more respectful of my feelings. My feelings are valid. I'm afraid, and that's perfectly—"

Kee!

"Stop acting like my dad! Let me speak and don't lecture me about how it's important that I do hard things or face my fears. It's okay to be afraid. Everyone's afraid of something."

Jip seems to accept my request as he stares at the mountains before us.

I take a deep breath.

I'm about to journey into a land no one has ever seen. There are no maps for this terrain or trails, only mysteries, secrets, and unknown dangers. I'm on another planet with different gravity, strange creatures, and perhaps an intelligent alien species. What lies ahead of me?

I wanted a mountain-exploring video game, so God threw me on an entirely new planet. Thanks, God. Just what I asked for. Remind me to never invite you to my birthday.

Beyond the smoke and ash, the sun shines upon the plains, as if promising ease and relaxation, but I know that's not true. Every step along the way, I'll have to avoid touching unknown poisonous plants that may cause my skin to fester and peel. I'll need to keep watch for undiscovered predators in the trees, behind rocks, and quite possibly in the ground. And what else? Are there killer bees here? Sinkholes? More volcanoes?

I can't believe I'm about to journey across an uncharted land. Anything could go wrong. I could wrench my ankle or get a searing gash in my arm, and I'd have no one to help me. I could break my leg and have to crawl the rest of my miserable life until I starve to death. I can't respawn or eat food to instantly heal like my avatar in *Minecraft*.

"Jesus, why in the world am I here?"

I used to have plans weeks and months in the future, and now I don't know what's coming in the next five minutes. One minute I could be walking and the next, lifted away by a pterodactyl only to find myself running from a volcano.

I'm like Joshua in the Bible. He probably felt the same way when he became the new leader of the Israelites, and God told him to enter an unknown land full of enemies. Talk about walking into danger. At least I'm only responsible for myself and Jip. I'd hate to have a few hundred thousand people depending on me and pressuring me.

I sit down, set Jip on the ground, and pull my Bible out of my dry bag. Reading it helped encourage me last school year; maybe it will help now.

Jip stares at me.

I glare back at him. "I'm only going to read a little. We have plenty of time before the fire reaches us."

I start at the beginning of the book of Joshua and stop when I reach verse 9. *"Be strong and courageous. Do not be afraid; do not be discouraged, for the* LORD *your God will be with you wherever you go."*

Do not be afraid?

"Jesus, I am afraid!" I yell. A gust of wind blows ashes into my face and mouth. I sputter as I spit them out and wipe my face. "I want to trust you, but I hate this. I don't understand why I'm here or why you let that portal pull me away from everything I love. It feels like you hate me. How can you tell me not to be afraid?"

I look back at the dark ash cloud and the raging fire. "It sure doesn't feel like you are with me after all that's happened."

But I am still alive.

The most I survived back on Earth was a few football jocks who were mad I didn't make their team win like my older brothers did during their high school years. My enemies here were trying to eat me, and I survived. Sure, I'm cut, bruised, exhausted, and my entire body aches from fighting to survive, but I still have all four limbs.

"Were you protecting me through all of that?"

Has God been with me this whole time?

But why would he bring me here in the first place? Joshua at least knew God was calling him to be a leader, and he was supposed to help the Israelites conquer their new home. What does God want me to be? Does he have a plan for me?

Lightning flashes off to the south where the smoke hasn't reached. A dark storm rolls across the distant plains, and a gray curtain of rain descends halfway down from the cloud.

God asked Joshua to trust in him. And God did deliver him from all the threats before him. Since I know how his story ended, it's easy to recognize he could've trusted God all along. But he didn't know how his story would end.

Isn't my situation like how Joshua's story started? He had no idea if God would protect them. He couldn't see the future, yet he stepped forward anyway.

Ugh. I hate this, but I climb to my feet.

"Okay, Jesus, I still don't believe you are making the best decisions, but I have no choice; I must go. If you really are good, please show me the way. I don't know what you want from me nor do I really care right now: I want to go home. And don't you dare expect me not to be afraid because that will never happen here."

With one last glance back at the black and burning land behind me, I pick up Jip and descend the other side of the mountain. Will I ever see Portal Mountain again? Will I ever see my family or friends? Will I ever get to tell Sophie I like her? Probably not, but my best chances at surviving this dreadful world are ahead of me.

So, one shaky step after another, I leave my home behind.

MONKEY-LION

LOOKS LIKE A COMPACT LION

CHAPTER 11

HUNTER

DAY 2

Snap!

I look up from the spear I'm whittling.

The sun is high in the beautiful teal sky but has started its trek down toward the western horizon. To the northeast, the volcano continues spewing dark smoke. The wind sweeps the smoke and ash eastward, leaving this part of the mountains pleasantly free of immediate death.

My bottom is numb from sitting with my back against a tree.

Something moves between the trees.

I grip my new spear. It isn't as sharp as I'd like. I only sat down twenty minutes ago to escape the midday heat and start working on it.

A scaly miniature deer ducks under a log downhill. It lifts its head and sniffs the air.

Food.

Energy courses through me. I don't care if it kills me, I have to eat something. I can already imagine the taste of the meat. Like a nice green-chile Lota Burger, except with a juicy steak to replace the hamburger patty.

The creature's floppy ears shoot up and grow to the size of

my hiking boot as it spots me. It bolts toward the stream at the bottom of the valley and through a small gap in the orange-leafed trees.

Suddenly, the ground clamps over it and lifts the creature into the air. The critter cries and wails as it thrashes about, sending cascades of dirt, sticks, and leaves to the ground. The forest debris falls away and reveals a green net. The more the deer fights the net, the more the cords tangle it up.

I use the tree to climb to my feet. Every movement aches with pain. Jip is still asleep in his sling, so I don't bother waking him. I check the area for danger, then hobble toward the scene with my spear and a can of bear spray clipped to my belt.

The net looks like a giant green spiderweb. The scale deer stops floundering in the net. It scans the area, as if expecting something to happen. Its gaze lands on me, but it moves on a second later as if I'm not the thing it's searching for.

Beyond the net, a brown blob crawls out of the ground. It's about two feet across, has six legs, and its skin is pock-marked like a sponge. It climbs a tree, then waltzes out onto the net and sinks its teeth deep into the scale deer. Green blood drips down the deer. It kicks and twists, but the blob doesn't let go. Slowly, the kicking stops, and the deer lies motionless.

The brown creature spots me with its four black eyes and gives a low growl.

I step forward. I have no idea what it is capable of, but I'm starving, and I need that scale deer. I lift my spear and aim, but it's too far for me to risk throwing my only weapon.

Wooop! Wooop! Wooop! Its whole jellylike body wobbles with each warning.

I freeze. Can it shoot poisonous toxins? Is it wicked fast? Can it launch a spike at me out of one of those holes in its body?

It's warning me rather than running away. Most birds fly

away when they feel threatened. That is, unless they're defending their young or know they'll put up a good fight.

Another brown blob climbs out of the hole and joins its friend up on the net.

Wooop! Wooop! Wooop! They take turns, each of them calling three times before the other takes over. Both of their bodies jiggle with each warning.

But I'm *really* hungry.

"Haww!" I raise both my arms and charge them.

They freeze, expand their bodies, and convulse, launching a blue dust from every pore in their bodies. I back up.

It's toxic. I know it.

Thankfully I'm far enough away that none of it gets on me.

When the dust clears, both blobs are trying to pull the deer into their hole. I lift my spear and hurl it at them. It skims one and lodges into the ground. Both blobs give gurgle-like cries before they scamper into the hole, leaving the scale deer behind.

It worked!

I almost shout for joy but stop as I remember other predators could be lurking nearby.

I rush around the contamination zone to the scale deer. The blue dust could be an escape tactic like a squid's ink, but I'm not risking it. Now I know to avoid any blue dust I may encounter.

The scale deer is covered in it. I grab big leaves and wrap them around two of the creature's legs so I can drag it to the river.

But I did it! I won a battle against the blobs and scored enough meat to feed me for days! Dad would be so proud.

My stomach rumbles at the thought of eating meat. Finally, something other than beetle-fruit. My mouth salivates. I can already smell the savory scent of it roasting over the fire.

The river is only thirty feet away, and the deer is easy to drag since it's a little smaller than a German shepherd. Each scale resembles a tiny mirror. They aren't perfectly reflective, but they do a great job at camouflaging it. Thankfully, I didn't have to be the one to kill the beautiful creature because I don't know if I would've gone through with it, and I doubt my spear could've punctured the tough scales.

The moment I drop the deer in the river, a blue cloud flows from it and drifts downstream. I shake it around to make certain all the dust is gone.

Then I lift the scale deer over my shoulders and lug it back toward my temporary camp, using my spear as a walking stick. It's not heavy, but I'm dangerously weak from hunger.

A flat rock wall comes into view between the trees. But its side is too flat to be natural. Even the corner is a straight vertical line. I stagger toward it.

It's a wall.

I lay down the scale deer and soften my steps as I approach with my spear ready.

The roof has caved in. A tree grows from inside the structure. The walls are made of metal just like the buildings in the city, but this structure is much older.

What happened to them? Did something more dangerous kill them? Or do they now live on a different part of the planet?

I've played enough *Halo* to know any encounter with aliens won't go well. Besides, I'd rather fight a dumb beast than an entire advanced civilization. But the mystery draws me.

It's not a big house, just thirty by twenty feet, but it has a triangular door like those in the city.

The foul odor of urine and poop assaults my extra hunger-sensitive nose. I scowl and stop within the doorway.

Grass and vines grow over the walled-off enclosure. Some

sort of animal scat hangs off the top of the wall and litters the larger vines.

I heft the scale deer onto my back and head to my temporary camp. But the discovery of the house hangs over me like a shadow. If something killed off its residents, what chance do I have?

As I approach, Jip's catlike ears flip up and angle toward me before he lifts his head. He treats my victorious hunting smile with total indifference. When I set the scale deer on the ground, he sniffs the air with his bunny nose, then settles back down.

With plenty of dry grass and sticks around, I don't need to use much fuel from my lighter to get a good fire going.

I don't have any ice or a refrigerator to keep the meat from spoiling, so I don't need to rush harvesting every bit of meat —just enough for today—but I feel like I could eat half of it now. I learned in one of my Trail Life camping trips about preserving meat through smoking it, but by the time I make a smoker out of sticks, the meat would spoil in this heat.

I find my four-inch knife in my bag and unsheathe it. Surprisingly, skinning the deer is exactly as I expected after hearing my dad and brothers talk about it and seeing people do it in movies and documentaries. The "gutless method" is what I heard my brothers call this technique of focusing on the legs and leaving the guts in the chest cavity. I cringe as I wrench the scale deer's leg to the side, pop it out of the socket, then cut it off.

"Sorry, deer."

With one leg done, I set the whole limb over the fire before I turn to the next leg, but I don't bother with the rest of the animal. I feel bad not using all the meat. It feels wasteful and irreverent of the animal's life, but two legs is more than enough to fill me. After reading *Hatchet,* I know not to eat too much. In it, Brian ate his fill, and it sat in him like a log until his body digested it.

As hungry as I am, I can't camp here. I'm sure those blobs will want vengeance, and I would never sleep knowing those nasty critters live two hundred feet away.

Once the meat is done cooking, I pull it off of my makeshift spit roast and replace it with the second skinned leg. I don't wait for the meat to cool before biting into it. It's amazing! I burn my mouth with each bite, but it's worth it. Each bite tastes like a juicy piece of steak. It doesn't taste like the gamey venison my dad and brothers always brought home. But that's probably my hunger talking.

Like magic, my strength returns. But my stomach feels just as empty. After my hunger abates, I force myself to put the rest of the leg away and pack up. I promise myself I'll stop in an hour or so and appease my raging stomach more.

I scatter the coals and smother them with dirt. As I stand, I feel like Superman. With my hunger-weakness gone and the lower gravity, I'm ready to take on anything. I strap the remaining cooked leg to my pack and head on. My backpack is heavier with the added weight, but this only makes me smile. That's good weight. I honestly wish it was heavier.

Dad often told me near hunting season that there's something special about hunting your own food. He said it brings a degree of pride to the soul and respect for the world and the animals around us.

I never doubted him, but this wasn't enough to convince me to camp out in cold weather and hike miles lugging a weapon just to kill a deer. What better setup could there be to let my dad down?

But now I know what he meant. Because now I'm a hunter like my dad. Actually, I'm a better hunter than my dad.

I smile. If Dad were here, I'd say, *You know, hunting is great and all, but there's something special about hunting with a weapon you made yourself.*

I'm more than a hunter; I'm now officially a survivalist.

BLOB

BROWN SKIN
LIKE A FROG

SKIN POCKMARKED
LIKE A SPONGE

FOUR
BLACK
EYES

CAN CLIMB
TREES

TOXIC BLUE
DUST CAN
BE EMITTED
FROM PORES

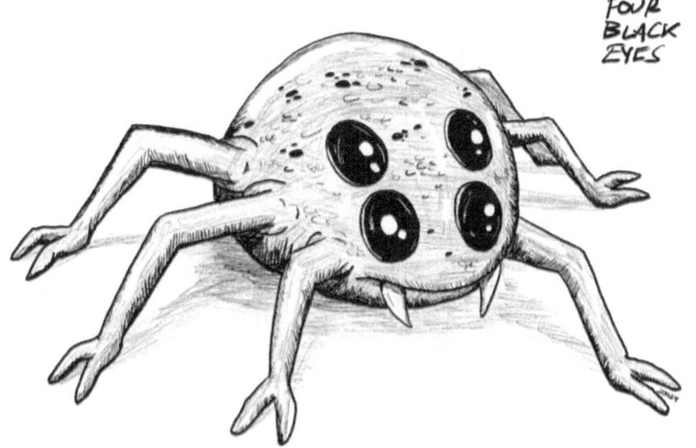

CHAPTER 12
THE PLAINS

DAY 4

The hot sun beams down on the plains before me. Even in the shade, the heat of the sun reflects off the ground. Beautiful white clouds dot the teal sky, but none appear threatening… yet. I blink as the breeze hits me. The hot wind does little to cool me. The humidity only makes it worse. I feel like I'm trapped under a hot blanket and can't escape.

I stand at the edge of the forest staring out over endless plains. This is the end of the shade.

Odd hills speckle the grasslands. They vary from fifty feet tall to hundreds of feet. Not a single tree grows out in the prairie, but the hills are covered with them. While the plains seem perfectly flat, each hill looks like an overturned bowl. What sort of erosion could've caused such formations?

Other than the hills, green, blue, and orange grass grows everywhere. Birds fly about, but there's no sign of ptero-dactyls. In the distance, a pack of animals stands around in a group. Every now and then a flock of turkey-sized creatures will hop above the grass and flap around before slowly drifting back into the grasses.

I feel safer already. I don't know what's waiting for me out there, but it must be better than what I'm leaving behind in the mountains.

It took three long days of travel to get here from Portal Mountain. Yesterday the small bit of meat I had left started to look and smell funny, so I didn't risk it and tossed it all away. Turns out, Jip likes meat too, and he hates it when I don't let him eat rotten scale deer.

I discovered ice-cold baths in the river during the noonday heat feel incredible and scale deer skin doubles as a well-insulated baking glove.

Jip walks better now and no longer needs the bandages now that the wound has scabbed over. He can't cover long distances, but he no longer squeals when he moves slowly. Which means he can now come and beg me for food every time I start cooking and claw me to death whenever I bring him near water.

How can he be so afraid of water when he spent his whole life drinking from a stream?

According to the sun, the river led me in a general southerly direction. According to my dad's compass, it's been leading me north.

Dad's compass also says the sun rises in the west and sets in the east, which is beyond disorienting. The magnetism of this planet must be upside down compared to Earth, or maybe the planet is spinning in the opposite direction. But what is up or down in space?

Since I'm already conditioned to the sun rising in the east and setting in the west, and it's far easier to use the sun than Dad's compass, I decided to orient east and west on the sun's movement. Which means the compass is now backward.

With the sun just past its height, I only have eight hours to travel about seven miles to the biggest hill before nightfall. It must be at least four hundred feet tall and easily a quarter mile across.

"Don't worry, Jip; we'll settle down on that hill. It's close enough to the mountains that we can easily find our way back. It's not far from the river, it has good visibility to spot any approaching predators while still providing a significant amount of shade, and there are enough trees and plants that we shouldn't run out of resources."

The moment I step out from the shade of the trees and into the grass, the humidity and heat slam into me. I glance back at the mountains. Do I really want to hike seven miles through this?

I hate hiking in the heat, but I hate dying more. Besides, I've hiked the past three days. If that hill is the end of my journey, why turn back now?

The height of the grass increases with every step until I'm surrounded by blades eight feet tall. I have to clear the path before me with every step.

In no time, I'm sweating fifty gallons of water an hour in the hot, muggy air. A small breeze tugs at the top of the grass, but I feel none of it down here.

My only relief comes in the form of puddles, which I douse my clothes in. The water is murky, but I'd rather smell bad than die of heat exhaustion.

I can't see anything more than three feet away, so I use the sun to make sure I'm still heading south. A predator could be feet away without me knowing, but I'd hear it, right?

Small bugs fly about. Occasionally I walk through what I can only describe as a cloud of them. I'm glad there aren't any mosquitoes, but this doesn't comfort me much. What might these other bugs do to me? Will one fly into my eye and release a toxin that poisons me? Will another explode into flames? Will the ground drop out from under me, revealing the teeth of a monster like a Sarlacc in *Star Wars*?

Who knows what's possible here?

After two hours of trudging through this unending grass, I stop and guzzle more water. The biggest threat here is dehydration. I've finished off two of my four Nalgene water bottles. It's a good thing I topped off my water before I headed into this sauna. My dad would've been proud of that decision.

Dad.

I take a deep breath as mixed thoughts fill my mind.

I miss him. A lot. But sometimes I'm glad he's not here. It's more peaceful not having him judge my decisions. But it would be nice to have him here.

Is he searching for me or waiting for the portal to open? Did he run back and get phone service to tell my mom and call in help?

My heart weighs heavy. My poor mom. And my brothers too. Are they all out looking for me?

I hang my head. Their search is pointless. If only I could tell them it will take another year for the portal to reopen.

As much as I worry for them, I can't change what they do, nor do their actions change my circumstances. It's best that I focus on what I need to do so I can survive and get back to them when the portal opens.

I push more grass aside and step through as sweat rolls down my cheek. "God, it would be real nice if you brought a few clouds or some rain to cool me."

Clouds are forming far off in the west, but I can't wait that long in this heat.

I stagger into a clearing. I'm standing in a large area of flattened grass about the size of a tennis court. To my left is a puddle about six feet across. I tear off my pack and stumble into it. Jip doesn't join me, so I splash him and go back to set up my pack to give him some shade.

As I reach the puddle again, a deep snort sounds nearby.

A super fat and stubby green animal stares at me. It has a thick horn like a rhino's on the bridge between its eyes. It backs away, angling toward a packed-down path through the tall grasses.

I step toward it.

It glares at me. A flap of skin around its neck flips forward to create a circle around its head. The flap turns a bright red and my world goes black.

My mom opens my door and strides into my room. She gives me an impatient look. Dark bags hang under her eyes from working a night shift the last three nights.

I pull off my headset.

"Jake, dinner's ready and everyone's waiting for you."

"I'm almost done with my game." The score is close, and we're pinned down. I lob a grenade over the bunker my team and I hide behind.

"No. I told you it would be ready fifteen minutes ago. That's plenty of time to finish a game."

True, but then I started another one. Matt and Oliver are on, and we barely lost our last game. I can't abandon them now. Especially with the score so close and the time almost up.

"Okay, give me a minute."

My team and I all make a break for the next cover.

"Jake!" My dad's deep voice isn't loud, but his tone makes my bones tremble. His barstool scrapes against the tile floor in the kitchen as he stands.

"Fine." I pull my headset back to my mouth. "Sorry, guys, I gotta go."

"What, you—?" Matt says before I exit the game. Dad appears in the doorway. I turn off the TV and am out of my gaming chair in an instant.

Dad and Mom give each other a look but say nothing. I ignore them and dance past them into the hallway.

"There he is." My brother Tyler smiles as he bounces his one-year-old son, Blake, in his thick arms.

"Hi, Jake!" Jennifer wraps me in a warm embrace before she takes her son from Tyler and nudges him to hug me too.

Tyler gives his wife a glance that says *I know*, before hugging me too. Anthony and Nathan follow soon after. But all three of their hugs are quick and feel forced.

"So, how was cross-country?" Anthony asks.

"It's okay." I shrug. "We didn't make it to state, but we did win our last race."

"Is Hanson still coach?"

"Unfortunately."

"What do you mean? Coach Hanson was the best!" Anthony grabs Nathan's shoulder. "Remember that one track practice he caught you peeing on the side of the track and made you run four laps?"

Tyler, Nathan, Anthony, and Dad all laugh.

I feel so small surrounded by their more-than-six-foot frames.

Nathan plops down on one of the barstools and reaches for a carrot from the veggie tray. "I swear, that was my fastest mile time."

"Probably because you were too embarrassed to notice how tired you were," Tyler says and they all laugh again.

I back out of the center of the group as they continue talking about their favorite coach. I've heard this story more than once. Not from Anthony or Nathan but from Coach Hanson himself, who has a never-ending supply of awesome stories about his favorite three athletes. My brothers loved him, but he *adored* them, especially Tyler. I don't call my brother to get updates on his professional football career as a running back with the Chargers because Coach Hanson keeps me more than informed.

My dad and brothers continue laughing about some other shared memory they all enjoyed, which I was probably too young to join. Would they notice if I slipped back into my room and continued playing with my friends? Probably not. But Dad would find out and then tomorrow he'd sit me down for another one of his talks about how I need to face the real world instead of escaping to my video games.

I join my sister-in-law who sits my nephew in his high chair.

I'm only six years younger than Nathan, nine younger than Anthony, and twelve younger than Tyler, but by the time I turned twelve, Nathan was already heading off to college.

"How's your bird-watching club?" Jennifer asks.

"It's okay." I let baby Blake grab my finger as he fights against the buckle. "We went on a walk last week up in the Jamez and managed to see a spotted owl."

"Wow, that's cool. Is that one of the rare birds?"

"Yeah. I've never seen one before. They're much more common to find on the West Coast or in Mexico."

"That's gr—"

"Okay, boys, it's time for dinner!" my mom yells over their next round of laughter.

They all come in and join us around the table. Dad sits at the head of the table with a joyful gleam in his eyes. Being around my brothers always brings that light back to his eyes.

"It's good to have the family back together." Dad reaches out to hold Mom's and Anthony's hands. The rest of us settle down and complete the circle before Dad leads us in prayer.

I open my eyes to a bunch of grass. I'm lying in a puddle.

Kee! Jip leaves the shade of my pack and hobbles toward me.

I sit up and rub my eyes. The side of my head throbs. A soft breeze tugs at the top of the grasses to accent the silence.

It was only a dream.

I slump back to the ground. My back splashes into the shallow water. I'm alone. Millions of miles separate me from my old life.

I'm going to die.

Jip stares at me from the edge of the puddle. He sits on his hind feet and bobs his head up and down. That's his way of telling me he wants something.

I'm in an area of packed-down grass with tall grass surrounding it. "What just happened, Jip?"

He shakes his head and wobbles, then squints like he's in pain.

"Do you have a headache too?" He must, but what would cause us both to have headaches?

"The rhino animal! Did he do that to us?" The last thing I remember was the creature opening up that red skin-mane thing. But the dream felt so real. No, it was real. That was Thanksgiving dinner last year. But I wasn't remembering it; I was reliving it.

I pour some water into a pot lid for Jip. He laps it up with his little red tongue.

"Did he hypnotize us somehow?"

Thunder rumbles in the distance. Large rain clouds loom in the west. The bottoms of the clouds are dark with rain. The sun is much lower in the sky. I check my watch.

We were out for two hours.

I quickly gather our supplies, latch on my backpack, and pick up my freeloader named Jip. He *kees* as I pull the sling strap over my shoulder.

"Sorry, buddy, but we need to go. I don't want to spend the night out here in this prairie, especially with that storm coming."

I can't see the hill with all this tall grass, so I pick a south-ward path made by the psychic rhino. I can cover more ground on this path and the psychic rhino—or psyno as I'll name it—must not eat meat because it didn't hurt me when I was unconscious.

Of course, if I don't find the hill, none of this matters.

I can't make a shelter in this grass, nor should I risk a fire. If I don't make it to the hill, I'll freeze tonight.

N
NE
E
SE
S
SW
W
NW
(Magnectic North)
PORTAL MOUNTAIN
ALIEN RUINS

CHAPTER 13
WET

DAY 4

The rain hits. Hard. It feels amazing. The muggy heat is gone in seconds. But the rain doesn't stop. No matter what I do, curtains of rain douse me, Jip, the grass, and my pack. The temperature drops.

To protect what little remains dry in my pack, I stop and wait out the last of the rain. I drape my raincoat over us. This gets us out of the rain, but we are drenched. Water drips off the sides of my coat and onto my already-soaked hiking boots.

At least an hour passes, and the rain shows no signs of stopping.

Jip nestles close to me on my lap as we both shiver.

Why couldn't the rain come after we reached the hill?

"Thank you, God, for answering my prayer for rain," I say sarcastically.

Hunger gnaws at my stomach. It's been almost a full thirty hours since I've eaten. Usually I can ignore the ache while I'm moving, but not when I'm sitting and doing nothing. All I think about is a nice, hot pepperoni-and-green-chile pizza from Dion's with a large Coke.

I adjust my legs to a more comfortable position.

Jip sinks his tiny claws into me.

"Stop it!"

He glares up at me and shivers.

"You know, your crabby attitude isn't helping. Being mad at me won't make you warmer or bring us food."

Kee!

"For the last time, no. If we pull out my dad's sleeping bag, it will get soaked. And if it's wet, there's no chance we'll survive the cold night."

Jip blinks and stares back out at the rain.

The small *taps*, *plips*, and *plats* of raindrops hitting my raincoat, puddles, and grass combine into a loud din of cascading water from the sky.

This isn't even a level in the video game. It's like a never-ending loading screen that can kill me.

How did things get so bad so fast? The last two days were great. I was starting to think I might survive. Now, I can hardly unclench my hands, and I'd give anything for a blazing fire.

Why do all my plans keep failing? How could I have predicted a psyno would hypnotize me and cost us hours out of the day?

This is why I hate the outdoors.

Sure, it's beautiful, fun to explore, and there are birds, but one wrong decision and death is right there ready to pounce.

The sky was clear when I walked out into the grassy field. I did nothing wrong.

Even if the rain stopped, I still probably wouldn't find the hill before night comes, and all the wood will be too wet to start a fire.

No matter what happens in the next few hours, I'm going to freeze to death.

The sky darkens into night, and still the temperature drops.

"J-Jesus, please h-help me." I shiver. "You've been there

for m-me so many t-t-times at school. Why aren't you here n-now?"

I pet Jip. His wet body trembles as he presses close to me for warmth.

"Heck, if you aren't even strong enough to k-keep me from appearing here, are you strong enough to p-protect me from this storm?"

My question stirs to life something my youth pastor said a few months ago: *"The Israelites likely believed God wasn't big enough to save them. Then God parted the Red Sea. Remember this the next time you doubt God."*

Trusting God was easy when I sat in a heated room with pizza on my paper plate. But here—in a place where I can't see or feel him—God feels light-years away.

"Okay then, J-Jesus, please part the r-rain."

Nothing changes.

"I thought so."

It makes sense now why the Israelites would get mad at Moses and God so quickly when they were cornered against the Red Sea. I know God let them be cornered so he could show how powerful he is to provide an escape. But they didn't know that at the time.

"How can I t-t-trust you when there's no w-way out of this?"

What would God have told the Israelites as the Egyptians surrounded them on the shore of the Red Sea?

Do not fear, for I am with you.

I let out a frustrated huff.

"Really, God? I'll follow and listen to y-you, but you can't tell me not to f-fear." My stomach rumbles. "I have the right to be afraid. I'm millions of miles away from h-home, I haven't eaten in over a day, I'm w-wet, cold, and I have nowhere to s-sleep tonight that will keep me from freezing to death."

Before I finish my rant, I already know God's response: Do not fear.

I roll my eyes. "Okay, God, what do you want m-me to do?"

The last time I asked God this question, I was walking to school. The cold winter air stung my face. Each breath puffed out a cloud of water vapor. I stood at the entrance to the football field. I could walk a quarter mile around it, but I was running late and had a test in my first class.

Coincidentally, a few football jocks chose that day to hang out at the field before school. If they bullied me in the hallways where a teacher could intervene at any moment, who knew what they'd do outside.

I asked Jesus what I should do. His answer: start walking.

So I did.

They noticed me and started calling me names like Fake Rogers. Several moved to cut me off, but then a popular girl rolled up in her dad's blue Mustang and asked if they wanted to go for a spin. With whoops and hollers, they left me alone and went with her.

Jip's little body trembles in my hands.

Start walking.

The words resonate within me as they did that day on the football field. I gaze out at the rain falling on the endless sea of grass.

"Why can't you ask me to do easy th-things?" But I either wait until I freeze to death here, or I hope for the best and walk.

I lift Jip off my lap. He glares at me and sinks his claws through my jacket and into my arm. I wince, but I don't let him win. I set him down outside my tiny raincoat shelter. His paws sink into a puddle. He stares at me like I'm the devil, then leaps back onto my lap, bringing a wave of muddy water with him.

I move an inch and he sinks his claws into me. "L-look, bud. I know you hate water, b-but I'm as wet as you."

I stand up and stretch my numb legs. A puddle quickly forms in the indentation of my bottom.

This is miserable.

I hang my raincoat over my head and backpack. I don't care how wet I get since I'm already soaked, but I can't let my pack get wetter.

Using the compass I failed to earn, we journey south—or north, according to it. The rain continues its depressing pitter-patter without change. With no more psyno paths to lead me south, tall blades of grass now *whap* me in the face and slide across my body like hundreds of wet dog tongues.

I hold Jip and reach forward to part the grass with my free arm before I step through. I repeat this process over and over as the gray sky darkens. Colors fade to shades, shades to silhouettes, and silhouettes to utter darkness. With the light of the stars blocked by thick storm clouds, it's so black I can't see my hand.

I would turn on my headlamp, but all I'd see is grass. I'd rather save what little remains of my battery for a time when it will be more useful.

Still the rain drums on.

"How c-can you d-do this to me?" I yell out at the endless abyss of darkness. "Do you know how much I hate this?"

God says nothing.

I clench my jaw and walk on. He told me to walk, and here I am wandering blind. According to my watch, I've been at this hopeless charade for over an hour now. And where is God? Nowhere.

I huff. Why do I still believe in God?

Something in the back of my mind triggers. As mad as I am and as impossible as my circumstances appear, I know he exists. He's talked with me and guided me.

But I'm still mad at him. He's done nothing but ruin my

life these past few days. Sure, I'm still alive, but my joints are frozen.

When I reach out my arm again, I don't find any grass. I step into the void and reach out again. Nothing.

Something feels off. There's no pitter-pattering of rain in front of me.

I step forward again and this time the rain stops. It still falls behind me, just not on me.

I quickly pull out my headlamp and click it on.

A small cave opens before me. It's about fifteen feet deep, twenty feet wide, and twenty feet high. It's shaped like someone came and took a giant scoop out of the hill. The floor is flat and covered with short grass. Best of all, the cave is warm!

The farther into the cave I step, the warmer it gets. The walls are all warm and soft to the touch. They feel more like dirt than rock. The rocks have weird patterns and splotches. I suppose that should make sense though since I'm on a different planet and there's no telling how these rocks formed.

I press myself against the wall and let its warmth seep into me. Either I'm one degree above frozen, or these walls are ninety degrees.

I may actually survive tonight.

My muscles relax. I breathe out slowly and slide my back down the wall until I'm sitting. I pull my damp legs close to my body and cradle Jip, who still shivers.

As the tension leaves my body, so does my anger. I hang my head in shame. "God, I'm so sorry. You knew all along where you were leading me. You cared about me the whole time, even when I yelled at you. I shouldn't have complained or been mad at you. I should've trusted you. Please forgive me."

He doesn't say anything, but I can picture his caring face. He watched me the entire time.

"Thank you for speaking to me and giving me the faith to start walking. Please help me to remember next time I'm in a scary situation that I can trust you and not freak out."

The moment the words leave my mouth, I remember I'm alone on a planet a billion light-years away from the closest human.

Joshua, chapter 1, verse 9 flows out of my mouth, "'Have I not commanded you? Be strong and courageous. Do not be afraid; do not be discouraged, for the LORD your God will be with you wherever you go.'"

All of this comes to mind as if God is saying, *Okay, Jake, since you asked, let me remind you that even on this dangerous and mysterious planet you don't need to be afraid. I am with you. Trust that I have a plan with your good in mind.*

I frown. "Don't use my prayer against me."

But didn't you ask me to remind you?

I shake my head and get up. "I don't care." I open my backpack and rummage through it for my dad's sleeping bag and some dry clothes. "You can't apply that to this situation. It's not fair. Being here on this planet is bad. It isn't for my good. It can't be your will, and I know you messed up."

I focus on getting ready for bed to drown out God's voice. I don't care what he has to say. I won't believe him. I won't stop fearing.

But a part of me doesn't believe my own words.

CHAPTER 14
DIGGING DEEP

DAY 5

I wake to the ground rumbling. The earth shook throughout the night, but this feels closer. Morning light filters into the cavern.

Jip jumps out of my arms, clawing my forearms in the process. He hobbles toward the cave exit with frightful *kees*.

I pull the sleeping bag off and stand. Wind blows between my legs, reminding me that I'm only wearing boxers.

Standing at the mouth of the cave, Jip calls for me frantically as the rumbling continues.

That's right; an earthquake could collapse the cave.

But my clothes and backpack!

I throw the sleeping bag and some of my clothes out of the cave and race back in for another load. Jip yells at me but doesn't dare enter the cave. Next I haul out my backpack. Then I go for my boots.

The moment I turn to leave with my hiking boots, the ground at the back of the cave bursts open.

I stumble toward the exit, but the ground rises under me. The mud springs out of the ground and fills the cave as it rolls outward. Much of it spills out of the cave, yet more continues to flow in, gradually lifting me toward the cave's ceiling.

I throw my boots out of the cave and flop forward to swim through the muck. It sucks me back the moment I stop pushing myself forward.

Outside, Jip cries out in concern and scampers on top of my backpack to escape the mudslide.

The mud keeps rising, and I still haven't moved more than…

My stomach drops.

I'll suffocate if the muck rises to the top of the cave before I escape.

The sludge sucks me back just as fast as I swim forward. The exit is only ten feet away, but I can't move!

I make eye contact with Jip. *Kee!* He hops off my bag and approaches the mud as if he's about to come rescue me. He tests the mud with his paw and immediately his ears flatten. We both know he'll never escape the mud if he enters it. He hops away, then turns back to the mudslide and cautiously approaches again.

Pax did the same thing once when a thunderstorm caught us by surprise. I took a shortcut home across the arroyo. The drainage canal only had a few inches of water, so I took off my shoes and carried her across. I told her to stay as I waded back to get my shoes and backpack. The moment I turned back to Pax, a wave of water rushed through, turning inches of slow water into a three-foot-deep gushing river.

If the current had caught me, it would have swept me away into the deadly torrents. Pax stepped toward the raging water once she saw my hesitation. If I went to the bridge a quarter mile downstream, she'd try crossing to me.

"Stay, Jip!" I yell as I try to push myself forward in the muck.

The cave's ceiling is only four feet above me now. I reach and grab a crack in the ceiling and pull. I move a few inches.

I reach forward and slide my fingers into another crevice of the rock and pull while kicking my feet like I'm swimming.

With something solid to anchor myself to, the suction can't pull me back.

As the mud rises, I flip onto my back.

Jip's muffled *kee* barely reaches me through the small gap between the rising mud and the rock ceiling.

"Stay there, buddy!" I yell as I find another notch in the rock and pull.

My fingers latch around the outer lip of the cave just before the mud rises and presses me against the ceiling. Jip's cries are cut off as mud fills my ears. I close my eyes and take one final breath. Mud rolls around the sides of my body to seal me against the top. It presses into every corner of my body.

Everything stops, but I can't move. The mud is tight around me.

My heart hammers from intense claustrophobia.

I'm dead. My cause of death: not outrunning the world's slowest mudslide.

I'm so close. Just three feet away from air. I grip the rock. My freedom. My survival.

With panic fueling me, I push my other hand out of the mud and grab the rock.

No matter how hard I pull, the most I manage is an inch of progress at a time. Just like crossing the flooding arroyo: one inch at a time. I couldn't slip because if I did, Pax would jump in after me, and we'd both drown. But I made it then, and I'll make it now.

My lungs rage for air, and my pulse pounds in my ear like a thousand drums. I focus on Jip.

In my mind, I see him pushing and pulling against the mud with wild eyes as it sucks him in more.

Please, God! Please help me!

I grit my teeth. My arms tremble.

Reaching farther out of the cave, my fingers latch on to a

tiny ledge between the grass. When I pull, the rock holds strong.

My arms feel weak, and my lungs burn.

Light blasts my closed eyelids. With one final pull, my head breaks free of the mud.

I gasp for air and open my eyes.

The mud still encases my body like an oddly comfortable, form-fitting mattress. "Jip?" I yell.

Kee!

I flop my head back against the mud and exhale.

Then I gag and nearly vomit as the stench of poop floods me.

I've smelled this stench of methane while trekking through the Rio Grande's muddy spillovers in Albuquerque. Knowing this must be swamp mud doesn't free me from the horrific stench.

I gag again.

Weak from hunger, I work for several minutes to haul myself out of the mud. I flop onto the grass and sigh. The cool early morning air chills my exposed body. My arms shake with exhaustion, but I manage to get up and stagger around and down the gentle slope beside the cave entrance.

Two feet into the mud, Jip is buried up to his chin. I pluck him out and hold him tight.

My chest heaves and my eyes water. I collapse to the ground. "I can't do this anymore, God!"

I'm exhausted, weak, starving, humiliated, lonely, and utterly defeated. My back aches from the pterodactyl and volcano incident, my clothes are wet from last night's bout with hypothermia, and now Jip and I are covered in poop-smelling mud.

Why can't I have a single day that goes according to plan?

I'm never safe here. It's like high school but worse; I don't know what threat will hit me next.

I need to guard myself against creatures attacking from

the sky, exploding volcanoes, suffocating mud, freezing rain, starvation, and who knows what else.

This is no video game; it's a torture chamber.

If God is supposed to bring me to good things, why does he keep letting me fall into all these hardships?

It's a good thing I had those bullies in school or else I'd never be strong enough to survive here.

A thought tugs at me. I push it away, but it comes right back.

"But—" I shake my head. "No, that doesn't make sense."

Except it does make sense, and I don't like it.

I throw my head into my hands and dig my fingers into my muddy hair. "You seriously want me to thank you for the football jocks?" I stand and pace.

How crazy must I look right now? I'm mostly naked, covered in mud, and yelling at the sky.

"God, I know they helped prepare me for this place, but they were a problem, not a blessing. And they definitely weren't your gift to me.

"And if you gave me them to prepare me for this, then why are you giving me these insane trials? Is this preparing me for something else?"

I freeze. My whole body goes cold. Goose bumps race across my skin as the truth sinks in: God *is* using these trials to prepare me. Which means…

Something much worse is coming.

CHAPTER 15
PINK BALLOONS

DAY 5

I sit up and gag at a horrendous smell. I'm on the ground shivering. Cold sweat covers my body. It's still early in the morning, and I'm covered in mud, which now hangs on me like a wet blanket.

I must've fainted.

At least I escaped the crudslide.

Jip is rolling in the wet grass to wipe away the mud. To the north rises the Portal Mountain range. The river I followed out of the mountains flows a quarter mile west of me. And I stand on the edge of a hill. There are dozens of other hills, but none of them are nearly the size of this one.

"I made it to the hill?" I must've hiked seventy miles by foot through uncharted terrain.

It feels unreal. I forgot my trek had an end destination.

My journey is over.

I let out the most relieved sigh of my life. I no longer have to keep wandering through unknown land. I don't have to hike fifteen miles today. After I bathe and find food, I can relax.

My whole life is about to get much easier.

I can't believe I did it.

All it takes is two steps toward my supplies before searing hunger hits me. Lifting each foot feels ten times harder. As much as the ravenous hunger tempts me to stuff my mouth with dirt just to fill my stomach with something, exhaustion makes me want to drop to the ground and sleep.

I gather my supplies and climb the hill as Jip slowly hobbles after me.

I put my hand against a strange palm tree to rest. It looks like a palm tree because the trunk is round and branchless, however it has only one big blue leaf. It's like the umbrella tree except this leaf is shaped like a funnel. The stump is six feet tall, and its long funnel-like leaf rises a story above the ground with an eight-foot diameter. The sun shines through the leaf. At the bottom of the funnel, sunlight ripples through a large pool of collected rainwater.

Perfect!

I cut a small slit in the bottom of the funnel leaf with my pocketknife. The water squirts out in a steady stream. It's not the cleanest water to shower with, but I'd take anything over this poop mud.

When I finish, I still smell like I rolled in a cow pie, but the mud is gone.

"That's better, but how long is that smell going to stick to us?" I search for Jip, but he's gone. "Jip?"

Birds sing their morning songs all around me. I listen for Jip through their calls, but one bird literally sounds like someone burping. Another makes a smacking noise in the tree to my right. I follow the noise. Sure enough, Jip's the smacking bird.

"What are you eating?" I sidestep to get a better view through the foliage. He sits on a branch at the top of a tree, munching on a pink ball about the size of his head. He stares down at me like he forgot I existed.

"Did you think to share?"

He pauses for a moment to mock me, then continues gorging himself.

"Don't you remember how I shared my scale deer with you?" But there's no point in reasoning with the stubborn critter. Unfortunately, the only pink fruit are at the top of the skinny tree.

The one Jip munches on is the smallest of them. Most are as big as a soccer ball, with some even bigger.

How in the world will I get up there? The branches are too small to hold me.

I shake the tree. Jip gives an annoyed *kee* and drops his fruit. Other than his fruit, nothing else falls. Except…

Several float into the sky like pink balloons.

What in the world?

"That's one way to spread seeds."

After it's clear the balloons won't come back down, I examine the fruit Jip dropped. The inside is hollow, but the thick skin is fleshy and seems tasty. I bite off a tiny piece. The sweet taste of mango floods my mouth. I'm so hungry I don't mind the waxy texture nor do I care that Jip ate half of it. I chow down on the little balloon fruit until it's gone.

I'm ravenous for more. Jip has another fruit in hand. This one's bigger. Again, I shake the tree.

Jip lets go of the fruit to grab the branch. He scolds me with a *kee*.

"Hey! Watch your language!"

He ignores me and continues reprimanding me with the K-word. After a final *kee*, he turns back to find another fruit.

The bigger fruit is waxier and less sweet. Still, it's food, and I'm starving. This one is also more hollow as if it is a balloon.

My stomach still aches with hunger after I finish the second fruit.

Should I shake the tree again? Jip would hate me, but it's

not like he's courteous enough to pick and drop a fruit for me of his own accord. So it's really his fault.

I look up at Jip, who holds his third fruit now. I want to let him finish eating, but if he gets full, he won't grab another one for me.

"Drop it, Jip."

Unsurprisingly, he doesn't understand the command. But I did get his attention. He glares at me as I put my hand on the tree. Just as I'm about to shake the tree, he lets go of the fruit and grips the branch with all four feet.

"Good boy!"

Because it's a bigger fruit and because Jip didn't bite into it, the balloon fruit he dropped slowly floats down to the ground like a three-day-old helium balloon. I bite into the fruit and suck in the gas like I did as a kid with balloons after a party ended.

"Hi, Jip!" My voice is a high-pitched squeak. I burst with laughter. "It *is* helium! I knew it!"

Jip gives me an odd glance before he searches for another balloon fruit.

The bigger the fruit gets, the hollower and waxier they become. This one tastes less like fruit and more like a flavorless stick of gum. And, like gum, it takes a lot of chewing before I can swallow.

Two bites into the fruit, the ground moves under me. I stumble and catch myself on a tree. Then the ground moves the other way. I stumble forward and fall. I catch myself with my hands, but the movement wrenches my back, bringing to life my injury after the pterodactyl dropped me.

I groan and roll to my back. The trees sway above me, but I don't feel any wind. Jip, on the other hand, is fine on his branch. The trees aren't moving in the same direction. They sway, swirl, and start falling to the ground before swinging around and standing back upright.

The ground rolls like a flag flapping in the wind. I close my eyes and try not to vomit.

Is it an earthquake?

I crawl, tumble, and crawl some more until I reach a tree. I wrap my arms and legs around it. But what if the tree falls? And what if the ground splits open under me?

I grab on tighter and close my eyes.

CHAPTER 16
FORT JAKE

DAY 5

Slowly, the earthquake fades. And somehow I hold down what little food I ate.

Jip watches me, his eyes wide with concern. His front two paws are on my leg as he leans forward and sniffs my arm. When we make eye contact, he gives me a little lick.

I release my death grip on the tree and roll to my back. My spine flares with pain. The trees tower above me like nothing happened. The sun flickers behind rustling green and orange leaves. And puffy clouds slowly glide across the teal sky in silent procession.

The ground still rolls every now and then, but it doesn't affect Jip.

Did I imagine it all?

As I sit up, Jip pushes off my leg and hops over to the balloon fruit I dropped when the quake started. He steps on it several times until all the helium is pressed out of it, then he picks up a side and starts nibbling.

The ground rolls under me. I set a hand down to stabilize myself. Jip is still on two feet holding the balloon fruit.

"Did you feel that?"

Jip stares at me like I'm a moron.

"Then why do *I* feel the ground shift?"

Is it the helium?

Breathing in the gas was the only thing I did differently from Jip, and he was pretty careful not to inhale the gas inside the balloon.

I stand slowly. Everything still moves around me, but it's tolerable now. As I bend down to pick up my backpack and the balloon fruit, Jip releases the fruit, jumps onto my pack, and then onto my back.

"Excuse me?" I laugh. "Am I a horse or something?"

I'm glad he's not digging his claws into my back, but he's also not getting off.

"You do know I need to carry my backpack, right?"

Since he doesn't move, I continue looping the straps over my arms. Jip settles on top of my left shoulder strap.

"Are you a parrot now?"

He faces forward in anticipation. Then he glances at me, as if curious why I haven't started moving.

"You're a strange creature." I reach over and pet his soft shoulder. He leans into my hand and nuzzles me like Pax used to do, his small ram's horn soft under my touch.

"What else will you start doing as you heal?" I smile and shake my head as I walk. It's much easier carrying him on my shoulder than in a sling.

I munch the balloon fruit as I journey up the north-facing side of the hill. Near the crest, I find a fallen log that lodged itself into the *Y* of another tree to create the perfect start of a lean-to.

Several guys in my Trail Life troop went on a camping trip to get the Survival Skills badge. They had to make a shelter and sleep in it with no sleeping bag or insulate pad. They could only use a space blanket. This sounded terrible at the time, but now I'd be happy just to have something over my head to keep the rain out and trap the heat in.

I smirk as I start gathering logs and sticks to create my lean-to. What would my younger self think of me now?

He'd think I'm so cool. I've slept outside without a tent or sleeping pad for five nights now. I have a rabbit-thing on my shoulder. I've fought off multiple predators, hunted, foraged, escaped a volcano, survived a crudslide. And *I flew with a pterodactyl!*

Would he even recognize me?

If I told him I was his older version, would he believe me?

Absolutely not.

Yet here I am! I never would've attempted any of these feats before because I thought they'd kill me.

I was so wrong about myself.

Despite what my dad thinks, I'm not worthless without him and my brothers.

I've done things I was never willing to do before. I still don't like being hungry, hot, or cold at night. I don't like having uncomfortable beds, but it's kind of cool here. It's exciting not knowing how I'll get my next meal. Constructing my new home with my own hands makes me feel accomplished and capable. And it's awesome to be exploring and seeing things no one has ever seen before.

Didn't Matt, Oliver, and I mention several times while exploring a *Minecraft* world that it would be cool to explore a new world in real life?

"God, I'm still mad at you for bringing me here. But it *is* kind of fun. Spending a year here is definitely too long, but if I only had to survive a week, I'd probably be okay with it."

How else have I been limiting myself?

If I've grown this much in less than a week, how much more will I grow? Who will I become? What other crazy dangers will I face?

I lean another long log against the fallen tree and look up. "I'm just now discovering I can do much more than I thought possible, but you've known all along. You know who I am and who I will be.

"I don't like all the difficulties but help me trust you. Help me appreciate all you've done for me. And when you ask me to do hard things, help me not to focus on who I know myself to be. Instead, help me focus on you and how you've been faithful to lead me in the past."

I step back and examine my lean-to. To one side of the fallen tree, I have several large logs and a bunch of other big branches piled against it. There's plenty of room under it for me to sleep. It's far from perfect and not really that great of a shelter. I'll still need to make the roof rainproof. I should also pile logs against the other side to trap the warmth more and to protect me from wild animals. But it's a great start. And it's something *I* made.

A gust of wind blows through the forest. Speckles of late-morning sunlight dance on the forest floor.

I decided to move to this hill, and I'm the one who charted the path to get here. I made these decisions, not my dad or brothers.

"I'll call it Fort Jake," I say to Jip, who never left my shoulder. "And after some work, it will go from being the best fort on the planet to the best fort in the universe."

Jip *kees* in agreement.

A warmth grows in my chest. I may just survive this year here.

Using Dad's compass to pinpoint magnetic south, I face north and the direction I'll need to go in a year to reach the portal.

I draw a big arrow in the dirt pointing the way home. When I turn back to my shelter, I hold up my compass. "If my dad could see me now, Jip, do you think he'd say I've earned this? Would he recognize that I did something, or would he focus on all my failures here as he's always done?"

Have I finally met the qualifications of manhood?

N
NE
E
SE
S
SW
W
NW
(Magnectic North)
PORTAL MOUNTAIN
ALIEN RUINS
VOLCANO
FORT JAKE
CANYON LAKE

CHAPTER 17
SETTLING IN

DAY 24

Burping birds—or burds as I've named them—break the peaceful quiet of night as the light of dawn grows on the horizon. Their rude songs echo through the forest every morning. I never thought I'd say this about a bird, but I genuinely hate them. They are too small to eat, their plumes are an ugly gray, they've pooped on me a dozen times, and they always wake me up too early. Is anything about them nice or pleasant? My official birder answer is no.

Jip looks up at me without moving his head. He stretches next to me in my dad's sleeping bag, as we both start our morning routines.

My timer reads thirty hours and twenty-five minutes. I reset the timer and start it again for the new day. Just for kicks and giggles, I check the time and date back on Earth: Saturday, September 10, 1:24 a.m.

A month has passed since I traveled through the portal.

If I were home, I'd have a cross-country meet in a few hours. Homecoming would be just a week or two away. Dad probably would've talked to me a half-dozen times about asking Sophie to the dance and facing my fears.

I laugh and sit up. My head is just inches from the top of

my shelter. It's hard to imagine being afraid of asking a girl to a dance when the fears I face daily center around survival.

I've definitely changed in the last month.

If I could go home right now, would I be scared to ask Sophie? Would she say yes?

Does she think of me as she picks fruit during practice runs? If I hadn't fallen through the portal, I wonder if I would've told her how I felt about her by now. Does she miss me on practice runs, or has she found someone else to run with? Does she still think about me?

The birder club would've started up by now too. I hope the first few meetings went well without me. Is Benny, the freshman who motivated me to keep the club going that first semester, still active in the club even though I'm not there?

Has everyone moved on without me?

What about my family? Are they still searching for me? I hope not. They must be heartbroken. Even worse, they probably think I'm dead.

I push the thought out of my head and step into the chilly open air. I'll never know the answers to those questions until I get home. And getting home requires staying focused.

As I climb out of our shelter, the large leaves that cover the entrance shuffle and slide back into place. The early rays of sunlight pierce horizontally through the foliage. The air smells humid, which may mean another evening of thunderstorms.

Jip hops past me and claws at the stone I set over my refrigerator, which is a simple hole I dug into the ground.

"Starting the day quick, huh? No time to breathe, just straight to snack time?" As I approach, he takes a few steps back and sits. His eyes lock on me as he stamps his little paws impatiently. I remove the rock weight and set aside the plank of tree bark before crawling into the hole. My body blocks most of the light coming through the entrance, but I don't need light to find what I stashed. Our breakfast today consists of two slices of dried squid fish—or squish as I call them. Despite their slimy, rubbery touch, they harden into crisp sheets when I smoke them over the fire.

I break off the tentacles and toss them to Jip. He loves them.

With the rain from last night, the coals in my firepit are cold. So I gather some kindling and use my lighter to get a small fire going. Once it's strong, I throw balloon-fruit pieces into a pot of water along with some leaves I picked from a tree that taste like cinnamon. While I wait for my tea to boil, I sit on my log and pull out my Bible as I do every morning.

I continue reading in Luke chapter 5 as I munch on the crispy squish. I don't think I would've ever eaten something like this for breakfast back home, but here the game isn't about taste; it's about survival.

Jip finishes his tentacles and curls into a ball on my lap. I pet him with one hand and hold my Bible with the other.

Verse 28 catches my attention: *"and Levi got up, left every-thing and followed him."*

Levi left everything to follow Jesus? Did he and the other disciples know how much their lives would change? Or that there was no going back?

Well, I suppose they could have gone back. And their choice to follow Jesus was theirs to make in the first place. Unlike my situation.

And God used them to do incredible things. But what's God going to do through me here? Give me PTSD? If I was too weak for God to do anything through me back on Earth, how could he possibly use me here?

The pot starts boiling. I pour out a serving of tea into my aluminum cup and add some cold water to cool it. My whole body relaxes as I sip the sweet and tangy tea. I've tried adding a few different ingredients, but this combination still wins. I inhale the sweet aroma and swirl the leaves and fruit pieces around in my cup. I was never a big tea or coffee person, but here it's nice to have a routine.

Here.

"God, why did they get to choose their path, but you forced me here?"

Do you really want to go back?

The question hits me in a way that I know it must be God speaking.

"Of course I want to go back. That's all I've wanted!"

Jip looks up at me from his spot on my lap. He blinks and lays his head back down.

I sip my tea. My perfected tea. To my left is our now fully rainproof shelter and slowly growing stockpile of food in my refrigerator.

I do want to go home, but the thought of leaving all of this —especially Jip—weighs on me. A part of me would be sad to give up this life I've built.

But I would leave… wouldn't I?

I put my Bible back inside my shelter and grab my backpack. I breathe a sigh of relief as I slide my arms through the straps. It's been twenty days since I reached Fort Jake, and I'm still grateful for the light pack. Now that I don't need to carry my sleeping bag, all my clothes, and my kitchen supplies, my pack weighs a fraction of what it did before.

I separate some of the less burned wood, pile all the coals into a little heap, and cover them with ashes to keep them warm. If I'm back by high noon to escape the midday heat, I shouldn't need to use my lighter to restart the fire.

"Come on, Jip."

He scampers over and hops beside me as we make our way to Canyon Lake.

I stop at the end of the trees and scan the skies. I thought these meadows were far enough from the pterodactyls, but I saw one circling overhead about a week ago. I was able to hide in the tall grasses until it left, but now my number one rule is: always check the skies.

Rule number two: always bring a knife and spear no matter how far I plan to go.

I haven't found any dangerous predators in these plains, but I'd hate to discover I'm wrong without my spear. And, well, my four-inch knife is always useful, especially if I have to throw my spear.

With the coast clear, I bend down for Jip to jump onto my shoulder. In one leap, he sticks the landing and settles onto his favorite spot on my backpack strap.

The cool morning air smells moist and crisp. Splotches of sunlight pierce through the trees on my hill to gently warm my exposed arms and face. A small warning that later today the sun will be much stronger.

I've walked this way so many times I've worn a thin trail through the grass, which is damp from the rain last night. But now I know to wear nylon pants and long sleeves whenever I enter the grass. I don't mind them getting wet because the afternoons are always hot.

Jip paws at my shoulder. *Kee!*

"Okay, but I won't throw you as much as I did yesterday. I'm still sore." He climbs into my hands. I lower him and wait until he's settled. "Ready?"

Once he stops moving, he gives the ready signal: a simple *kee*—like all of his other forms of communication. I throw him as high as I can.

He spreads his four legs and catches the small breeze to glide. He circles, dips, and rises in the breeze like an expert fighter pilot.

What must it be like to soar through the air like a bird?

I've caught myself plotting how I may ride a pterodactyl safely. I'd have to start with a hatchling and raise it so it wouldn't eat me.

After a good twenty-second flight, Jip glides closer. A

second before he reaches me, he curls in his tail and collapses the skin flaps between his front and hind legs to make an expert landing on my shoulder.

I thought he only had a puffy bunny-like tail until he started flying. When he glides, his tail unfurls into a perfect five-inch rudder, which he flicks to direct himself.

Before I take two steps, he paws at my shoulder again.

"Fine, but you better keep up because I'm not waiting for you." I launch him into the air again. He starts his aerial acrobatics as I walk on.

We do this over and over until we reach Canyon Lake. Jip lands on my shoulder, and I set him on the edge of the canyon before I continue down to the water.

It's not much of a canyon now that it's filled with water, but the ground split open right where the river ran only a week ago during a particularly bad earthquake. The river poured down from a waterfall to the north and had already filled the bottom when I found it the next morning. The canyon was about two hundred feet deep and forty feet wide. Since then, the water eroded the walls. Now it's only thirty feet deep with the water filling it and five hundred feet wide. I haven't walked its full length, but it's at least three miles long.

It's unnerving that a massive canyon split open less than a mile from Fort Jake, but this lake is perfect for fishing. Some huge squish swim here. I can only catch the little ones that wander close to the shore.

I'm still a beginner at this survival video game, so I can only fish from shore, but soon I'll level up and learn the skills needed to build a boat and catch the bigger squish in the middle of the lake. I need to learn soon because I'll have to catch bigger squish to stockpile enough food before I reach the winter level of this game called Jake Rogers' Planet.

Do I really want to leave this place?

I miss my birder club and my friends, especially Sophie,

Matt, and Oliver. But is seeing them again worth returning home to my dad? I'll miss my mom and the little bits of time we got to spend together, but is that worth always being compared to my legendary brothers at school?

I don't have to worry about that on this planet. Here, it's not about what my brothers did or what jobs I'm able to apply for ten years from now. Here, I focus on today and prepping for the winter. I know what I need to do each day. I make my own decisions. I have my own life.

I find the anchor stick in the side of the sandy bank and slowly pull the paracord attached to it. My woven grass basket emerges from the water. As the water drains out, three medium-sized squish flop around inside. I grin. That's one to eat and two more to add to the stockpile. Their slimy tentacles twist around my arm, then slide off as I toss them into a small holding puddle I dug beside the lake.

That's odd. The lake is lower. Not by much. Just four or five inches. It used to be only a foot from my puddle, but now it's almost three feet away.

I stand up. Something is off. Other than the lake being lower, everything appears the same. Everything is as quiet as normal. An occasional prairie flier calls, and the wind rustles the colorful grasses. But something is different.

In the book *Hatchet*, Brian developed this same sense. Sometimes he knew something was off before he recognized what it was.

I walk back up to Jip and sit down to think it through.

There are a lot of prairie fliers out this morning. That or else they are calling to each other more. The grass also sounds louder in the gentle breeze. It's not windier than usual, but for some reason, I hear it better.

"Am I being paranoid?"

Jip climbs onto my lap and stares out across the lake like I'm his portable watchtower.

"Why couldn't I hear this well before?"

Jip cranes his neck to glance back at me before flicking his pointy ears forward.

"The waterfall!"

Jip jumps at my sudden outburst.

Normally, the sound of the river pouring into the lake drowns out most of the surrounding noise.

What happened to the waterfall?

I place Jip on my shoulder and race along the ridge. Worn river rocks and sand cascade down the canyon with each step.

We round the corner of the canyon. Where the waterfall once was is now mud.

How can a river vanish?

Ten minutes later, we reach the place where the waterfall used to be. There are a few puddles in the riverbed, and the rocks and soil are still wet. Only yesterday the water was flowing through here full force.

"I'm no riverologist, Jip, but I don't think this can happen naturally."

He looks at me and sniffs my nose before he gives me a quick lick on the cheek.

"Thank you." But I can't tear my eyes from the empty riverbed.

A hollow feeling grows in my chest. My new sense is picking up something again. Something is dangerously wrong. At the very least, my water supply is gone and soon Canyon Lake will dry up.

I don't want to walk miles up the riverbed to see what happened, but if I go back to Fort Jake and climb a tree on top of the hill, I'd be high enough to see far up the riverbed.

Jip grips my shoulder strap with his claws as we journey back.

I stop at my holding pool and pull out my pump and water bottles to fill them from the lake.

What happened to the river? And what does its disappearance mean?

I gut the squish in my holding pool and throw the intestines in my submerged basket as bait for the next group. I string the squish on a small loop of my paracord and hang them over my shoulder.

Did another earthquake create a new Canyon Lake farther upstream?

With the heavy smell of gutted squish in the air, I grip my wooden spear and head back to my hill.

I search the grass on each side of the trail for any sign of reed raptors.

They're fast, quiet, and tricky too. They run on two legs and have clawed hands like raptors. Their teeth are sharp. Good thing they're the size of a chicken, or I'd be screwed. They move too fast for me to get a good look at them, and it doesn't help that they have some kind of green and blue fur that blends in with the grass around me.

I've only ever encountered them while traveling with squish, gutted or not.

The wind is calm today, which helps me hear the reed raptors before they attack. Even so, I do a full turn every ten steps.

Halfway back, I find my first thief. He stands thirty feet behind me and cocks his head to watch me out of one eye.

"Haw!" I raise my spear and charge at it.

Jip joins in by giving a firm *kee* of his own.

With a quick flick of its tail, it vanishes into the grass. *Gluck, gluck, gluck!* It calls as it runs away.

I smirk and continue on my way. Good thing they're scared little critters.

As I rest my hand on my squish line, my smile vanishes. One's gone!

"How in the world?" I spin back to find the thief. A second reed raptor disappears into the grass to my left with my squish in its mouth.

I huff and guard my last two as I race back to my hill.

I stash the two squishes in the refrigerator and make sure the rock weight is in place before I journey farther uphill and climb the tallest tree. I stop ten feet from the top at the last of the biggest branches. This places me above all the other trees.

The plains spread out for miles in all directions. A new river flows east of my hill.

I cock my head. That doesn't make sense. I trace the river back up to the north where it flows from the Portal Mountains.

"So, it's the same river?"

Jip glances at me from my shoulder and blinks before sniffing the air.

"How's this possible, Jip? Rivers don't move. At least, not on their own."

I nearly lose my grip on the tree as the realization hits.

I have a much bigger problem than a moving river.

Shifting ground can move rivers. Some animals divert them. But most often, intelligent life redirects flowing water.

A chill runs down my spine.

What if the creatures that built the portal tower and the abandoned city aren't dead or gone? What if they diverted the water?

Just because I haven't seen them doesn't mean they haven't spotted me.

A deep ache grows in my chest.

I might've spent a month here, but I know nothing of this world. Anything could change on me, and I'd never see it coming.

"Yeah, God, I definitely want to go home."

CHAPTER 18
HOSTILES

DAY 41

Something is wrong. I've been thinking this for weeks now, but I can't shake the feeling today.

I pump the Canyon Lake water through my filter and into my water bottles. The sun is bright and there's not a cloud in the sky… yet. I've learned that lesson. Even if the sky is clear, a storm can come within an hour.

It's already warm out. Normally I make this trek for water in the morning right after breakfast, but I still had some left-over water from the rainy day yesterday. So I focused on building my crow's nest until I drank the rest.

I check my watch. The sun rose five hours ago.

Jip stares at me from far up on the bank. His fear of water prevents him from coming any closer.

At least I understand why he acts this way. What I don't get is why the river is moving. Every day it slides farther from me. It's now two miles east of Fort Jake.

The other mystery that bothers me is why I keep waking up far back in my shelter. It's annoying because the back of my shelter is where the ceiling is lowest. Each time I slide to the back, I have to scoot toward the door to sit up. I don't typically move much in my sleep, so why did I start now?

I'm being paranoid. Maybe my shelter was never truly level. Or I packed down the dirt on one side more than the other. Yet something about this small problem feels significant.

I put my water bottles back in my pack and reset the squish trap.

"Okay, let's go, buddy."

Jip perks up.

I place Jip on my shoulder and hold the squish I caught to my chest. It's the only way to keep them secure from the reed raptors. I keep up a brisk pace. I'm not even breathing hard by the time I reach the base of the Fort Jake hill. I guess I'm in better shape now.

But wait...

I was sweating up a storm on my way to the lake. Why was going that way so hard? That wasn't the case before. The ground is flat...

Or, the ground *was* flat.

I stop dead in my tracks. My heart thuds.

Can it be? Is this whole plain lifting to one side?

I inhale and nearly drop the squish.

The river. Waking up farther back in my shelter. The lifting plains. It's all connected. The river is shifting eastward, and I'm sliding to the eastern side of my shelter because the west side of the grasslands is rising.

But why?

Is there a super volcano? Are the tectonic plates shifting? Both would explain the frequent earthquakes.

Great. I didn't need something new to worry about.

Kee! Jip says impatiently.

I keep walking but my mind races. Once I get comfortable with my food and water routine, everything changes. How do I prepare for a massive volcanic eruption or the ground lifting into the air?

We reach Fort Jake and I start slicing up the squish to set

in my smoker rack above the fire. After I lay down a few green branches, I step away. The thick smoke rises.

Jip stands at the base of Crow's Nest Tree waiting for me to follow.

"Yeah, I was thinking the same thing."

I tie up the next bundle of wood for the crow's nest and loop it over my back. Jip climbs ahead of me, eagerly *kee*ing down at me.

"Give me a break, dude. I wasn't born with claws like you." I duck under a branch and watch to make sure none of the logs on my back snag. "If you were hauling all this wood, you wouldn't make it a foot up this tree."

Jip continues *kee*ing.

At the top I stare out over the orange-blue-and-green-splotched blanket of grass that stretches into the horizon. The smoke from my smoker rises through the trees and drifts eastward in the calm air. The river is now a mere thread in the distance. The land seems as flat as ever with the Portal Mountains rising to the north. How can it all tilt and still appear exactly the same?

I tighten the straps on my backpack and then tie myself and my backpack to a tether attached to the tree.

I have about twenty feet of bark-rope that I made during the long rain yesterday. My hands ache from the repetitive motion of twisting and wrapping the three cords together. I should be grateful though; the bark fiber is both plentiful at Fort Jake and easy to harvest. It peels off the tree in long strands, and it's ready immediately for twisting together.

But how do I construct a crow's nest on the top of a tree?

I have a basic frame that reminds me of the tree stand my dad used for hunting. It's all lashed together using my bark-rope. I've tested the rope, and one cord alone holds my weight. So three braided together should be more than enough. But I'm more concerned about the rope or knots slipping. If one of the support-beam knots comes undone, I'll fall forty feet.

Jip settles down and watches me from a branch above my construction project. He scans the sky for pterodactyls.

I secure another lashing under the bottom support beams. I hate knots. Every time I tie a branch into place, I feel like my dad, forcing the piece of wood to do what I want.

"If only I had nails and a hammer."

Jip cocks his head at me.

"If you knew my past, you wouldn't judge me."

Jip *kees*.

"Okay, but if I tell you, you better not make fun of me."

He blinks.

"I've never told someone this before, so I'm trusting you."

Jip licks his paw and runs it over his face.

"When I was fifteen, my dad and I went on a Trail Bridge camping trip. I was nervous because Dad and I would be alone on a team working to build our bridge with only ropes and logs. We had a wonderful time together. To top it off, our bridge came in first place. It was my favorite memory with him."

I check my tether again and wrap my rope around the other support log.

"For Father's Day, I printed and framed a picture of us on the bridge. I gave it to him to hang in his office. You know what an office is, right, Jip?"

Jip flicks his catlike ear.

"Good. Well, he loved the gift and said he'd hang it up with the other pictures he had of my brothers. A year later, I toured his work with my mom. I felt like a legend when I saw the picture on his wall surrounded by many pictures of my brothers. Dad was finally talking about me at work. Everything was great, until I had to go back in and get the water bottle I left in his office.

"From across the office space and through his open door, I

saw my dad remove my picture and replace it with one of Nathan holding his bachelor's degree."

I yank the next knot tight.

"Jip, he only put it up for me to see. My favorite memory with him wasn't good enough to make it on his wall. That's why I hate knots. Because they always remind me of that picture."

Kee!

"I know! How can—"

Jip's gaze is locked on something in the sky.

Something flies high above the ground. "Is it a pterodactyl?"

Kee! Jip answers.

It grows quickly. As it approaches, another dot appears in the sky next to it. They are too far away to see any flapping wings.

"That's a fast pterodactyl."

The dots don't fly straight. The front one curves and the second follows it.

Crack! The sound is muffled from the distance.

A dark cloud poofs off the front dot. A second later, another *crack* splits the air. A high-pitched whine carries to us through the wind.

It sounds less like a pterodactyl and more like an…

Airplane.

"Jip, get down!"

I race down the tree and hide under my crow's nest. More *cracks* sound as the whirring noise grows. I peer around the platform. The back dot is firing at the front one.

The smoke from my smoker stings my eyes as it drifts past me and out into the open air like a giant beacon giving away my presence. I take a step down the tree to put it out but stop. Anything I do to the fire now will only make it smoke more.

"God, please don't let them spot me or the smoke."

The two planes are nearly overhead. Neither has wings,

which means they must have some kind of jet engine. The front one zigzags in the sky as the back one trails it. *Cracks* and *booms* fill the air as the back plane unleashes one blast after another. Most explode in the air near the front plane.

Both aircraft are brown and oval. They're about the size of a car and definitely not human-made.

Before they reach me, they turn south. Soon after, a small orange fireball explodes on the front jet. Black smoke streams behind as it wobbles in the air, then spirals downward. The other craft slows and follows the first.

More than seven miles to the south, the jet crashes into the prairie but doesn't explode.

From this distance, the back plane appears to stop in midair. It unleashes a volley of missiles, destroying the crashed plane before it turns back to the west and speeds off into the horizon.

I give Jip a dumbfounded look. "So we aren't alone."

Jip blinks at me and returns to his perch to keep watch.

Not only are the aliens who built the portal still alive, they're also hostile.

This changes everything.

This isn't the next level; this is an entirely new video game.

RABBIT THING
"JIP"

CHAPTER 19
CHANGES

DAY 49

The evening sun blazes down on me. There's no wind to help with the scorching conditions. I haven't spotted any more alien aircraft, but knowing they are out there is almost worse. I wish I could find that crashed airship, but it's hopeless. I barely found a hill in these tall grasses; finding a wrecked aircraft will be impossible.

I wipe the sweat from my brow and grip both sides of my rock shovel before I slam it into the wall of sediment. Dirt and round river rocks cascade down the side of the pit and add to the growing pile of loose soil around my feet.

My back aches and my shoulders are killing me, but I lift the rock again and bash it into the wall.

"Ugh!" I drop the rock and lean against the pit's wall. "I never thought I'd miss a shovel so much."

Jip glares at me from the other side of the hole before he settles his head back down into a cute little ball of fur.

"You need to stop pouting, mister. If you don't want to be here with me, you can go home by yourself and become the main course at a reed-raptor feast."

Jip glares at me one more time, then adjusts his sleeping

position, making sure to exaggerate his discomfort in the heat.

The reed raptors haven't targeted Jip with their cunning thievery, but he'd be a perfect meal for them, and I don't want to learn I'm wrong the hard way.

"Besides, I'm almost done for the day, and then we can go back for dinner."

Jip perks up at that word. He loves dinner, breakfast, lunch, snack time, and midday-nap time.

"But first I need to finish here."

The hole is about eight feet long and five feet deep. It spans the full width of a psyno path, which is about five feet wide. It's taken me four grueling days to reach this point. A pit this big better be large enough to kill a psyno, because I'm burnt out. I would've quit two days ago if it wasn't so important. But I need a psyno hide or two before winter hits.

My little fort keeps most of the rain out, but it's still cold and drafty inside. Every day the temperatures swing drastically. The now seventeen-hour days easily reach an average high of a hundred degrees, and the thirteen-hour-long nights must be dropping down to the forties. If this is how cold it is in the waning summer, how cold will it be if I have ten-hour days and twenty-hour nights in the winter?

I need a psyno skin to winterize my shelter.

The heavy weight of fear settles on me, and I get back up to dig out the hole. I grab both sides of the thin, foot-and-a-half-long rock. It's shaped like a massive fingernail and is far better at moving dirt than my bare hands.

I jam the stone shovel back into the soil, but my heart feels empty. Fear has been about as close of a companion as Jip. Even as it propels me to action, it numbs me.

"Our situation wouldn't be so terrifying if I knew what was coming." Jip doesn't stir. He's heard enough of my complaining for the day.

"If I knew an Albuquerque winter was on its way, that

would be one thing. Or even a Colorado winter. But I've never seen winter here. Will the sky rain down knifelike icicles? Will the snow pile fifteen feet high? Will the temperature drop below negative fifty?

"You've seen winters here, Jip. What are they like?"

He ignores me.

If only he could talk.

"What else is going to change? The river moved, the ground is tilting, and we share this planet with mysterious aliens. How can I prepare for winter when I have no idea what else this planet will throw at us?" What if the ground is tilting because the whole prairie is a super volcano and the magma is building and about to erupt? Do I need to build turrets to prep for an alien attack?

I drop my shovel, slump to the ground, and hang my head between my knees. "I can't do it, Jesus. Sure, I can keep myself alive day by day, but I can't bear the weight of knowing my entire situation could change in an instant. I might feel great one moment, but the instant something unexpected happens, I realize once again that everything here is unknown, and all I've done could fall apart in a second."

I want to give up. Surviving this winter and the planet feels impossible. I flop onto the dirt pile I made and gaze up at the sky.

Fluffy clouds float by lazily without a care in the world.

What a dream. If only I had a life like that.

"I'd love to let go of this fear and find rest in you. But how? Do I just tell myself to stop fearing?"

Yeah, right.

"You know what, Jesus? If you want me to stop fearing things, then maybe you should stop throwing me into terrifying situations!"

Jesus doesn't answer.

I smirk. Did I outsmart Jesus by coming up with a flaw in

his plan? Probably not, but I feel as if I did, and that's all that counts.

With this small win, I stand and square myself up to my current number one enemy: my rock shovel. When I finish here, I'm going to throw Mr. Rock into the lake so I'll never have to see him again.

Except, what if I need him to dig another hole in the future? As tired as I am from hefting him into the air again and again, he helps me dig much faster.

A thought clicks in my mind: My shovel is like my circumstances. My weariness is like my fear. I hate my circumstances because of my fear, just like I hate my shovel because of my exhaustion. Even though I hate my shovel, it still helps me. I only have a hard time seeing that because of my exhaustion. In fact, it isn't the shovel that's my problem but my fatigue.

No, that's a terrible analogy. Because that would mean my fear is the problem, not my situation. And that would also mean my circumstances are enabling me to progress faster. But what would they help me to progress in? Not being afraid?

I stop and gawk at the sky as I realize what Jesus did.

"That's not fair, Jesus." I shake my head. "You let me think I won only to use my own thoughts to prove your point! Isn't that some kind of manipulation?"

In some bizarre way, I feel God's warm laugh.

I pick up my shovel and work at the hole again, but I can't fight my growing smile.

"Okay, that was pretty clever." I laugh.

Kee!

I look up from heaving another shovelful of dirt out of the hole. There aren't any psynos up or down the trail. No reed raptors are peeking out from the tall grasses. "What's up, little guy?"

Jip stares at me and shivers in the shade.

"Buddy, you aren't going to fool me. It's probably eighty-five degrees right now. Plus, you have a fur coat. There's no way you're cold."

He doesn't break eye contact and gives me the most help-less expression I've ever seen.

I laugh. The whole trap is covered in shade now. The sun is about an hour above the horizon.

"Okay, that's enough for today. Hopefully, we'll finish the trap tomorrow."

The moment I set down the shovel, Jip leaps out of the hole with ease and waits for me impatiently. I grab my pack and climb out after him. As he climbs onto my shoulder, I make sure the sky is clear of pterodactyls.

We journey east toward Fort Jake, which is now downhill. I intentionally found a psyno trail through the grass west of our hill because if we do catch a psyno, I'd rather lug it downhill.

I stop at Canyon Lake and take a bath. I slide into a clean set of my worn-out clothes and sigh. As always, I sport one of my three pairs of nylon pants and a long-sleeve shirt. When there's so little I control, it's a relief to be clean.

After we eat back at Fort Jake, we climb to the top of Crow's Nest Tree and watch the sun set. I'm still hesitant to trust the rickety platform I built, but Jip isn't. He climbs right out to the edge while I sit propped up against the trunk scan-ning the skies for pterodactyls or alien aircraft.

The sun paints the clouds a soft yellow, contrasting beautifully with the teal sky. As the sun dips below the horizon, it lights the western slopes of the mountains to the north a soft orange. To the south, the four bright stars that make the wings of the pterodactyl constellation are barely visible. When the sky darkens, the remaining ten stars that form me and my shield hanging from the pterodactyl will appear.

"And soon, Jip, we will be the mighty psyno hunters that the sky already tells about." I point to the east where the

Mighty Survivalists Jip and Jake constellation should be rising soon.

Jip stares out to the east.

"I know you don't think it looks like us, but it's like the clouds: You have to give meaning to the shapes."

Jip ignores me. Suddenly, he goes rigid. His ears focus forward and away from me.

Kee!

I follow his gaze. The plains stretch unbroken into the horizon. Except there's a glow in the sky. "What's that?"

Jip glances back at me nervously.

As the sky darkens, one patch of sky on the eastern horizon stays lit.

"Could it be a fire in a distant forest?" If so, that would be a huge fire.

Jip crawls back across the platform to sit in my lap. He shakes, but he doesn't feel cold.

The lighter patch on the horizon reminds me of light pollution from distant city lights. I saw something similar many times when stargazing with friends east of the Sandia Mountains. The distant Albuquerque city lights lit up the sky exactly like this.

"But that light wasn't there last night, was it? So it can't be an alien city."

Jip looks up at me for a moment, fear evident in his eyes.

I groan. "What new challenge is heading our way?"

N
NE
E
SE
S
(Magneetic North)
SW
W
NW
PORTAL MOUNTAIN
ALIEN RUINS
VOLCANO
FORT JAKE
CANYON LAKE

CHAPTER 20
PSYNO HUNT

DAY 52

Burds croak in the distance as the morning light grows in the east. How do their annoying calls carry so far? I'm at least a half mile from Fort Jake.

Jip is fast asleep in my coat snuggled up against my chest as I sit in my psyno blind. I shiver. An hour of sitting motionless in the cold is enough to freeze any man, especially my slim self. But it will all be worth it. It has to be.

Psynos apparently aren't very active during the day or at dusk, or at least they aren't on the trail I dug my trap on. Hopefully, the reason I haven't seen any psynos on it is because they use it early in the morning when I'm not here.

I did make sure this was a psyno path before I built my trap on it, right? I want to face-palm.

Either way, I'm committed to this trap now.

The glow I first spotted in the eastern sky a few days ago keeps growing brighter... or closer. Is it a giant moving alien city? Jip is terrified of it, and it's probably a good idea for me to catch my psyno before it gets any brighter.

Grass rustles to my left.

I hold my breath. *Please, Jesus, please.*

The noise is too deep to be a reed raptor.

Something big exhales.

One slow footstep falls after another. Rhythmic chewing draws closer.

The chills in my body vanish.

In the growing light of dawn, a large creature moves down the path and passes my blind without stopping. A good ten feet of thick grass separate me from the creature, so all I see are a few glimpses of movement. Now the psyno is between me and the trap.

To my right, I created a narrow path that angles toward the psyno trail so I can see the trap. Once I see the creature down my chute, I'll run at it.

My aching legs don't get the message that I need to wait. I fidget in place.

I force myself to take long, slow breaths.

Patience.

A dark mass steps into view down my narrow path. It's huge!

It stands as tall as a horse. Its thick chest is only a foot or two above the ground. Its head is low as it sniffs.

I was right. I'll need to scare it into my trap. At this slow pace, it will spot or smell my trap before reaching it.

Just three more steps. My pulse pounds in my ears.

The rear of the creature comes into view, and I jump from my seat.

"Roooaaaarrr!" I yell. I hold Jip close in my coat as I lift my other arm high in the air and charge.

Rmmmff! The animal starts, then runs with a brief glance backward. The psyno's haunches heave as it pounds down the trail, and I double my speed.

Its front feet fall through the thin cover of grasses I set over the top of my trap. It flips headfirst into the hole. The grass flies over the psyno, hiding it from view.

"Yes!" I fist pound the sky with sheer joy and almost forget I have Jip in my coat.

Roooommff! bellows the beast.

It moves under the grass. Sticks snap. Larger sticks—which must be my spears—break.

It isn't dead.

I detach my bear spray from my belt loop.

Its head pops out of the trap. Then a leg. It turns to face me with a low growl. The sharp horn on its nose is pointed straight at me. I stagger backward.

The red flap pops out of its green neck like an umbrella to circle its head.

The psyno and trap vanish as my vision goes black.

"Did you decide on a high-adventure program for the summer?" Dad says from the passenger seat the moment he shuts the door to his Ford truck.

I set my Trail Life Handbook on the center console and buckle my seat belt. Cory waves goodbye from his car. I wave back, then start the truck. "Yes, I want to do Boundary Waters."

"Aren't several of the boys going to do the Pacific Crest Adventure?"

"Yes..." I glance over at Dad as I pull out of the church's parking lot. What is he getting at?

One of the streetlights illuminates his calm face as we pass underneath. "Your brothers did the Pacific Crest Adventure and loved it."

"And because my brothers did it, therefore I should do it too?" I snap.

"No, but if—"

"If they enjoyed it, then I will probably enjoy it too?" I grip the steering wheel.

"Well, yes. Why are you so mad about that?" Dad grabs the handle above the window. "Slow down, Jake!"

I take my foot off the accelerator and watch the

speedometer slowly lower from sixty to forty-five.

"Why are you so upset?" Dad shifts into the intentionally calm voice he uses when he's frustrated but doesn't want to elevate the conversation. "I was only trying to give you ideas for what you can do next summer."

"Thank you for suggesting one more way I can walk in my brothers' footsteps," I mutter.

"Is that what this is about?"

If only that's all it was about. Does he still have no idea?

As the road slopes upward and over I-40, I check my rearview mirror. City lights stretch into the distance with nothing but the dark sky hanging over them. I put on my left turn signal and merge.

"Where are you going?"

"Home." I slow as we approach the red light.

"Then why are you taking I-40 east?" His tone sharpens like it did when I told him I was quitting football to join the cross-country team.

"Because it's faster." The arrow turns green, and I take the opportunity before he questions me further.

"Wait, Jake. Hold on!"

I turn left onto the on-ramp.

"I told you to wait!"

"Why?" I roll my eyes. "I'm driving. Doesn't that mean I get to make the decisions?"

"First of all, you only have your permit, so you don't get to make all the decisions. Secondly, I'm teaching you, which means you need to listen to me when I give instructions."

"Unless your instructions are wrong." The engine roars as I accelerate and merge onto the highway.

"What's going on?" Dad raises his voice. "It's faster to go right and take I-40 to I-25. We always take that route. *You* always take that route."

"Not tonight."

"Why?"

"Because I decided to go this way." My hands are sweaty on the wheel.

Dad lets out a pent-up breath and leans back into his seat. "Did I say something wrong?"

"No. You thought something wrong." Will he ever understand? How many times before have I tried to communicate my thoughts only to walk away misunderstood?

Dad straightens up. "What did I think wrong?"

"Me."

He sits in silence for a moment and drums the tips of his fingers on the door before turning to me. "What do you mean by that, Jake?" he says in a sincere tone.

I'm not sure what I meant.

I bite my lip and wipe my sweaty hands on my pants. "Dad, did you ever yell at my brothers for taking this route home after a Trail Life meeting?"

"No. They never took this route."

"But if they did, would you have second-guessed them as you did me?"

"I don't know. They always turned right onto I-40."

"Because *you* always turned right."

"Yes, it's faster." He gives me a confused look.

"But what's the problem with going this way?"

"Nothing, it's just slower and wastes gas."

"That's the problem. You think this way is bad because it's different from the one you and my brothers took."

"Well, it is a bad route."

"No, you *think* it's a bad route."

"The other way is better. This way is slower. It's not a matter of opinion; it's a fact."

Something within me breaks. "Just because I like and do different things doesn't mean the path I'm taking is worse than the one you and my brothers took!"

Dad opens his mouth, then closes it again. He lets his

hand fall from the handle above the window to his lap. "So that's what this is about."

I swallow.

"Jake, like this route you're taking home, some life paths are better than others. As your father, it's my job to help you make the best decisions. And it's best for you to go to college even if you don't know what you want to study yet."

"But what if you're wrong? What if I *know* you're wrong?" I merge onto the exit ramp to turn north onto Tramway Boulevard.

"I'm not wrong. College is statistically proven to be beneficial no matter where you go afterward."

"But it's my decision, and what you think to be best isn't always best."

"Why do you say that?"

"Because of the Balloon Fiesta."

He throws up his hands. "What does that have to do with this?"

I tighten my grip on the wheel. "The AfterGlow fireworks already ended tonight. I looked when we were crossing over I-40 on Wyoming."

"But what—" Dad cuts himself short as his eyes widen. "Oh..."

I clear my throat and relax my grip on the wheel. "Do you remember last year when we took your way back from Trail Life and got caught in twenty minutes of traffic? This way we avoid the whole problem."

"I'm so sorry, Jake." Dad turns to me. His face softens. "I remember, and yes, you're right. I should've trusted you."

Kee! Kee!

I rub my head. Morning sunlight casts long shadows through the grasses.

Kee! Jip stamps his foot on my chest. His fur stands on end.

Kheeekh!

I bolt upright. Small feet scuttle on the trail. A reed raptor vanishes into the dense undergrowth. The grass quivers in two other spots. There must've been three of them.

"What happened, Jip?" My head throbs as I climb to my feet.

Jip's fur settles down. He presses his face against mine.

On the path ahead, the grass is ruffled up.

My trap! The psyno! And… my dad? No, that was a psyno-induced memory of him.

But the psyno. It's gone!

Thank God it didn't trample or gore me. My watch says I was out for a good two hours. Psynos must prefer to use their psychic power defensively to run and hide instead of fight.

I race to the trap and pull out the grass. Most of the thick spears I spent an entire day whittling to a point are snapped in half or lying on their sides. I buried the base of each one a good two feet in the ground. The psyno must have crazy thick skin to dislodge or break the six-inch-thick spears.

I count three broken spearheads and three more lying intact on the ground, but I made eight. Did my trap work?

On the far side of the trap, there's a splotch of blue goo. "It worked!" I turn to Jip. "We did it!"

Jip stares at me and wipes his front paws over his face.

I race back to my blind for my day pack and then help Jip up to my shoulder. I make a quick stop at the trap to grab one of the unbroken spears, then charge down the trail of blood.

I've heard more than enough large-game hunting stories from my dad and older brothers to know this is how most hunts go. First you hit and wound the animal, then you wait an hour or two for the animal to run off, bed down, and bleed out. I waited accidentally by reliving that drive with Dad, but now it's time to find my psyno.

I can't believe my plan—not my dad's or my brothers' plan—worked! And I know if Dad were here, he would've told me digging this pit was a stupid idea.

"We aren't going to die, Jip!"

I round a slow bend in the trail and stop dead in my tracks. A patch of tall green grass is disturbed on the right. It's partially trampled but not all of it. This isn't a regular psyno trail, but a psyno did make this new path recently.

I lift my spear and slowly step through the haphazard trail. All the grass the psyno didn't break still stands eight feet tall and obstructs my view. At most, I see ten feet down the trail.

"This creature is smart," I whisper. "It ran past all the orange and blue grass because it knew its green skin would blend in with this green patch. We need to be careful. It might be trying to ambush us." I check behind me and to my sides, listening.

It could be anywhere.

Jip crouches on my shoulder as we slowly press forward.

Large, sticky globs of blue blood hang from broken blades of grass.

I creep through the trail as it curves to the right and through a patch of all-green grass. I place each foot where the psyno stepped to minimize the sound.

After a few minutes of tense silence and slow progress, I push past another bunch of unbroken grass and freeze.

A green mass lies five feet ahead. It doesn't move.

"Haw!" I yell, pointing my spear at it.

It still doesn't budge.

I throw my spear at it, but it bounces off the tough hide and disappears into the grass.

The creature lies motionless.

I approach, taking one careful step at a time, then reach out and touch the rough skin and pull my hand back instinctively.

Nothing.

"I actually did it," I whisper. I step around the side of the creature to see the psyno's glassy, lifeless eyes. It looks like it was ready to pounce on something, except there's nothing ahead of—

Three feet beyond the wall of grass in its face, I see the trail it made: The trail I followed.

My chest tightens. I stumble back.

It was waiting for me.

It made this new trail, then circled back to see what would follow it so it could launch a surprise attack on its pursuer.

Everything stills at the revelation.

To be that close to death without knowing, to see the plan put in action, and to have walked right into the ambush— A chill races down my spine.

If my trap to slay this animal hadn't worked, it would've killed me.

But I won. My plan prevailed in this game called survival. And now I have what I need to endure this winter.

"Thank you, God!"

Man, what would Dad say now? This rivals all of my brothers' hunting stories. I got this kill by carving sticks and digging a hole. "Take that, Nathan! This puts your seven-by-seven-bull-elk story to shame."

Even better, no one is here to nitpick what I did or tell me I was doing it wrong. No one is here to compare me to my brothers.

I did this myself in my own way and with my own ideas. And I'd say my way worked out pretty well.

If I had a camera, I'd take a picture with this beast. I'd blow it up forty times its original size and hang it on every wall in my room. I'd hang it on my brothers' walls and plaster it onto every truck my family owns. I'd get a life-sized mount of the creature and set it at the foot of my bed. My mom would hate it, but Dad wouldn't be able to enter my room without seeing something I accomplished with my own hands.

"I did it!" I scream at the top of my lungs.

Several birds startle and fly away from their invisible perches.

I'm not worthless without my dad or brothers.

Who would've thought I'd love hunting so much? I always said no to my dad when he invited me hunting because I knew I'd inevitably mess something up.

And who would've thought I'd actually enjoy being here? I thought I hated backpacking and camping, but was that all because of my dad? Is this why I loved reading adventure books, playing survival video games, and watching nature documentaries?

I pull out my large knife and unsheathe it.

It takes a ton of work to roll the thick beast onto its side.

When I complete my mission, I find my two missing spears. Each one is lodged three feet deep into the psyno's neck and chest. The hide on this guy is thick too. Cutting through it with my knife is brutal. But I don't mind. This is the happiest work I've done in weeks. That is, until I gut the psyno.

I reel back and scrunch my nose as I finally break through to the intestines. The stench of guts mixed with poop floods my senses. And I thought the crudslide smelled bad.

I hold my breath as I dig my arms deep into the chest cavity to pull out the intestines. If I don't gut the giant animal, the meat won't cool and will spoil before I can smoke and preserve it.

An hour later, I finally finish skinning and break off one leg. One front leg alone weighs at least fifty pounds. I heft it over my shoulder and lug it home. At least it's all downhill.

As I turn east onto my path, I nearly drop the leg. My muscles tense. I blink, but it's still there.

"Jip, are you seeing this too?"

His gaze follows the direction I'm pointing. His eyes grow wide, and his ears flatten. He gives a soft whine and presses closer to my head. One of his ram horns pokes my neck

Above the eastern horizon rises a massive red rainbow.

But it's not a rainbow.

It's a huge crescent moon.

It must be twenty times the size of Earth's moon, but this is just the tip. I fully extend my arm and spread my fingers. I line up the tips of my fingers with the outline of the moon. When fully risen, this moon will be the size of my extended hand.

It must be a hundred times bigger than Earth's moon.

"So this moon is what caused the eastern horizon to glow. Is it also what's causing the gravity to shift?"

I've only seen planets in the sky like this in video games and movies. Seeing it in real life is beautiful and… terrifying. At least I don't have to worry about a giant moving alien city.

If Earth's moon rises and lowers tides by two feet and impacts Earth's weather, what will this gigantic moon do? Will it tear the planet apart or cause four-hundred-mile-an-hour windstorms?

"What does this mean, Jip?"

One look at my cowering friend and I know.

This moon is about to change everything.

CHAPTER 21

ADULTHOOD

DAY 57

The top rim of the massive moon glows red as the sun rises above it. It's way bigger than I thought. Now that it's fully risen, it's about the size of an extra-large pizza!

It's beautiful. Terrifying, but beautiful.

The crackling of my fire breaks me free from the awe-inspiring moon. It doesn't seem real.

Jip and I sit near our fort eating a late breakfast. A sweet aroma fills the air from my tea boiling on the fire. This time I cut up half a balloon fruit to add, along with three small cinnamon leaves and an inch-long piece of sweetheart that Jip helped me discover the other day. He dug up the sweet-tasting root for himself from a tree with heart-shaped leaves.

I bite off a chewy piece of psyno jerky.

Every morning this moon has eclipsed the sun for over an hour. Today, the last of the moon rose above the horizon. It took five days to rise. Only the illuminated crescent is visible right now, but I can't wait for this evening!

Since the moon sits nearly stationary in the sky, it goes through every phase every day. Right now, it's a new moon. This afternoon it will be a half-moon, and this evening it will be a glorious full moon in the teal sky. Last night, it was so bright I could feel its warmth.

It casts an orange glow on everything, similar to when the sun sets and lights all the clouds a bright orange. It's about that bright too. The darkest part of the day is no longer night but the daily solar eclipse.

Now that the fire is strong, I grab the white rocks I found at Canyon Lake and continue outlining the arrow I drew pointing toward Portal Mountain. I don't need the arrow to know where Portal Mountain is, but adding these small rocks to the arrow is part of my morning routine. I'll likely finish the outline tomorrow and then I can start filling it in.

I also add a rock to my day counter. "Fifty-seven days. Jip, we've survived nearly two months." I rest my hands on my hips. "Does that mean we're one sixth of the way through a year? Or is a year longer here?"

Jip licks a paw and wipes it over his face before he snatches up his squish tentacle and hops on top of our fort.

"Either way, it's progress. I'm closer to going home than ever before."

I won't live here forever. I will return home one day. I may be millions of light-years from Earth, but I'm only a four-day journey from home.

When winter passes and daytime stretches to eighteen hours long, I'll know a full year has passed and the portal is about to open.

"Speaking of orbital periods, we still haven't solved the moon riddle."

I walk back to our fire and pick up the remaining half of the balloon fruit and squash it into a ball. Like wax, it holds together. "Okay, Jip, let's say this balloon fruit is the moon, and my rock chair is our planet. If our planet spins fast enough that we see the sun rise every thirty hours, how is it that we haven't seen this moon until now?"

This question has haunted me the past several days, but I

was too busy preserving hundreds of pounds of psyno meat and lugging an impossibly heavy hide back to our fort. Now that I'm done with the psyno, I can crack this puzzle.

Jip, who has a double doctorate in astrophysics, watches me between bites from the ridge of our shelter. His teaching technique is very hands-off. He likes to let me arrive at the answers by myself.

"The only way this could happen is if the moon is orbiting around us about as fast as our planet rotates. But that would mean the moon orbits us once every thirty hours." I pace around the fire. "That's way too fast for a moon this size. Is that even possible, Dr. Jip?"

Jip finishes his tentacle, leaps off the fort, and glides over to me. He jumps up against my leg with large pleading eyes.

I bend down and pet his little forehead before I hand him another tentacle. He snatches it with his mouth and scampers back up the psyno hide I fitted over the top of our shelter. With the hide in place, this perch has become his favorite spot in our camp.

"How do I know you hold a double doctorate if you won't tell me anything or help me solve this puzzle?"

Jip glances at me, lifts a leg to scratch behind his ear, then picks his tentacle back up.

"Sorry, I didn't mean to doubt you."

Though I don't have the same prestigious education as Jip, Oliver was part of the astronomy club and always talked about it.

Oliver often mentioned how Earth's moon does something similar. It's tidally locked to Earth, which means it always shows the same face to the earth.

From the moon's perspective, one side never faces Earth, while the other side always sees Earth fixed in one place in the sky. If someone spent their whole life on the dark side of the moon, as they call it, they'd never know Earth existed.

"So, wait." I peer at the moon through a break in the trees.

"If the moon is slowly rising over the span of several days, then that means this planet is almost tidally locked to the moon. That's why it took so long for me to finally see it."

Jip *kee*s his praise of my conclusion and glides over to congratulate me on solving the puzzle. Then he begs for another tentacle.

"Okay, but this is the last one, Professor." I toss him another tentacle and he snatches it out of the air before climbing back up to his perch.

"So that's the solution to why I didn't see the moon until day fifty-two. But if we are almost tidally locked, then each day would last as long as a full orbit around the moon. Just like with Earth's moon, each day on it lasts a month because that's how long it takes to orbit Earth and spin one full time."

I tap my foot on the ground. "So we must orbit this moon every thirty hours. But orbiting another planet or moon every thirty hours is crazy fast. If we are close enough to orbit that fast, we must be dangerously close to the Roche limit."

Jip stops chewing and looks at me. *Kee!*

"Don't be so surprised I know about the Roche limit, Dr. Jip. I'm a smart guy. And it's Oliver's favorite astronomy topic. He loved the idea of moons and planets crumbling because they got too close to another celestial body."

I pull the kettle out of the fire and pour myself a cup of tea. I take a sip, then add another piece of sweetheart. The root spins as I swirl the tea.

I stare at the giant red moon. "Is it tidally locked to this planet too? Because those three dark-orange streaks across the moon haven't moved much, if at all. Oliver said the smaller celestial body is always first to become tidally locked to the bigger one, but if both of these bodies are slowing at the same pace, then they must be about the same size.

"There's no way a moon could orbit a planet every thirty hours. But if they were both planets and they orbited each other, the total orbit would be much smaller and quicker."

I jump to my feet. "That must be it, Jip! We didn't see this planet for over fifty days because we are almost tidally locked to it. And each day isn't created by how fast our planet rotates, but by how fast we orbit this other orange planet."

Jip startles and glances between me and his squish tentacle.

"Really? Are you telling me you didn't think of this, Professor?"

Jip pauses for a moment, then licks his front paws and runs them over his face and nose.

"Well, it seems you've underestimated me."

As soon as the words escape, I freeze.

I've never said those words before.

I smile.

If my dad and brothers saw me now, would they be surprised with how well I'm surviving here?

I check my watch. "Just a little longer until a very special day starts back on Earth. Which means we'd better start moving if we're going to be ready in time."

Jip follows at my heels as I grab my day pack, supplies, and spear. As I start heading down the hill, he scampers ahead and climbs a tree. Once I pass by, he leaps, glides, and lands on my shoulder. We start down the path to Canyon Lake.

The morning is still cool even though the sun is reaching its peak. An hour solar eclipse each day is enough to keep the air cool later into the day.

"Now that we know the planet isn't a moon, we need to name it. Calling it Planet sounds weird. It's giant and orange. It causes lots of problems here on this planet, like all the earthquakes, volcanoes, and the shifting gravity.

"What about Garfield?"

Jip *kees* as if he's laughing at me.

"Seriously, think about it. Garfield is orange with darker stripes, and Garfield also ruins everything. And"—I laugh—

"when this planet is full in the evening, we can call it a full Garfield!"

Jip gives me an are-you-kidding-me type look, then uses his little left horn to scratch his backside.

"It's a perfect name."

Jip *kees* in protest.

"Hey, Professor. I'm the one who discovered this is a dual planet system, so I reserve the right to give it a name, and I choose Garfield."

Jip's body goes rigid. The hairs on his back go up. He searches the sky.

I follow his gaze. Seconds later, a high-pitched whistle fills the air.

"What is—"

A pterodactyl!

It's diving toward us.

The whistle grows stronger.

I'm too far from the hill to shelter in the trees and too far from the lake to dive underwater in time. Poop towers! The one time I forgot to check the skies.

I can try to hide in the grass, but that will only tangle me up and give the pterodactyl a direct shot at me. Here on the trail, I have better footing. I raise my spear and square myself off to the predator.

It spreads its wings some and turns its dive into a swift glide toward us.

"Get out of here, Jip!"

Jip jumps off to my side.

I toss off my backpack and anchor myself. "Come and get me."

The pterodactyl opens its claws, and I run at it.

I throw the spear and duck under its talons. I roll back up to my feet and face it.

The pterodactyl flaps, but its efforts are uncoordinated. It turns back toward me. As it lands, it folds its wings and uses the joint in its wings to land on all fours. Without skipping a beat, the pterodactyl charges me.

My spear is lodged in its side. I race to my bag and fumble with the zipper. My hand closes on my knife. I roll through the grass right as the pterodactyl speeds past.

I unsheathe the knife and hold it before me.

Rau! The bird bellows. Even on all fours, the skinny creature is taller than the eight-foot grass.

I glance left and right. There's nowhere to hide. Fighting is my only way out. I take a step back and set my feet.

The pterodactyl slowly approaches me, as if knowing there's no hope for me. It stops a few feet away and slashes at me with its sharp talons that protrude on the joint of its bat-like wing.

I take another step back.

It swipes at me again and I duck. Its claw catches my shoulder and throws me to the right. I hit the ground and quickly scramble to my feet.

I rise in time to connect with its next strike. The blow flings me to the left like a rag doll. I land hard on my back and groan.

I gasp, but the wind is knocked out of me.

How can I beat this monster?

The pterodactyl pounces on me. Green blood splatters down on me from the spear in its side.

God, help me!

It lifts its head and goes to stab me with its beak. I raise my left hand to protect myself. Its beak pierces my left forearm and rams into the ground just right of my head. My vision flashes white.

Before it pulls back, I lunge forward with my right arm and slash blindly at it with my knife. I strike something, and warm liquid spills onto me.

Rau! The pterodactyl bellows, then releases me. It reels back, a fresh gash on its neck oozing blood.

The pterodactyl collapses to the ground, twitching.

I drop my knife, grip my left forearm, and clench my teeth. Blood seeps out. I yank off my shirt and tie it over the wound to slow the bleeding. Blood also trails down my right shoulder from where it clawed me. My back aches. The old pain from when I landed on my shield after the volcano eruption flares up again.

I gulp in air.

Jip finds me in the tall grass. He doesn't say anything but glances from me to the dying bird.

The twitching pterodactyl stills.

I nearly died.

Two minutes ago, we were fine, and now I'm barely walking away from a pterodactyl attack.

Pain in my back flares as I bend down and pick up my knife. I wipe off the blood on my shirt, then slide it back into its sheath.

"Holy smokes," I mutter as I apply pressure to my shirt wrapped over my forearm. Warm blood seeps through. "That was insane."

Jip and I cautiously approach the dead bird.

My spear sticks out of its stomach. Green blood covers its entire body and much of the orange and blue grass.

I exhale and look at Jip. "We defeated a pterodactyl."

But it came at a huge cost. How much blood will I lose? Will my arm ever fully heal?

At least I'm alive.

A smile creeps across my face.

I, Jake Rogers, killed an eight-foot pterodactyl with nothing but a spear and a knife.

How is this real?

"We're going to need a bigger refrigerator."

Beep! Beep! Beep!

I jump, then realize the noise came from my watch. I slap the button to stop the alarm I set this morning.

That's right.

"Jip, it's now officially October 22 in Albuquerque."

He cocks his head.

"Are you kidding? You forgot my birthday?"

Jip gives me an I-don't-care-about-your-petty-day-of-birth-celebration type look.

"But this one is special. I'm eighteen now!"

Which also means, I officially will never become a Freedom Ranger.

An invisible weight lifts off me.

Finally, it's set in stone. I didn't do something my dad and brothers urged me to do.

And I didn't fail to accomplish this because of my inadequacy but out of choice.

I chose a different path, and now there's no going back. I will forever be different.

Come to think of it, my choice not to become a Freedom Ranger is what led me here. If I'd never told my dad I was quitting Trail Life, we never would've had the argument that caused me to storm off to our tent. If I hadn't been near the tent, I never would've fallen through the portal.

I'm here because of a choice I made to be different. And now look at me.

I poke the pterodactyl in the bridge of its beak.

I didn't just survive flying with a pterodactyl, I killed one.

With the psyno pelt, I'm set for winter. With the lake, my traps, and my growing foraging skills, I'll have food to survive the winter.

And now... I'm strong enough.

I almost stumble at the realization.

My hands are dirty, rugged, calloused, and coated with green and red blood. Though I left the Portal Mountains to find a place less dangerous where I could "level up" my strength. I never thought I'd actually do it.

Am I strong enough now to go back to Portal Mountain

and defeat the threats I was too weak to face before? But I barely survived this one, and how much of my victory came about by luck? And what about the aliens? Am I ready to face them?

Besides, if I go back home, as proud as my dad might be of me, he'll still hit me with the what-do-you-want-to-be question. He'll expect me to go to college and become successful like him and my three older brothers.

My spirit sinks.

Something about success, good jobs, and making money makes me sick. I don't care about them, and even if I did it to make him happy, he'd want me to get married, have kids, and then who knows what else.

"Ugh." Sometimes I hate thinking about home. But I don't have to worry about that right now. This pterodactyl kill is my victory, and my future here is whatever I want it to be.

I smile. "You know what, God? I guess bringing me here wasn't such a bad idea after all."

CHAPTER 22
THE GARFIELD PROBLEM

DAY 89

A light as bright as the sun wakes me. I blink and squint. Jip stretches beside me in my dad's sleeping bag. The blinding light flashes again.

"What in the world is that?"

With the psyno hide over my shelter, everything is dark. The light shines through the hole I had to make above the door to let in some light.

I jump out of my bed. Jip startles and hops away from me.

"Sorry, buddy." I crawl over my bed to the door.

The light is as warm as the sun, but my door opens to the west and there's no way I slept through the whole day.

The timer on my watch shows 31:24. I suppose I did sleep in, but only an hour. I reset the timer for the new day and throw open the flap of psyno hide.

Brilliant sunlight floods me.

I stumble back and fall onto the sleeping bag, hitting my head on one of the branches that make up the wall of my shelter. I sit back up and blink.

"I... I... I don't understand."

The sun is in the wrong spot, but that's not possible. I

timed the last day, so I know I only slept ten hours. But somehow the sun is now in the west.

Jip curls up on the sleeping bag where the sunlight bathes him.

"Could Garfield cause this to happen?"

Jip stares at me and stretches again in the patch of light.

I don't need Professor Jip's input to know that's an absurd idea.

"Did our planet decide to start rotating backward?"

Jip hops out of our shelter as I start tying my boots.

"Wait, what happened to the burds?" Usually, they wake me up before dawn. I'm not at all upset that they let me have the extra rest, but why did they go silent?

Change. I hate change. It's the one thing that prevents me from going home this spring.

First the sun, now the burds. What's going on? Could some alien tech do this?

In the absence of the burds' constant belching, I hear everything. Something scuttles outside our fort. In the distance, a boom bird blows up a tree limb in search of food. Wind rushes over the tops of the trees. Distant waves lap against a shore.

Wait. Waves?

A reed raptor scurries away the moment I leave the fort. Strange, they typically don't leave the tall grasses.

A massive, waning Garfield floats directly overhead.

It doesn't feel like morning at all. The backward shadows tell me it should be evening. The air doesn't smell like dew; neither is it chilly as it always is in the morning. Instead, the strong wind feels warm and humid and carries a slight taste of salt. Puffy clouds fill the sky.

A loud splash sounds to the east—or is it west now?

I follow the sun through the trees and down the side of the hill. Jip hops along beside me and gives a frustrated *kee,* which translates to "Why aren't you feeding me?" Halfway down the hill, I freeze.

Beyond the trees, sunlight reflects off rippling water that stretches far into the distance.

My stomach tightens.

I blink, utterly dumbfounded.

I cautiously approach the water. "Am I dreaming?"

The lapping of waves grows louder as we near the bottom of the hill. Jip eventually perks up as he notices the change. We stop at the edge of the water. It's not just a lake; it's a sea… maybe even an ocean. Water stretches out to the horizon.

Yesterday, it was all grassland.

I can't wrap my head around it. What did I miss? Did this all happen overnight?

I suppose it does make sense. If the moon raises Earth's tides by as much as several feet, then a planet much closer could raise tides hundreds or even thousands of feet. So this must be high tide since Garfield is nearing the highest point in the sky.

Some of the other smaller hills pop above the water. Beyond them, mountains rise off in the east.

"Huh, that's odd. I've never seen those—" The words catch in my throat as a terrible thought comes to mind.

"Try to keep up, buddy." I set Jip down and race back to camp.

Running uphill is easy now. With Garfield at the highest point in the sky, his gravity has decreased my perceived weight to be half that of what it would be on Earth.

Jip also bounds up the hill with ease.

We reach our shelter, and I waste no time climbing Crow's Nest Tree.

I cradle my left forearm as I scale the tree. The wound from the pterodactyl attack a month ago has mostly healed. I can grip things in my left hand again, but my grip is weak and there's still an ache each time I use that hand to pull myself higher in the tree.

Jip climbs beside me.

At the top, my heart stops.

With my 360-degree view, there's only one mountain range in sight. It's miles off to the northeast—according to the sun.

I pull out my dad's compass from under my shirt and lift the string over my head. With the needle pointing due south to compensate for the planet's reversed magnetism, the sun is rising in the east as usual.

Jip climbs up beside me and gives me a quick lick on the nose.

"So it's not the sun that changed. It's our hill." I pet Jip's soft blue-and-black fur before he climbs farther up the tree. "Our hill must be floating. That's why I thought the sun rose in the west, because Fort Jake spun to face the other way."

My breath catches. "Our hill is floating away," I whisper.

I gulp.

"Away from the portal."

My home. My family. Sophie. Matt and Oliver. Those distant peaks are my only way back. If I lose them in the distance, I'll be trapped here forever.

I'll never see another human again.

My fingers tingle and the sides of my vision darken.

No. I can't faint.

I need to build a boat. I have to paddle to those mountains before we lose them forever.

I lie down on the platform on the top of the tree, push down any thoughts of drifting away, and focus on my bed at home. My safe and comfortable bed. Where I didn't have to worry about anything other than my dad trying to make me be more like him. Where everything I did was compared to the impossible success of my brothers.

My vision fades as my lungs race for air.

My bed. The place where I could escape into my video games and be who I wanted to be. Where I could enjoy life with my friends and accomplish wonders like slaying thousands of invading aliens.

I force myself to take deep breaths, but the darkness closes in.

CHAPTER 23

THE OCEAN

The half-full Garfield floats above like a giant *D*. The sun is only an hour from setting, and my raft is looking pretty... terrible.

I tie my last bark-rope lashing. I ran out of paracord halfway through and had to finish the job with some bark-rope. I didn't have time to braid it to make it stronger. The twisted rope should last... I hope. Every knot I tie feels like a new chain wrapped around my heart. But I have to go. This is my last chance.

I can stay on this island and continue living this new life, but if I stay, I'll never find the portal. Once those mountains leave my sight, I'll have to search this entire planet to find them again.

The soft sea breeze tugs at my now semilong brown hair. The sun warms my tan, semimuscular arms. Scratches and scars cover my forearms. My hands are rough and calloused. I'm a different person now because of this place. A person I'm proud of. A person I never thought existed.

Do I really want to go home?

I've learned so much here.

I no longer see wild animals and wonder what their lives

are like because I'm one of them. We are fellow runners in the same race to stay one step ahead of the oncoming winter.

The weather isn't a slight flavor to mix up each day as it was in my old life. It's a fluid dance between the hot sun, the warm Garfield, and the cold night. It's part of me, and I'm part of it.

It's all so rich and vibrant.

And now I must choose.

Waves lap against the side of my floating island.

Poor Jip. He's curled up on a sunny patch of grass. He stares out across the ocean, squinting as the sun gleams off the water.

Should I leave him here? He absolutely hates water.

A large shadow passes over us as another massive bird flies past the sun. Dozens of them scatter the sky. Their wingspans are easily over three hundred feet across. They have a similar shape to stingrays but without the long tail. The skyrays must migrate with the ocean—where Garfield decreases gravity to half that of Earth's—because there's no way these creatures can fly otherwise.

Unless they are giant alien aircraft.

I shudder.

No, it can't be aliens. These things fly like animals.

But if these skyrays are animals, what do they eat?

If they eat meat, floating out on a raft is like giving them dinner on a plate. Whether they are animals or aircraft, my only hope of surviving will be reaching the mountains under the cover of night. I'll have about thirteen hours before the sun rises and betrays me to the skyrays.

I bury my face in my hands.

I have to go. For the sake of my family and my friends, I have to make it back home.

"'Be strong and courageous. Do not be afraid; do not be discouraged, for the LORD your God will be with you wherever you go,'" I whisper from memory.

"I can't let fear hold me back from doing what I need to do, right, God?"

I lie back on the raft and stare at the sky. Jip hops over and nestles against my side.

How could I leave my only friend here? But how can I take him on this dangerous journey?

The thought of saying goodbye to him is too much for me.

Jip hops up on my chest and licks my cheek.

"I love you, Jip." I pick him up and set him beside me. "I'm sorry, buddy, but we can't snuggle right now." I run back to Fort Jake. Jip races at my heels. Hopping and gliding between each lunge.

Reed raptors race away from us. We even spot a psyno. They must've run to safety on this island when the water came.

Inside our fort, I pack my dad's sleeping bag. I stuff it down inside my bag along with my emotions.

Jip sits to the side and cocks his head.

After all that hard work. After killing the psyno and winterizing my fort, I'm leaving this soon? I could keep surviving here. My food stocks are high and lots of animals are around if I need more food. Even in this big salty ocean, I can still get fresh water from the funnel palms that collect the rain.

But I have to go home.

I seal my Bible and other books into the dry bag, close my backpack, and grab my can of bear spray. As I head to my underground refrigerator, I pass my firepit. How many fires have I started in there? How many squishes have I fried over it? Now, it's cold and lifeless.

Jip again follows me with total devotion.

A sick feeling grows in my stomach. Does he know what I plan to do?

"Do you want me to stay, God?"

No. I shake my head. What an absurd thought. Of course I

need to go. I planned to stay here only for a season. My real home lies on the other side of the portal. Now that I'm strong enough, I can survive closer to the portal until it opens.

The familiar dusty scent greets me as I crawl into my enlarged refrigerator hole. I stuff two dozen large slices of psyno jerky and what little remains of our balloon fruit and dried squish into the brain of my backpack.

When I finish backing out of the hole, Jip jumps up on my leg. I toss him one of the last squish tentacles. I already have the large, flat rock lid in hand before I realize I don't need to seal my refrigerator anymore.

It's not my fault I have to leave. It's this stupid hill. The stupid ocean. And stupid Garfield.

In the fading sunlight, I storm past my shelter to the arrow pointing home. It lied to me. It promised me I could live here until it was time to go home. We could've done it too. We stood a chance at surviving the winter. It would've been fun with Jip. Comfortable even.

Now I need to start over, and either I abandon Jip or he'll hate me for bringing him.

I kick the white rocks I used to fill in the arrow. I stomp on it. Jump on it. And when the ground is so mixed up that it's impossible to tell there was ever an arrow there, I spit on it.

"This is your fault, God! You knew this would happen, and you didn't warn me."

I collapse to the ground and hang my head.

"Why are you doing this to me, God? I'm not ready to leave this life with Jip."

An evening breeze *swooshes* through the tops of the trees. Down here, a gust drifts past me.

"*I never said to go,*" comes a soft whisper. This time, I swear the words are audible.

I scoff. "You're forcing me to go!"

Only the wind above responds.

I huff and stand up. "Right, I suppose I could stay and never see my family, friends, or home again. No big deal."

For a brief second the idea of living here with Jip glimmers in my mind, but I push it away.

Absurd. It was always my plan to go home. I can't give up on that plan now. What would Dad think if I stayed? I can't stand the thought of my family and friends thinking I'm dead.

The ground jolts under me. I stumble to the side and land hard on my bottom. Jip also falls to his side. Above, the last of the season's balloon fruits float away.

Again, the ground moves under us.

Pop! Snap!

The sound continues to the north, like a giant creature chewing a tree.

Jip runs to me and jumps into my arms. His body trembles.

I brace myself against a nearby tree and stagger northward, which used to be the south side of my hill. I nearly fall each time the ground moves. As we near the bottom of the hill, I slide to a stop.

Through the few trees ahead, another island floats. It's almost as large as ours. The sound comes from dozens of trees snapping as our island slides onto the other. In the middle of the island is a long, gray rock. Its wet surface gleams in the fading sunlight. It resembles a giant slug.

The rock turns.

On the far end of the rock, a massive eye blinks.

I gasp and fall back as the ground moves and slides up farther onto the island.

It's not a rock, it's an animal. But it's not just the rock. It's the island.

I'm on an animal!

That's why it floats. That's why the hills seemed so out of

place when I first left the mountains. That's why the cave was so warm that rainy—

My mouth drops open.

"Gross! That's why the crudslide smelled like poop. It *was* poop! I spent the night in this creature's…" I can't even bring myself to say it.

Jip *kee*s in disgust.

I gag.

The ground rocks under us. I grab a branch to keep myself from falling. "We need to go, Jip."

Stay, Jake.

I glance behind me, but no one's there.

I swipe God's words aside.

No way. Not with this being a giant turtle-mountain! What if it took a dive? Or what if…

Even as I think my concerns, I know they're empty. These thick, old trees are proof that these turtle-mountains have been a suitable environment for life for many years.

Still. This hill being a massive creature is just one more reason I must leave. Why risk it when it means losing the portal?

Be strong and courageous.

"Shut up, God!"

I hold Jip in the crook of my arm like he's a football and run back to the fort. With my pack over my shoulder, my spear in my right hand, and Jip holding on to my shoulder strap for dear life, I bolt for the raft.

I set Jip and my supplies on the raft, then push it down the hill.

The ground moves under me. Suddenly, the ground slides into the water. The raft floats and I go from pushing to holding on. Water splashes everywhere.

Kee! Kee!

I quickly pull myself on board.

Jip jumps for the island, but I lunge forward and pluck him out of midair.

He *kee*s again and fights against me. His sharp claws slice my forearms, but I keep a tight grip on him. "It's okay, Jip! We're going home."

The ocean waves sweep us farther from Fort Jake.

Our turtle-mountain—turtain—is halfway on top of the other one. The other turtain's colossal head rises above the water and lets out a deep bellow as it reaches back to bite at our attacking turtain.

The giant ocean waves splash over us.

Jip *kee*s again and fights to get free.

Now that we're far enough from the island, I set him down on the raft. Jip turns from the turtains and glares at me. Not a playful you-better-feed-me type glare, but a who-are-you look.

I glance away.

My gut twists, but I push the guilt down.

The last rays of sunlight cast a dark red glow on the puffy clouds, while Garfield stains me, the raft, and the water with an orangish red.

To the west, the Portal Mountains peek above the horizon. I pull out the paddle I made and kneel on my bag. I fix my attention on the mountains and plunge the paddle into the water.

I'm going home.

CHAPTER 24
THE RED NIGHT

DAY 89

My muscles ache. I grit my teeth and spear the water with my paddle.

Another wave crashes over the top of our raft, dousing me and Jip with salt water.

I wipe my face with my sleeve, plunge my paddle into the dark water, and push us forward just in time to collide with another wave. I set my jaw and fight on.

Every wave is massive.

I hate Garfield. He's swept me away from the portal, and now it's because of his decreased gravity that these waves tower over us.

But he won't win. These waves won't win.

At the crest of the next wave, I focus on the distant mountains.

My home. My old life. My family. Sophie.

I've failed many things in my life, but I won't fail tonight. I *will* reach those mountains.

A giant wave races at us like a rolling hill of water.

"Hold on, Jip!" I grip the side of the raft and lean forward. Despite our raft tilting nearly vertical, we level out.

As we slide down the backside of the rolling hill, I sigh; the next few waves are much smaller.

The mountains glow a dark red in Garfield's light. The sky is dark but lit enough by Garfield to feel like it's still twilight. The turbulent water is black except where Garfield's massive red body reflects in patches and specks on the rolling waves.

A shadow passes over us as a skyray glides silently through the night, blocking out Garfield.

Right, and if I don't make it to the mountains before sunrise, one of the monstrous creatures will eat me.

Jip glares at me. His claws are lodged deep into one of the raft's logs. He isn't shivering, but he must be freezing. Usually, he'd stare at me and shiver so I'd show pity on him. Now it's as if he doesn't want my pity.

He doesn't want anything to do with me.

"I had to, Jip." I heave my paddle back into the water and pull again. "For your own safety, I had to bring you."

My arms ache, my stomach growls, and my throat burns for the taste of fresh water. But to stop and rest, eat, or drink would mean giving up any progress I've made to the relentless wind and waves.

After two hours of paddling, it seems as if the mountains are no closer. In fact, they may be farther away.

I can't accept that.

I can't give up.

I picture my mom's glowing face the night I won the piano contest and urge the feeling of her warm embrace to resurrect my strength. The thought of never seeing my mom, dad, and brothers again feels unreal.

I have had good times playing board games with my family or *Halo* with my brothers. In fact, those early days of playing *Halo* are what got me hooked on the game and video games in general. Even though I've endured so much pain because of my family, I know they love me and will always be there for me when I need them most.

Jip still glares at me. He hasn't *keed* since we left. Or, rather, since I kept him from leaping back to the island. I've never seen him this mad at me. Sure, he's scratched me several times, but he was always quick to forgive me. Not this time.

Was leaving the island a mistake?

No. This is the only way home.

But I feel guilty.

I drown my second-guessing thoughts and focus on the goal. If I don't want to spend the rest of my life here, those mountains are my only option.

The rest of my life spent here?

My pulse pounds in my ears.

I'd never talk to another human again. I'd never get to hold Sophie's hand or enjoy a meal with friends and family. Every Christmas, Thanksgiving, or holiday, I'd spend by myself. My voice would be the only one I'd hear. And if I broke an ankle or my leg, no one would be here to help me.

On top of all this, my family would never know what happened to me.

Sure, I may have Jip with me now, but what about when he dies? I doubt he'll live more than five years. And then what would I do with the next sixty years of my life here?

My nose stings. And I throw myself even harder against the waves.

The mountains are so far ahead of me, but no matter what I do, I don't get any closer.

"Agh!" I yell at the waves and press into my next stroke.

The image of my dad in a canyon flashes through my mind. He and my three older brothers are ahead of me on the trail. I've been falling behind for the past two miles.

I find a rock and collapse onto it.

"Jake, it's okay. Just one more mile until the falls and the swimming hole." He holds my hand and stares into my eyes.

His face blurs as tears spring up.

"I can't do it," my eleven-year-old self says.

"Yes, you can," he tells my younger self.

"But then we still have to walk another six miles back to camp," I mutter as I hide my tears from my older brothers who wait impatiently farther up the trail.

"We can worry about that after we reach the swimming hole."

My feet ache from my new shoes. My legs quake.

"No, Dad. I'm staying here."

I blink away the memory as another wave tosses us, dousing me and Jip with salt water. I spit and plunge my paddle in again.

My shoulders are weak and my back aches. I can't tell in this light if I'm bleeding, but my palms feel rubbed raw.

As I rise over a wave, I locate the three highest mountain peaks popping above the horizon.

I stop with my paddle hanging above the water.

"No"—I shake my head—"it can't be."

The mountains are much farther away than when I started.

I drop my paddle and bury my face in my hands as the horrible truth sinks in.

The wind and ocean current won.

I'm not good enough, just like in the canyon.

It was because of me that my dad stayed behind as my brothers went on ahead and enjoyed the incredible waterfall. They talked about it for hours at the campfire that night. The moss-covered rocks that provided a slide, the twenty-foot cliff they dove off, the perfect temperature, and the beautiful blue water.

As the conversation continued, I watched Dad's frustration grow. His fierce grip on his marshmallow stick as we sat around the fire.

I sank lower in my seat and retreated deep into myself.

Something changed that day. I could see it in his eyes. He was ashamed of me because I was too weak. Unlike my brothers, I was a failure. He was proud of them and not me because they were better. Stronger.

So I swore never to go on another boys' trip. I grew to hate the outdoors because every hike reminded me of my failure and insignificance.

I collapse onto my raft and roll to face up. Garfield's massive face grins at me. My chest feels hollow, and what little remains of my strength leaves me.

I failed again. I thought I had it in me, but I haven't changed at all.

Another wave tosses us like a hopeless piece of driftwood. The wind and waves will take us where they wish.

I lost. And now I will die alone.

"God," is all I get out.

He knows what I mean. Not only does he know, but he knew all this was coming.

And he let it happen.

Maybe he even caused it to happen.

My heart shatters. Tears spring from my eyes. And I let it all flow out of me. My frustration, my fear, my disappointment, my confusion.

"Why would you let this happen?" I whisper. "You said I didn't need to fear because you'd be with me."

If I were home, my mom, dad, or youth pastor would tell me that God leads us through hard times for a reason. But why don't I get a say in the matter? Or does God force people around against their will like…

"Like my dad has always done to me," I whisper.

I can't breathe.

God. My God who's always been there to help me. The God I've depended on in so many situations. He's just like…

Deep sobs seize me.

…my dad.

I grip one of the weak lashings I made from bark.

My body shakes.

I stare up at the stars that shine trillions of miles away. I'm just like one of them; a speck lost in the sea of space.

"How can this be, Jip? I thought God was good."

I clench my eyes shut. Garfield is gone; the waves, a distant memory.

It's true.

God even admits to it. He's the potter; I'm the clay. I have no choice. He will make decisions for me. And he will force me to become who he wants me to be.

God is worse than my dad. Dad apologized. But God proclaims this plan like it's good.

"Is God evil?"

Jip doesn't reply. I open my eyes and roll my head toward him. Jip looks both terrified and angry.

I release my death grip on the cords and reach for him.

Jip snaps his head to the side and bites me.

I don't react. I'm too numb to feel the pain.

Jip releases my finger. Blood seeps through the wound and slowly drips from my pointer and ring fingers.

"Jip," I mutter. My voice sounds weak. "I'm trying to help. You might not understand, but I had to take you from that island. This is for your own good."

Too weak to gasp, I take a long breath.

Deep tremors run through me.

How many times has my dad said those exact words to me when he pushed me to do something I didn't want to do? How many times did I lash out or run away as Jip did?

A cutting pain pierces me.

"Jip, I'm so sorry." My voice sounds far away.

An ache too deep to produce tears encloses my heart. Changing my heart. Killing my heart.

I've defied the deepest principle I vowed to live by.

Worse than being stuck out on this open ocean awaiting death once the sun rises. Worse than knowing I failed again and will never go home. Worse than discovering God is manipulating me.

I've become just like my dad.

CHAPTER 25
THE OCEAN CURRENT

DAY 90

The skyrays are coming.

Their massive bodies block out whole patches of stars. They are so big they almost block out all of Garfield's light when they pass in front of him.

At least we didn't freeze to death. The warm water must've kept the temperature from dropping as much as usual. But it's still cold and we are drenched.

The stars fade as the dawn brightens the teal sky.

Another large wave tosses us.

"I'm so sorry, Jip." I can't stand the thought of dying with him still mad at me. I try to pet him. My shoulder, arm, and back all burn from the long night of rowing. He glares at me, and the corners of his mouth curl as he makes a clicking noise.

I yank my hand back. He's never made that sound before.

"I shouldn't have forced you to come with me." My dry throat makes my words raspy. "I was blinded by my selfish desire to go home. I'm sorry I threw you into terrible danger with me. I was wrong to assume I knew what was best for you."

Jip doesn't respond, just as I didn't respond many times when my dad treated me this way.

Since day one, I've had Jip by my side. His little licks as he passed me, or his stretches in the morning pressed up against my side. I've lost so much in the past few hours. It pains me now to think of losing tiny moments like those.

Will he ever trust me again?

At such a low angle, the sun illuminates the skyrays' brown, leathery bellies in golden light. Flecks of light dance around the animals like snow.

And like snow, the specks descend. They flicker in and out. Thousands of them. As they lower, they grow. They swirl in the air, giving form to the hidden winds. It's mesmerizing.

As one of the orbs grows close enough, I notice it doesn't blink in and out but pulses like a balloon inflating and deflating. Each time it deflates, it plummets toward the water. When it inflates, it slows and starts ascending once more.

One floats directly over us, then deflates. The dark speck seems to hang in the air, then it grows.

I quickly roll to my side and up to my knees. My sore muscles scream in protest.

The raft shudders as something smacks into it.

Jip jumps off, and I barely catch him before he's out of reach. As I turn back to the raft, I nearly jump off myself.

A three-foot-tall mosquito-like creature is busy pulling its needle beak out of the log right where I was lying a moment before. My skin crawls. Its beak is about a foot and a half long. Its six spindly legs and body take up half the raft.

I grab one of my paracord lashings as a wave lifts us. We slide over the top of the wave, and I set Jip down. Before the next wave hits, I stumble forward and snatch my paddle. The moment the massive mosquito pulls its beak out of the wood, I whack it into the ocean. And then drop into a push-up position as another wave throws us.

"That was terrifying."

Jip glances at me, then settles back into his petrified state.

Sploosh!

I spin back to where the massquito landed. A ten-foot-tall balloon launches out of the water. Under it, the massquito rises. Its black eyes glare at me, but it keeps its beak straight down, as if ready to deflate the balloon and spear me again.

Is that the intelligent alien race? It doesn't appear intelligent. Maybe it's a pet of the aliens or a soldier creature the aliens send out?

A hundred feet away, a blur of a massquito slices into the water without a splash. Farther away, dozens more massquitos spear the water.

Seconds later, they rise from the water by the balloons on their tails. Several of them successfully speared a fish and now carry them skyward.

Are they worker ants for the aliens? Or do they have a symbiotic relationship with the skyrays? If the skyrays send these critters down to hunt food for them, what do the massquitos get in return? A shelter in the sky?

My mind swirls with all the possibilities and unknowns.

Will the massquitos report back to the aliens about my presence?

The sky is polka-dotted with massquitos. And each one is a spear ready to kill me.

"Jip, we have to get out of here."

But where do we go? The sun peeks above the horizon. My mountains… are gone.

I drop to my knees and grab both my bag and the raft as a wave crashes over us.

A balloon deflates right above me. I crawl to the side. The whole raft shakes as the massquito spears it. I swing my paddle at the creature's neck. The giant insect's skinny body arcs into the water, leaving its spear-like beak lodged into the raft.

The raft lashings won't be able to survive many more impacts like that.

I prop my foot against the lodged massquito beak to brace myself against the next wave.

As we crest the wave, a mountain range rises in the west.

Finally, something's going my way!

These are much smaller than the Portal Mountains in the east, but they're only a few miles away.

I jump to the side as another massquito spears my raft. I shatter its beak with my paddle.

Clack, clack! The creature cries as it gives me a deadly stare. It puffs out its balloon and lifts away from us.

With the slow breeze and the tall waves, it won't take long to reach the mountains, but even a minute out here exposed to these massquitos is too long.

I've been lucky so far, but it's hard to know where they're targeting when all I see is a spot falling on us. And what if they target Jip? He won't let me move him.

Another wave throws us. Poor Jip gets doused.

We can't die out here.

Pax died because of my mistake. Jip can't die the same way.

If the massquitos attack from directly above, then I only need to defend myself from one direction: up.

I need something big enough to hide me from above.

Jip glances at me, then stares straight ahead as another wave comes. He doesn't seem to recognize the danger lurking above. He must not have encountered these creatures before. Probably because he's never been stranded on the water. Or is it because of this ocean that he's petrified of water?

I look down. He made the right call to stay on the island, but I forced him to deny his conscience.

"We won't die today, Jip," I say as much to myself as to him.

As another balloon deflates above me, I crawl to the other side of the raft.

The raft shudders as a massquito spears a log just inches from me.

This time, I don't bat the creature away. It doesn't appear to have any means of attacking its prey other than falling, so I let it dislodge its beak.

The moment it's free, I charge.

Its balloon inflates in the blink of an eye.

I lunge and grab its beak and one of its legs before it launches out of reach. The massquito squirms in my grip.

Clack, clack!

It thrashes its head to dislodge my grip, but I hold strong. The massquito balloon overshadows our entire raft.

"See, everything is going to be all right."

The massquitos withhold their attack. From their perspective, all they must see is one of their own kind trying to rise in the air.

With the immediate threat passed, I focus on the mountains. The current is pulling us toward a valley. We're moving fast.

To the south, a forested island pokes above the water. On top of the island is a tall tree with a nest. I squint to get a better look.

My jaw drops.

It's not a bird's nest, but the crow's nest I built.

"That's our island, Jip!" Our food, supplies, and cozy shelter, it's all within—

"Wait, it's here?"

Ugh… I hate myself.

If I'd stayed on the island, I would've made it to the same spot with much less stress and exertion.

The turtain is a good half mile south of us, but—if I learned one thing in the last twenty hours—I cannot fight this ocean current. Even lifting the paddle in my weakened state feels impossible.

First, I need to land on the mountains and escape these massquitos. Only then will I let myself dare to dream of possibly returning to Fort Jake.

The tan massquito fights in my grip again. One of its toeless feet tries to push my hand off its beak. For a moment, I make eye contact with its empty, black eyes. A chill runs down my arms and back.

It's disgusting holding this creature, but it is working.

As we approach the valley, the current strengthens.

The mountain range here is odd. It's narrow and long. Beyond these mountains is either flatland or the ocean. The current pulls us toward a valley that cuts through the mountain range separating it into two islands.

Why is the current growing stronger? Shouldn't it weaken as we approach land?

We crest a large wave, and the river flowing through the valley comes into view. It's three hundred feet wide.

But unlike normal rivers that flow into the ocean, this river flows *from* the ocean.

How does that make sense?

This mountain range must act like a funnel. The ocean is following Garfield westward, but with a north and south mountain range, the water must move north or south around the mountains, except here. In this little bottleneck, millions of gallons of seawater careen through this narrow valley to reach the other side.

The speed of the current picks up. The closest mountain is still a good hundred feet away to the north.

Sploosh!

The sound comes from farther downstream, where dozens of huge boulders break from the cliff and fall as the current erodes the mountain.

It's a death trap.

I release the massquito and paddle northward. Every stroke ignites my sore body with invisible fire. I grit my teeth and press on. My strokes are weak and seem to do nothing, but I force the thought away.

One hundred feet. That's it. Just one hundred feet and I'll never have to paddle this torturous raft again.

I'm at the mouth of the river. If I allow the river to carry me too far, I won't be able to get out as the banks turn into cliffs.

As we tip over the beginning of the river, rapids come into view. They cover every inch of the river.

Our speed doubles.

I paddle with all my might. My muscles ache in protest from the night before.

Kee! Jip flinches as a rapid splashes him.

I war against the current, but it's slow progress. Rapids toss us, interrupting my efforts.

Fifteen feet from the shore, our raft crashes into a boulder. The front end lifts onto the rock as water spills over the back, causing the raft to tilt more.

A bark-fiber lashing snaps. The raging waters tear the raft apart.

I grab my backpack and turn to Jip.

One more lashing fails, and the raft gives way to the torrents of water.

Kee! His shrill cry pierces the hammering rapids as I fall into the cold water.

No!

Desperation fuels my exhausted muscles as I surge to the surface.

"Jip!" is all I get out before the water whips my feet out from under me and sweeps me around the rock.

I'm thrown against another boulder, but my fingers find a ledge on the rock. I find a three-inch lip with my foot and push myself out of the river, dragging my backpack with me.

I shiver and wipe the water from my face.

The raft's logs race downstream, but Jip is nowhere to be seen.

"Jip!" I yell. I throw my backpack on and jump to the next boulder downstream. My landing is softer with the decreased gravity.

"Jip!"

Jumping from boulder to boulder, I search the turbulent water for blue-and-black-striped fur.

My throat burns as I scream his name.

My knees shake under me.

Jip.

I promised I'd take care of him.

My best and only friend here on this wretched planet.

And I didn't save him.

A familiar ache rises in my chest.

I stagger and crouch on the rock before I lose my balance.

I'm not like my dad; I'm worse than him.

When Dad tried to dive through the portal and save me, he chose me over his own well-being. But I didn't risk my life for Jip. I couldn't even choose him over my supplies!

And now he's lost somewhere in the water.

CHAPTER 26
PAX

DAY 90

My body trembles like it did when I held Pax on the street and watched her life fade from her eyes.

I did it again.

I stumble from one boulder to the next. Jaw quivering and tears stinging my eyes.

How could I?

I take off my backpack and throw it at the cliff. It lands on the rocky shore ten feet away.

But it wasn't my backpack's fault.

Maybe my dad was right. Maybe I am a failure.

I can't make it home. I can't take care of my animal friend.

No wonder he was ashamed of me and God discarded me on this planet; I'm useless.

On the next boulder, I stop and fall to my knees. My strength drips from me like water from my soaking clothes.

I hang my head.

The puddle slowly forming under me reflects the silhouette of my head against the vast teal sky. My features hidden in the shadow.

My dad's last question to me resurfaces. *What do you want to be, Jake?*

I slap the puddle so the gathered water splashes off the rock.

I am nothing and I will always be nothing.

Water drips from my hands as I hold them out in front of me. It glistens on my palms, like Pax's blood did on that dreadful day.

I clench my eyes shut.

Why do I always kill the things I love?

Tears shower my palms. I keel over as sobbing rocks my core.

Pax, the friend I could always count on. The friend who listened to all my frustrations and understood me for who I was. Even when so many others loved my brothers more, she always put me first.

I just wanted to play my new game.

I forgot to close the gate after I parked my bike on the side of the house and went through the back door. Only when I set my helmet on my desk did I realize the gate was still open.

Later, I told myself a second before I opened the game on my Xbox and forgot all about it.

Why didn't I take a break from the game when Pax whined for me to play fetch with her like we did every day after school? I pushed her off my lap dozens of times to keep playing until I couldn't stand it any longer and put her outside.

The cursed image of Pax staring at me from the other side of the sliding-glass door. Her head cocked. *"You aren't coming?"* her expression said.

The simple sadness of a dog's unmet desire to spend time with her owner burns in my memory.

And I turned away from my little buddy.

I shake my head and clench my eyes to send the memory back into the past, but it hangs over me like a dark cloud.

"Jip," I mutter.

I stand on trembling legs.

He needs me. Just as Pax needed me when I turned my back to her and ran to continue my game.

I forgot all about her as I fell into my own world. The puzzles. The action. The perceived freedom. Defeating enemy after enemy. Until I noticed my bike helmet on my desk twenty minutes later.

My joy dissolved like a mirage. Darkness gripped me as reality struck.

I dropped my controller, raced for the back door, and shouted Pax's name. Nothing. No ruffled fur. No limping gait. No wagging tail. And that was when I knew.

Without seeing it, I knew what I'd done, just as I do now.

Jip can't swim. The water's too dark to see the bottom. The horrifying image of Jip tumbling along the river bottom gnaws at me.

The river stretches ahead, like the road in front of my house.

And I see it all over again. Pax perks up from sniffing one of the shrubs at the edge of our front yard, but she doesn't see me.

Her gaze is fixed across the street where my neighbor walks her white husky; the white husky Pax has barked at for years from our living room couch behind the large window. Except now there's no window between them.

Her dream come true.

She bolts to meet it as a car comes into view.

"No." I rub my eyes. "That's the past." Jip is in danger.

"God." I hesitate. It hurts to pray. Do I even trust him? "If you are good, if you truly love me, please prove it right now by helping me find Jip."

The logs from my raft float a hundred feet downstream. They bob up and down in the rapids. Perhaps Jip is still clinging to one of them?

It's a slim hope, but it's a hope nonetheless.

I chase after the logs, jumping from one rock to the next.

Toward where the river narrows, and the cliffs rise… and the rocks fall.

Toward the car and the screeching brakes. But I'm not fast enough.

Pax lopes across the road, slowed by her stiff legs.

Brakes screech, but it's too late.

Pax's high-pitched whines fill the air, my ears, and my soul. Her cries of pain make a home in my mind, no matter how hard I try to forget.

I gulp and focus on the river.

Not again. Not this time.

The last of the shore ends, leaving the cliffs and the falling rocks. One boulder crashes into the water ahead of the logs. It throws them in the air. One of them tumbles, and—for a moment—I spot blue-and-black fur latched on to its underside before it splashes back in the water.

"Jip!" I yell before diving into the water.

I don't look up. I don't care if a rock hits me. If Jip dies because of my mistake, then…

I take a deep breath and swim.

I feel Pax's warm body. Her wet fur. Her tiny pulsing heart. I'm beside her on the street. Holding what's left of her. Telling her she'll be okay so her last moments won't be so terrible.

Worst of all, she believes me. Confident I'd never betray her.

My last words to her were lies; her last act toward me was trust.

Then her heart stops. Her body goes limp in my hands. Her head slumps to the side, and my world blurs, twists, and spins.

I vowed I'd never again let my selfishness hurt anyone.

Yet here I am.

I throw my arms at the water and gasp for air. I'm gaining on the logs.

Not again. Never again.

I promised.

My hand touches a log. I grab it and pull myself out of the water.

Up ahead, mist rises over some edge in the river.

A waterfall.

I roll the log over. Nothing.

I scramble to the next. Nothing.

One hundred feet left. And still five more logs.

Dipping my head into the water, I slide over a log and pull myself through the water to the next one.

I grasp the next log and pull myself above the water. The waterfall roars fifty feet away.

But I see him! Just thirty feet ahead of me on a log. "Jip!"

He doesn't look back. My voice is drowned out by the roaring waterfall.

His wet little body trembles with fear and cold as he faces his terrible death.

"Jip, I'm sorry!"

I hardly hear my own words.

"Please forgive me!"

His log tips over the edge, and his blue-and-black pelt vanishes.

"Jip!" My chest throbs as if I got shot.

My friend. My only friend is…

Dead.

Again.

And it's my fault.

As I reach the edge, the thundering of the waterfall engulfs me.

A large lake opens up forty feet below the falls. A patch of blue flies out over the lake toward the shore.

Jip?

Then I'm falling.

CHAPTER 27
THE LOST ONE

DAY 90

"Jip!" I yell.

Birds call from all directions. The waterfall rumbles in the distance.

The day is warm now, and I'm sweating from every pore on my body. The sun is high in the teal sky and just thirty minutes away from being eclipsed by Garfield. The puffy clouds have been growing, which means a storm may be rolling in soon.

Another mountain range rises to the west, blocking out much of the western sky. If a storm does come, I'll have little notice.

I'm in a long valley between the two mountain ridges. Each line of mountains rises thousands of feet above me. The valley floor is about a mile wide and lush with orange-, green-, and blue-leafed trees.

I've walked the entire length on this side of the lake several times. But I can't search the other side right now. I can hardly walk, let alone swim across the lake or the river flowing from it. I'd either drown or get swept out to sea.

Every step triggers tiny jolts of lightning through my sore body. My feet are soggy and ache. My stomach rumbles for food. My hands are raw with golf-ball-sized blisters. Some of which have popped and now ooze yellow pus.

But I can't stop. The slim hope of finding Jip is the only thing keeping my soul alive.

How did everything change so fast?

I first discovered the ocean yesterday. It feels like months have passed since then.

In one day, I've lost my shelter, my hope for returning home, and now my only friend.

If God cared about me, why would he let all this happen?

I'm glad God's silent. I don't want to talk to him.

But he doesn't need to answer. I know what he'd say. Much of this was my fault. Jip would still be fine if I had listened when he spoke. I'd still have my shelter and all my stored food.

I'm the one I shouldn't trust.

I betrayed Jip. I broke my promise to take care of him when I forced him onto the raft. I could've saved him when we hit the rock and the raft broke apart, but I chose my backpack instead. I'm weak and powerless on this insane planet. Trusting myself is what brought me here and cost me everything.

Who then should I trust?

A miniature bird or a large insect leaps off a leaf to my right.

I jump.

The creature flies away with a *kli-ki-ki-ki*. When it lands, I notice a soft humming filling the forest around me. The air smells of mud with a slight hint of sweet flowers.

"Jip?" I yell.

Nothing responds but the soft *whoosh-woosh* of a boom bird's wings as it flaps overhead.

I step over a fallen log and wince as my muscles scream in protest.

Even if Jip hears me, will he respond? He didn't respond

when I called to him on the raft. I picture his round eyes glaring up at me, confused and hurting. His expression saying, *Why did you do this? I thought you loved me.*

"I do love you, Jip," I mutter as I swipe a branch aside and step between two close trees.

But I trusted you, and you abandoned me.

My eyes sting with tears. "I was right there with you at the falls; you just didn't see or hear me."

You abandoned me.

In my mind, I see my poor, lost Jip. He's curled up in the nook of a tree shivering. Alone. Afraid.

I wish I could somehow let him know that I'm right here. That I'm caring for him even though he can't see me. That I know and feel his pain, and that I'm going to do everything in my power to help him.

I hang my head. I can't believe I did it again.

The memory of my room fills my mind. I'm crying on my bed an hour after Pax's death.

The soundtrack of my new video game still plays on my TV to remind me what I'd done.

My door opens and shuts. "I'm so sorry, Jake," Dad says.

I bury my face deeper into my pillows.

"It's going to be okay."

I picture Pax's dying gaze as I spoke that same lie.

Dad sits next to me on my bed. "Pax had a happy and long life, and now she's no longer in pain."

"Because she's dead!" My raspy voice scratches my dry throat.

"She had diabetes, was partially blind, and was showing signs of cancer. She didn't have much longer to live."

"You only say that because you hated her!"

Dad takes a slow breath. "You gave her a happy life, Jake."

"And then I killed her!"

He puts a comforting hand on my shoulder, and I shake it

off. "It was an accident, Jake. Everyone knows you loved that dog. You never would've willingly put her in danger."

That dog? Is that all she is to him an hour after her death?

"This Saturday we can go down to the pet shop and get a new dog."

I glare at him.

I get up and race out of my room and out the back door. I drop onto the patio bench and pick up Pax's tattered, blue rabbit toy. The toy I threw for her every day for years. Dad always wanted to buy a new toy because this one was so ugly. But Pax loved it.

It wasn't about what was prettier, newer, better, or younger; that rabbit was her favorite. She played with it every day. She'd bring it inside and snuggle it every night if Dad let her. And now she's gone, and all he wants to do is get a new one as if nothing was ever lost.

Just because she wasn't the dog he wanted. Just because she couldn't hunt with him or be a trail dog like our other dogs. Just because she wasn't pretty and big and strong like them.

Just like… me.

I lean against a tree in this foreign forest and let my grief roll out of me, leaving behind an emptiness in my chest.

The forest grows a tinge darker as the sun slides behind Garfield.

When Jip came into my life, he revived a part of me that had died with Pax.

I'm lost without Jip.

Giving up on finding him means giving up on myself and who I am.

My dad would say I was right to force him on the raft with me, and I was right to grab my bag first. He'd say Jip isn't important and that my survival should be my priority.

But he also said my bird-watching club wasn't important.

I need Jip. He's the side of me I can't lose. He's the side of me my dad doesn't like: the side that distinguishes me from him and my brothers. The side that makes me, me.

I try to stand up straight. My pulse hammers in my hands, feet, and ears like rhythmic thunder.

The last of the sun vanishes behind the dark disk of Garfield. Unlike the sunset, where it's still light for nearly an hour afterward, this darkness is immediate.

The forest stills. Birds stop their calls and nestle down to wait. Animals stop their pursuit of food and water to find shelter and hide as predators will likely take advantage of the midday eclipse.

Darkness fills the valley like a black flood, leaving a deathly silence in its wake.

But where can I go? I have no home. I'm alone. Hopeless. Hungry. Directionless. Broken.

Without Jip, I'm the lost one.

CHAPTER 28

THE RETURN

DAY 90

Garfield eclipses the sun every day, but this one is different. The trees are thicker here than at Fort Jake, and the approaching storm blocks out most of the starlight.

The darkness is so complete I feel it pressing in on me. Normally, I spent the eclipses eating lunch with Jip by our fire.

Now I don't have food, fire, or Jip.

"Jip!" I call for the hundredth time.

My words echo back to me empty and unanswered. The waterfall rumbles in the distance.

I sit with my back against a tree trunk. Its rough bark pokes me. I pull my knees to my chest and cross my arms over them so my blistering hands aren't touching anything. I drop my head into my arms.

"I'm sorry, God. It wasn't right of me to be mad at you. If I had listened to you, everything would've been very different. Please forgive me."

Nothing changes. My words are swallowed up by the black void.

So this is what life will be now. I'll never get Jip back. I'll never laugh again. I'll never have another friend. My family will never know what happened to me.

"I give up, God. I've tried to enjoy it here, but everything I built is gone. Everything I've worked toward has failed. I have nothing. I am nothing. I'll never be anything."

The darkness creeps into me. The chill of the eclipse settles on me.

"I've tried to be strong and courageous, and many times I believed you were here with me. But where are you now? I can't bring myself to hope anymore. I don't know if I can muster an ounce of faith."

The first of the raindrops patter on the canopy above. Mist-like rain speckles my exposed arms.

"I—" The words catch in my parched throat. My heart throbs. "I don't understand. Why have you abandoned me?"

I again picture Jip trembling and afraid, nestled in a tree, thinking these same thoughts about me as the patter of the rain grows louder.

You abandoned me, he says in my mind.

He didn't know I was right behind him before he fell over the waterfall, nor could he hear my voice. He still doesn't know I'm searching for him. He doesn't know how much I ache to hold him in my arms and never let him go.

"God, is this how you see me? Have you been here all along hoping I'd turn around and see you? Am I your Jip?"

I open my eyes. My legs cast a faint shadow. I look up. Blue moss glows on the trees all around me. The flowers on one tree glow a soft pink. A glowing green bird swoops through the forest, then darts back up above the canopy. Was that a night angel like the ones that flew in the Portal Mountains?

How long has all this beauty surrounded me without me knowing?

Slowly, the pieces fit together. The truth grows inside me.

I don't hear the words audibly, but I feel them being

written on my soul: *I've always been with you. I've been at work caring for you even when you couldn't see it. You are not the one searching in this forest for something you lost. You've been running. I'm the one calling for the lost one I love, longing for you to respond to my call and return to me once more.*

Of course God would love me more than I love Jip, but it's hard to believe.

A night angel lands on the tree to my left. Its large eyes glow a soft orange. It doesn't have feathers, just a smooth glossy body. But it doesn't resemble a bat either. Each foot has four rounded toes. It opens its mouth and out shoots a glowing red tongue that licks its eyeball. It reminds me of a salamander. Then it leaps off the tree and flies away.

This forest is stunning.

"But, God, if you've cared so much, why am I here on this planet thousands of light-years from home? And why didn't you warn me about the ocean that would carry me away from the portal?"

"Jake." The word hums through the forest. This time the voice is definitely audible. The authority in God's tone pushes away the cold breeze and dark shadows, leaving a warm love that makes the air come alive with energy. "My ways are higher than your ways, and my thoughts are higher than your thoughts. Whenever you think, realize I know." The words shake the ground and plants, like every cell, molecule, and atom is listening to their Creator's wisdom.

"I knew your path on the raft would be futile and full of pain, so I warned you. I'm not like your dad because I truly know you. I brought you to this world because I knew this journey would heal you. I sent you Jip because I knew he would bring you life. I know your heart and your future. Out of billions of people on Earth, I chose to bring you to this world because I know the decision that only you can make, and all the lives your decisions will impact.

"Jake." The way he says my name makes the flickering

flame in my chest grow. "You are not here by accident. Nor is everything that's about to happen an accident."

Now that the rain has stopped, only the soft sound of water dripping off leaves breaks the silence. Even here in the darkest night, God's beauty is abundant.

"Much is about to change. New dangers are coming, and the cost may seem unbearable, but even when all appears lost, trust in me. Do not look back. Follow me."

"But, God…" How dare I ask such a powerful being a question. "Does all this mean Jip is dead?"

"Be strong and courageous. Do not be afraid; do not be discouraged, for I will be with you wherever you go."

The static in the air fades.

I take a slow breath. "Be strong and courageous." I savor the sound of his words in my ears, committing the vibration and love to memory.

The forest is still dark, but it isn't threatening or ominous anymore.

My chest warms.

God hasn't forgotten me. He cares for me. I may not see or hear him now, like Jip couldn't see or hear me, but God is here.

I perk up as I remember God's words. "Wait, what decision? What new dangers?"

God doesn't answer.

Every muscle in my body aches as I use the tree trunk to stand up. So, what do I do now? Do I keep searching for Jip?

God, what do you want me to do?

In the soft glow of the blue moss, a movement catches my eye from the right.

A massive shadow leaps at me out of the underbrush with a low, rumbling growl.

MONKEY-LION

LOOKS LIKE A COMPACT LION

CHAPTER 29
A FRIEND

DAY 90

I drop to the ground as the shadow creature flies over me.

The foliage rustles as I scurry to the side.

Thump, thump, thump. The sound grows closer.

A weight lands on me. Searing white fire ignites in my back as claws dig into my shoulder blades.

I scream.

The creature lets go with a cry of its own.

My scream echoes through the valley, but it sounds different. It's louder and more shrill. It grows louder.

The beast shrieks and howls as it rolls in a patch of glowing blue moss.

And still the echo of my scream grows. Except it's not my scream. It's coming from my left. From the other side of the beast.

I scramble several more feet and dive behind a tree.

The shrill cry pauses occasionally, then continues. It's loud, but not deafening, though it must be for the creature writhing in the grass.

I peek out from behind the tree to see the beast rolling and squirming like a million bees are stinging it.

Backlit by the luminous moss, a dark shape steps out from

behind a tree fifty feet away. It's about six feet tall and moves slowly toward the beast. It seems to walk upright. It's big and bulky but not long.

It stops beside the howling shadow beast. The noise rises to a crescendo, then stops. Before the beast composes itself, the walking form swings something down at it with a heavy *thwak!*

The beast roars.

The shadow continues hacking away at the beast, but the way it does so looks very… human.

It can't be!

Lots of blue moss glowing behind the form confirms the impossible.

For a moment, the beast is able to gather itself and dash away from its pursuer, but it stumbles. The attacker is on it again. And with one more powerful *thwomp*, the beast falls to the ground motionless.

The forest stills. And the standing shape breathes heavily for a few moments. Its head turns, as if searching. Then silence.

"I believe now is when you say, 'thank you,'" a masculine voice says.

I gasp.

The man's head turns toward me. "I know you're there, and I know you can talk. That wrinkleface and I both heard you talking to yourself a minute ago." He takes a step toward me.

I back away.

Like a curtain being pulled back in a dark room, the sun peeks out from behind Garfield. Black turns to gray, and gray to muted colors. In seconds, the forest is lit with a soft glow from the sliver of sun.

My cover is gone.

Before me stands a literal caveman. He has long brown hair

that looks like it's been months since he last combed or washed it. Below his face hangs an equally unkempt beard. Streaks of silver glide through both. He wears some kind of leather overalls with no shirt. Around his neck hang several tools or weapons. Blue blood speckles his clothes, face, and covers his wooden club.

His eyes are wild and a little crazy. But he is indeed a human.

A *human*!

"Are you real?" The words slide out of my mouth.

The man laughs. "I could ask you the same thing."

Words! He said real words. And I understand him.

A deep laugh rumbles through his chest. "Did you think you were the only one to ever fall through that portal west of the Grand Tetons?"

His laughter continues a bit too long. The tone twists to some sort of crazed pitch and rhythm.

The wild man and I stare at each other as if to fully wrap our minds around the fact that we aren't the only humans here.

I stagger to my feet. My legs feel like rubber. I stumble. "So, umm…" What do I say? How are you doing? It's a beautiful day? Are you from around here?

"You're young," he says.

"Yeah. I am." I cringe. Why am I so awkward right now?

"Sorry, it's hard to survive here. I'm surprised you're alive." He bites his cheek. "I mean, I'm glad you are alive. Good job, I guess. You must've been a big outdoors guy before you came here."

"Not really. I'm just lucky I—" My legs give out as fatigue hits me. I collapse to my knees as a searing pain flares in my back. I touch it and then look at my hand. It's covered in blood.

The man's eyes grow wide seconds before everything goes black.

———

I wake to rhythmic rocking.

As my vision clears, I see bushes and grass flash under me.

The soft rocking quickly becomes a jostling and pounding motion. Is the man carrying me?

He's running. With each step, my back flares with pain. My vision fades again.

———

A cold, burning sensation jolts me back awake.

I scream.

"It's okay, stay still," the man says with a gruff voice.

The burning fades as a chilling sensation grows.

I'm in a small cabin. A fire burns in a fireplace, and a wooden table sits on the other end. I'm on something soft and hairy. His bed perhaps? I try to push myself up.

He holds me down. "Stay still. You need to let the solvent dry."

Too weak and sore to resist, I flop back onto the bed. "What did you do to me?"

"It's my miracle solvent. Just a bit of water and some crushed miracle leaves. It will clean the wound and function as a temporary scab to stop the bleeding."

"Thank you," I mutter.

The man laughs. "You had me scared there. When you fainted, I thought you were bleeding out. But I see that wrinkleface didn't get you too bad. Do you faint at the sight of blood?"

"Sometimes. I kind of faint all the time."

The man raises his eyebrow. "And you're still alive?"

I blush.

"My name's Kirk Drayford," the wild man says.

From my face-down position, I awkwardly extend my hand. "I'm Jake Rogers."

The man stares at me and then my hand with a confused look in his eyes. A flash of recognition sweeps across his face, and he jumps forward. He grips my hand and shakes it, but the motion is jerky and unnatural.

I cringe as my blisters burn.

He glances down for a moment. "Sorry, it's been a long time since I've shaken a hand."

"No, it's my blisters."

"Oh." He releases my hand suddenly.

Thankfully the new scabs haven't cracked and started bleeding again. "So, how long have you been here?"

He gives a sorrowful expression and turns away. After several seconds, he still doesn't reply. Did I offend him?

"Sorry, I—"

Kirk jumps. "Oh, I forgot you were here." His gaze falls to the ground. "My brain started down a rabbit path." He glances back up at me. "Forgive me! Where are my manners?" He turns and walks to the other side of the cabin and starts rummaging through some supplies.

I wait, but he doesn't turn back to me. I clear my throat.

He jumps and spins to me. "I apologize, again. It really has been a good while since I've had company."

"Yes, how long has it been?"

"Oh, right. I was about to answer, but I realized you must be starving and thirsty. I have food and water and, er, I don't have any extra dry clothes your size." He gestures to my wet clothes hanging near the fireplace.

My pulse spikes, but as I reach down to my side, I find my boxers still on. Good. But the thought of this stranger removing my pants...

That's awkward.

"These are the only clothes I have," Kirk continues, completely oblivious to my moment of panic. "All my clothes wore out several years ago, and I don't know how to do more than a basic sewing job. But hey!" He gestures to the brown-and-black-speckled hide he wears like overalls. "At least I can make this!"

Now that I'm stuck on this planet, is this what I'll be like in several years?

Kirk grabs a rod that sticks out from the wall and rises up to the ceiling. He pulls down on it and it bends like rubber. As he pulls, water flows out of it and into his wooden cup. "The soup will take a few more minutes to heat up."

He hands me the cup and turns to the stone pot over the fire. He pulls off the stone lid and stirs the soup.

I down the water. It tastes stale, but I can't complain; the water from my pump was starting to taste bad anyway.

I watch Kirk get lost in his work of stirring the soup. How did he learn this recipe? I tried making soup, but it never tasted good, so I stuck with teas and cooked meat or jerky. Jip never liked my soups either.

Jip.

Is he alive? Is he okay?

"Here you go."

I startle and turn from staring at the cabin rafters to find Kirk beside me holding out a bowl of soup.

"So it seems I'm not the only one who forgets other humans exist." A wide smile breaks through his messy beard.

I give an awkward laugh and accept the soup. Kirk helps prop me up by sliding a rolled-up animal skin under my chest so I can eat while lying on my stomach. Bolts of fire race up and down my back and sore arms from every little movement.

I stir the soup with the wooden spoon and blow on it to cool it down. It smells delicious.

"Who's Jip?"

I give him a curious look.

"You were talking to yourself."

Interesting.

I hesitate for a moment. Can I trust this man? He's a stranger after all, and some part of him feels a little unhinged. Besides, a stranger in this world is vastly different from a stranger on Earth. Who knows what he's had to do to survive and what else he's willing to do to gain the advantage against this bizarre planet? But what can he gain from killing me? Wouldn't it be more advantageous if we helped each other?

But he can kill me in my sleep or attack me when I'm not watching.

I stop my train of thought. This planet's made me too paranoid. Kirk saved me from the wrinkleface after all.

"So..." Kirk prompts.

"Oh, sorry. Jip is my friend."

Kirk's eyes widen. "A human friend?"

"No."

He nods. "I thought so. I had one of them too." A tinge of sorrow flashes in his eyes. "Which creature did you befriend?"

"He's a..." I pause, embarrassed of the name I gave his kind. I stare at the bowl of soup as I continue to swirl it. "I call them rabbit-things."

Kirk explodes with laughter.

I look away. He's right. It is a dumb name, but I never thought I'd have to tell it to someone.

"No, no, don't be embarrassed. I've come up with funny names too." Kirk grabs the carved chair in front of the fireplace and pulls it closer to me. "There are long-haired monkey-like animals that I call pit-lickers—or lickers for short—because they love licking their armpits."

I give a short laugh. My abs burn. The pain absorbs the laugh and leaves me wincing.

"So, what are these rabbit-things like?"

"They are like large flying squirrels, but they hop like

rabbits and are about the size of a rabbit too. They come in all sorts of colors, but Jip has blue fur with black streaks."

"And how'd you lose him?"

I bite my lip. "He hates the water and tried to fly away as we fell over the waterfall. I never saw where he went or if he made it to shore."

"He means a lot to you, doesn't he?" Kirk runs his thick hands through his long hair.

I focus on the fire and nod. A deep ache in my chest grows at the thought.

"So, what do you think, Jake?"

Kirk is staring at me expectantly.

"What do I think about what?"

He cocks his head and gives a confused look. Then slumps his shoulders. "I did it again, didn't I?" He scratches the back of his head. "Sorry, I haven't needed to distinguish between thoughts and real words for years now. I must accidentally think instead of speak my words."

"Okay…" I slurp down some of the soup. It sears my tongue, but it tastes great. It has a beefy taste, and something that gives it a slight zing like a lemon. I resist devouring the food to spare my tongue and throat.

"What I meant to say is that the high-ocean often brings lots of rain in the afternoon. But if you feel well after this rain passes, I can leave you here to rest while I search for your friend."

Only now do I notice the soft patter of rain outside the cabin. It must be nice to have an enclosed home big enough to move around in. When it rained for hours, Fort Jake started feeling more like a coffin than a shelter.

"We can search for your friend together if you want, but that will need to wait until tomorrow so we can make sure the solvent worked and your wounds are healing properly. Even then, you'll need to take it very slow to prevent opening the wounds on your back. Or you can stay here tomorrow while I search, since I'll be able to cover much more ground on my own."

It's very kind of him to want to help me find Jip, but why does he want to search for Jip by himself?

No, I'm being too paranoid. Now that he's so established, he probably doesn't have much to do. Besides, he's right. What good will I be in finding Jip in this condition?

I carefully hold the spoon so it's not touching my blisters and slurp down some of the soup. It's still hot, but it no longer burns my tongue.

"Fought against the ocean current, didn't you?" Kirk gestures to my hands.

I nod.

"Everyone does."

"Everyone?" I say around the food in my mouth. "You've met others?"

"Sorry, no, just you. I meant everyone as in the animals. I guess everyone only refers to people, doesn't it?"

I nod, but I'm not sure I believe his cover-up. But again, why shouldn't I trust him? Isn't he as relieved to see another human as I am?

"That's why I built my cabin near that lake. A lot of animals are caught by surprise when the ocean rises. Some died too long ago to eat, but their hides are still good. That is, if the spear birds don't snatch them up first and lift them to their sky homes."

I swallow a mouthful and laugh. "Spear birds? Is that what you call them?"

"Yeah. Do you have a better name?" His blue eyes shine bright in contrast with his tan skin and long brown beard.

"I call them massquitos and skyrays."

"Ha! I like your creativity, but I've been calling them spear birds and sky homes for years, so it'll be hard to change their names in my head. How long ago did you name them?"

"Just this morning."

I finish the bowl of soup and take a nice, slow breath. I'm far from full, but it feels good not to be starving. I set the spoon inside and move the bowl to the edge of the firm bed.

"Do you want some more?"

"Yes, please."

Kirk laughs as he grabs the bowl and heads to the fireplace. "I think we'll have to stick with my names for these ones. Besides, the spear birds are nothing like mosquitos. They don't suck your blood, and they aren't insects."

"But they do look like massive mosquitos."

He grimaces as he spoons some more soup into my bowl. "You're right. Never thought about that. That's one more reason to hate them. Though their gas pouches do make great water-storage bins." He gestures with his head to the water tube sticking out of the wall. "So they aren't all bad."

"How long ago did you name them?" I ask hoping to get a roundabout answer to my earlier question.

"About six summers ago, but I didn't name them." He sets the full bowl before me.

"Really? Who did?" Steam rises as I swirl the soup.

Kirk's piercing blue eyes lock on me. His hand freezes midstroke through combing his hair. Two seconds later, he relaxes and slowly exhales. "My daughter Ellie."

"You have a daughter?"

Kirk looks down. He blinks away a tear.

"Before I came here, I had three daughters and one son. I believe my son and eldest daughter are back on Earth with my ex-wife. Or so I hope. I was taking all four of them out backpacking when the portal opened under me and my two youngest girls. We were sleeping at the time." His chin quivers as two tears roll down his bare cheek and disappear into his beard.

"By the time we crawled out of the tent and back to the tower, the portal had already closed. I don't know what happened to the two oldest, but I hope they made it back home safely."

"I'm so sorry. What happened to the two youngest?"

Kirk bends over and squeezes his eyes shut. "Dead. Both of them," he says between silent sobs. "One from a wrinkle-face on our second day and the other from the Rakken three years ago."

I hold back from asking about the Rakken. Are they the intelligent species I saw? "I'm so sorry."

He shakes his head. "No, it's okay. That was years ago, and you didn't know." He locks eyes with me and fakes a smile. "Besides, you are here now, so everything will be better."

I pause with the spoon an inch from my mouth. Everything will be better? Is that what he's hoping for out of me? A new child to replace those he lost?

My intestines knot up inside me. Something is off about this guy. I'm relieved he wants to care for me, but do I want another dad, let alone him?

CHAPTER 30
THE ANCIENTS

DAY 91

"Welcome back to daylight!" Kirk gives a wide grin as I step out the door. He closes and latches it behind me. "After all that sleep you got yesterday, you could stay awake for a week."

I force a smile at his lame joke, but nothing feels funny. A dark hollowness fills my chest: Kirk came back empty-handed from his search for Jip on the other side of the lake.

I want to trust all those wonderful things God said yesterday, but living without Jip feels impossible. Everything about this world now serves as a reminder of the mistake I made.

The air is chilly this morning, but the sun is bright. Birds squawk from all directions in this valley. The scent of dew wafts around me. Gray clouds peel over the peaks to the west and south of us, but they dissipate shortly after like steam from a hot tub on a cold day.

I focus on the ground. Jip loved getting thrown up into the sky on days like this. Somehow, on cold and humid days he was able to fly longer.

Kirk walks past me, then turns back to his house with a proud expression. "I know you might think Betty is a bit gloomy, but on the outside, she's quite a cheery lady."

"Betty?"

"My beautiful home, of course! Look at her."

I turn, being extra careful not to twist my back much.

The only decently nice thing about the log cabin is the roof. It's covered with grass and flowers like some cottage I might've seen in a Norwegian documentary. It's about fifteen feet long and wide, but it felt much bigger on the inside.

"Why 'Betty'?"

"Hey, don't make fun of the name. It felt like a homey title. Besides, she's a sweet gal. You don't need to worry about her. It's Duke you have to keep your eyes out for."

"Duke?"

"Ah, you'll meet him soon enough." With a gleam in his eyes, Kirk continues down the path away from the home.

A garden sprawls out around the house. Some of the plants are wiry, some tall, and one plant has some sort of purple fruit that has to be tethered to the ground to keep it from floating away.

We walk a narrow path through the garden.

Ree, Ree.

I jump and spin. A spotted, six-legged wolf glares at me.

I back away, but all it does is jiggle. Its legs wobble above the ground.

Kirk's laugh fills the air. "Don't worry, that's Duke. He won't bite you. But he sure is noisy."

It isn't a real animal, but the skin is. Where the eyes should be, there's an empty gap, same with its mouth and nose. Looking in from the mouth, the whole thing is hollow. It's just an animal hide draped over a wooden frame. The frame is supposed to make the animal appear real, but it's grotesque. Like someone scrambled up the bones inside this poor creature, then told it to walk in place.

"Aren't you a good boy!" Kirk scratches the creepy animal skin's shoulder and rubs his cheek against Duke's forehead.

"He's the best guard dog on the planet. He scares off all the blue weasels and the grass mongers."

"*Ree, ree,*" Duke says as another breeze blows. He jiggles again.

The noise doesn't come from his mouth, but from the center of his body. On a rod above him is a small makeshift windmill. As the wind spins it, it pulls a rope that causes the lumpy creature to move and make the sound.

"Did you catch anything today?" Kirk bends down and gazes into its hollow eyes as he rubs it behind the ears. "Nothing? Well, you're still a good boy and there's a lot of day left. At least you protected our garden."

I feel something trickle down my back. I reach back and touch it. Blood. I must've twisted my back too much when I first heard Duke.

Kirk startles a little at my movement. "Do you want to come meet our new friend?"

Based off the tone, I'm not sure if he's talking to me or his animal hide.

"Okay, well, when you're ready, don't be a stranger. I'll be back later with your food if you can't catch anything." Kirk steps away. "No, it's okay, he won't hurt you."

As Kirk turns to me, he jumps. "Sorry, I'm still not used to seeing humans."

"But you were just talking about me to your—"

"Yeah, don't mind him. He acts tough at first, but he'll warm up to you."

"But he's..." I hesitate. Is it insensitive to tell him the animal skin isn't alive?

"I know he's not alive. He was a great friend up until one of those terrible wrinklefaces got him." His eyes grow dull with sorrow. "Gosh, I hate those things." Kirk gives a sly smile. "But none of that stops Duke from being a bit feisty at first." He laughs and shakes his head. "That dog."

I cock my head. He must see the inconsistency in his words.

Kirk continues down the trail and I follow.

Will I become like Kirk if we never find Jip?

As we leave the garden, a foul odor fills my nose. I scowl.

"Oh, sorry, that's the poo-rimiter. You gotta scare off the big beasts somehow, and with no one else around, it really doesn't matter where you drop the day's leftovers."

He seems oddly proud of his "creative" solution.

The smell only grows worse until we cross what is very obviously his poo-rimiter. I plug my nose and follow the trail through the narrow break in the poo-rimiter.

Several steps later, Kirk stops and looks back. He gives a satisfied sigh. "So, what do you think about your new home?"

My new home? I don't know how I feel about that. But my parents taught me better manners than to share my true thoughts about Duke, the name Betty, and especially the poo-rimiter. "It's very nice. Thank you for letting me stay with you."

"Of course, no problem. And once I finish tanning yesterday's wrinkleface hide, I'll make you a proper set of survivalist overalls like my own." Kirk points at a frame hanging ten feet above the ground in the shadow of a tree. On the frame is the hide, with the fur side down. It slowly turns in the wind.

"That was last night's wrinkleface?" It's weird to see the creature's hide in the daylight. It isn't nearly as threatening as I pictured when all I saw was a dark blur.

As the wind spins the frame, the monkey-like face comes into view. I tilt my head. It has an orange pelt too. "It's a monkey-lion."

"You've seen one of these before?" Kirk looks intrigued.

"Yeah, it attacked Jip my first day here." I saved him that time, unlike yesterday. I notice the horn hanging from Kirk's neck with his dozen or so other trinkets. "How did you defeat it during yesterday's eclipse?"

"Now, that's the right question." Kirk gives a big smile and folds his arms over his chest as a proud glimmer dances in his eyes. "But if we want to find your friend before today's eclipse, we'll need to walk while we talk." He leads me southward down a path through the trees.

"I hate those monsters," he says over his shoulder. "It took me years to figure it out. The key was realizing sound attracts them. I don't understand those gross folds on their face, but somehow, they must help them hear better. I caught one in a trap and started doing some tests on it. It's not every noise that drives them into a mad frenzy, but something about a dream rhino's horn really sets them off."

"Interesting."

"Indeed." Kirk nods. "The animals here are different from the ones on Earth. Some have a sense I like to call *connecting*."

"Connecting?"

"Yes, the dream rhinos give you visions. They connect with your brain by sending you back into your past. Or the flying rabbit creatures—like your pet, Jip—connect by reading your emotions, especially in regard to your intentions toward them. I think they use it to quickly determine whether you are a friend or an enemy."

My jaw drops. "Really? How do you know this?"

"Ellie used to have a syllo—that's what she called them— as a pet. They don't like me though. I've eaten too many of them. They know I think of them as food."

I always thought Jip was trusting, but could he read my intentions? Is that why he couldn't trust me after I forced him on the raft?

"Do you know of any others that have the connecting sense?" I say.

"The stupid pit-lickers." Kirk shakes his head with frustration. "They connect by sending you emotions. Either they'll hit you with crippling depression or flood you with sympathy if they know they can't escape. To kill them, you gotta hit them before they see you. And hopefully you land it well because you won't have the strength to follow them if they survive. Makes you wonder why they can't give you so much joy that you don't care about hunting them. But no, it must be depression. Maybe that's because they are depressed, or maybe sending depression is easier." His tone darkens. "There's an awful lot to be depressed about here." Kirk fiddles with a smaller necklace that has a few decorative beads. One of them has an *E* inscribed on it.

I nod. And the conversation falls to silence.

Out of habit, I glance back to make sure Jip is still following me. The path is empty, and the emptiness inside me aches once again.

God, if you want me to trust you and not fear, I'll need your strength.

But how do I stop worrying? I need Jip. Or at least I need to redeem our relationship. If he's dead, how can I ever forgive myself?

Kirk walks with his head hung low. What would it be like to lose a daughter here—or two in Kirk's case?

"What about the Rakken? Can they connect?"

A cold look crosses Kirk's eyes. He glances at me, then back to the path. "No, they are different. I don't think they're from here. They're like mammal versions of ants, but smart. They have advanced technology and communicate with clicks or by stomping their feet."

"Oh," I mutter as the pieces in my mind fit together. "I saw a small airplane fly over my camp and shoot down another airplane. Do you think that was them?"

Kirk scratches his beard. "Probably. That must've been one of their scouting ships. But what did they shoot down? The Rakken are pretty unified. I can't imagine they'd shoot down one of their own. Hmm… maybe they aren't as unified as I thought." The idea seems to get his gears turning.

"And the skyrays and massquitos. Are they connected with the Rakken?"

"I haven't thought of that." Kirk grips the *E* necklace. "I don't think so, but maybe that is how the Rakken feed themselves? They do rely heavily on animals to support their race."

"And the Rakken built the portal structure, right?"

"No. Not that I can tell. They do know how to control the portals, but I don't think they built them."

"Portals?" I stop and stare at Kirk. "There's more than one of them?" Why have I never considered this before? If the ancients could build one portal, why not two or twenty?

"Oh yes. I don't know how many, but there are likely hundreds of them."

"And they all go to Earth?"

"No, not to Earth, unfortunately. They all go to different worlds. My guess is this whole planet is like a big, crumbling train station." Kirk gestures for me to keep walking as he heads down the trail.

I can't move.

Different worlds? Hundreds of worlds? I thought I was alone on this planet a month ago. Now there's Kirk, the Rakken, another race, and hundreds of worlds? I'm an ant in comparison. This planet is like a giant train station. And it's crumbling?

The ground seems to shift under me. "This planet is falling apart?" I stumble forward and rush to catch up to him.

"With each ocean cycle, the water rises higher. The waterfall, for example, wasn't there two years ago. The earthquakes are growing more violent. That monstrous moon up there must be drifting closer, and it will eventually tear this planet to pieces."

My lips part, but no words come out.

I'll die if I stay here.

As we round a corner in the trail, the trees end abruptly. The lake spreads out before us fifty feet down the path.

"Eh, it's not a big deal. It will be at least several more years. It just makes living here a little more interesting."

His answer doesn't calm me.

We step out onto the shore of the lake, but this must be a different lake because there's no waterfall.

"No, it's the same lake," Kirk says, reading my expression. "The high-ocean has passed on to the west. This waterfall only flows when the ocean's at its peak." He continues walking me down along the edge of the lake toward the river, which is much smaller now.

"So, if the Rakken didn't build the portals, who did?"

"Not sure. I've never met them. From what I've seen, that intelligent race vanished a long time ago."

"What happened to them?"

Kirk gives me a didn't-you-hear-me glare. "How am I supposed to know? I can't read their language or work their tech. Heck, I've never even met them."

"Then why do you think the Rakken didn't build the portals?"

Kirk shrugs. "It doesn't seem like their form of tech. And..." Kirk wraps his thick right arm over my shoulder. His horrendous body odor assaults me. He brings his head close to mine and points with his right hand down to where the stream flows between the mountains.

I follow his finger. Beyond the mountains, where the much lower ocean still covers the ground, I spot hundreds of giant skyscrapers rising above the water. Unlike the buildings I found near the portal, these are easily three times bigger than the tallest building on Earth. They appear broken and crumbling. Some have fallen; others lean against the more-intact buildings.

I can't see much from this distance, but they are old and have gone years—perhaps hundreds of years—without any maintenance.

"Because whatever advanced civilization built those towers, also built the portals," Kirk continues. "And by the looks of it, they've been gone a *very* long time."

The city by the portal tower is nothing compared to these monstrous structures. "I wonder how they built the portals and these impossible skyscrapers?"

"The better question is, why?" Kirk says in an ominous tone. "Why build portals to hundreds of other planets? Were they searching for something?"

CHAPTER 31

MYSTERIES

DAY 95

The air is cool as the late-morning sun rises. It's about three hours away from being eclipsed by Garfield. Puffy white clouds contrast the beautiful teal sky, but none of them are big enough to threaten rain. The wind tastes salty as it blows over the muddy plains. The sky is reflected in the hundreds of large lakes that got left behind like muddy tide pools by the fleeing ocean.

Kirk paddles at the front of his scrap-metal boat. We row toward the giant skyscrapers, which stand in the middle of this lake.

I'd offer to paddle, but he won't let me since my back is still healing. Kirk's miracle solvent worked wonders; I should be back to normal in a few days.

Kirk pauses and points down to the bear spray clipped to my belt loop. "So that's how you survived then?"

"Kinda." The canister is so scratched and worn that its original label is impossible to read, but it hasn't depressurized. I feel much safer now that I have it back. "Thank you again for taking me up the cliff to get my backpack."

"No problem. I was wondering how someone like you could fight off all those wrinklefaces."

I glare at Kirk and fold my arms, but he's staring off at the skyscrapers.

"I only had to use it once. Besides, I knew it wouldn't be smart to live around the monkey-lions, so I moved south of the Portal Mountains to the plains."

Kirk levels his eyes on me. "Are you calling me stupid?"

I hold his gaze. "Are you calling me weak?"

Kirk lets out a burst of laughter. As his laughter subsides and he glances back at me, the lines on his face soften, but there's another look in his eyes. Remorse? "You've got wit, kid. And I admit, you surviving here puzzles me. Someone of your age, stature, and experience shouldn't have lasted the first night, let alone ninety-four. I've never believed in God, but either you've got a brain more inventive than Leonardo da Vinci, or your God is real, and I may need to reconsider."

I open my mouth, but I can't find the words to say. Is he right? I'm definitely not as smart as da Vinci, but is my survival proof of God's existence?

"Either way," he continues paddling, "I'm sure your parents would be very proud of you if they could see you right now."

I peer over the side of our makeshift boat and watch the water ripple. My distorted reflection flickers in the waves. "I'm not so sure of that. My dad would probably—"

"Jake, stop that thought right there."

I slowly look up.

Kirk's eyes are warm and serious. "You have no idea what it's like to be a dad. I know I'm a bit crazy around the edges, but I'd do anything for my kids. I wish the wrinkleface had killed me or that the Rakken took me instead. And I bet your dad wishes he fell into the portal instead of you. There isn't a thing in the world—this world or Earth—that a father wouldn't do for his child."

Kirk pauses for a second, then continues in a sincere tone.

"I can promise your father is proud of you. Heck, I'm proud of you, Jake, and I've only known you a few days."

I glance back up. His warm expression pierces me. I focus back on the cloud-spotted horizon as my chest tightens. Does he mean it?

Would Dad really be proud of me if he saw all the decisions I've made? I hope so, but I'll never know now.

If I was of any importance, why would God throw me into this world like a discarded banana peel into a trash can?

If only Kirk's words were true.

Lines cover the steely buildings like those on the portal tower. Kirk must be right that the same civilization built both. The towering skyscrapers creak and groan in the soft breeze as we draw closer. They are so tall it feels like we are already under them, but their bases are still a quarter mile away.

"Are you sure this is safe?" It feels weird to sit by as Kirk does all the paddling, but my arms and blistered hands are still recovering from my last ocean adventure.

"Absolutely, these towers only fall when Garfield..." He pauses and winks at me with laughter in his eyes.

He'll never let me live down that name.

"...nears the horizon. With him doing all this funny stuff to our gravity, it's only when Garfield is high in the sky that I dare journey to these skyscrapers. If they can withstand his sideways pull, then they will stand strong when weighing 20 percent less."

I can hardly sit still at the thought of exploring these skyscrapers. I always longed to roam through ancient ruins. Investigating the abandoned city near the portal was awesome, but this is far grander than I ever could've imagined. And something about rowing a boat through the buildings makes it even more exciting. Even on my last hike with my dad, I wondered what ancient mysteries were waiting to be discovered in the Grand Tetons. And here I am. A mystery no one knows the answer to. An entire race or civilization, gone. What caused it? Did they die? Where did they go?

Is this why you brought me here, God? Because you knew I loved things like this? And because you knew that, deep down, I loved the outdoors, even though I convinced myself otherwise?

I want to hope this is true, but then there's Jip. We've spent almost every hour of sunlight searching for him and haven't found so much as a trace. But he can't be dead.

I push the dark cloud out of my mind.

We reach the towers, and Kirk expertly guides the boat between their enormous bases. Each tower must be two football fields wide.

A cool shadow falls over us as the structures block the sunlight. The air is damp and tastes salty. Ahead is a maze of buildings. The gaps between them aren't straight; they stagger so the farthest ahead we can see is a mile.

My dad once took me and my brothers into some slot canyons in Utah where the walls rose a hundred feet above us, yet I could reach out and touch both sides at once. These buildings feel similar, only they're much taller than those canyon walls.

The sky above is a mere sliver between the skyscrapers. Each paddle stroke echoes off the lifeless buildings. The waves splash against the immovable structures before returning to us.

The walls of the buildings are covered in blueish dust. About forty feet up, the dust gives way to the dark gray of the skyscrapers. Is that how high the ocean reached?

Craaaakakaka! a big white bird calls as it drops off a ledge high above and flies away. Its cry echoes through the metal jungle. A white feather falls from it. Its slow descent contrasts with the eerie stillness that holds this abandoned city captive.

Small waves ripple away from our boat, interrupting the glass-like water ahead of us. Water drips in every direction. I can't see the droplets, but the echoing *blip*s and *bloop*s high-light the lifelessness of this place.

The unknown draws me. Like unheard voices beckoning me to answer their fading cries.

"What happened here?" I whisper, but my voice carries through the still air.

"I don't know." Kirk paddles slowly, each stroke breaking the silence.

"It couldn't have been war." I point at the walls. "Or else we'd see more damage to the buildings. It definitely wasn't a natural disaster because the buildings wouldn't be standing. Maybe a plague killed them off? Or famine?"

"Creepy, isn't it?" Kirk says softly, as if speaking too loud will awaken the old city.

I nod, but I love it!

When the building to our right curves away from us, Kirk turns to follow it.

Are these buildings all shaped like hexagons? It's hard to tell since they're so big and I can only see three or four build-ings at a time.

A darker shadow falls over us now that we are blocked off from the entrance. Light shines in from the sides of some buildings, but it feels like we are in a cave. Ahead is a clear-ing. Small structures rise above the water, but most appear to be statues. A courtyard? Across the space, a crumbling skyscraper has fallen all the way over the large clearing and now leans against a sturdier skyscraper.

Sploosh!

I jump and turn to find ripples on the other side of the channel.

"It's just a fish." Kirk chuckles. He steers our boat closer to the building on our right. "Now, watch this." He presses the paddle against the building to stop next to it. He searches around, then wipes away the blue muck on the wall. He slides four of his fingers into small holes in the wall.

A light grows around us. Hexagonal shapes engraved in the building above us light up a soft blue. They are spaced thirty feet apart and wrap around the building as far as I can see.

"The real spectacle is about to come. But before it does, I want you to see something else." Kirk steps off the boat and into a triangular doorway that must've opened when he turned on the lights. The door is the exact same shape as the ones I saw in the city by the portal. He takes the rope tied to the front of the boat and loops it around a metal shard.

I follow him inside.

As I step into the large doorway, I find myself in a ten-foot-long hallway that opens up into a large arched room. It's lit by hexagons like the exterior and is about twenty stories high. Platforms line one wall, with small grooves leading up into holes in the ceiling. The air smells musky and dripping water fills the silence.

"Are those elevators?" My words echo in the large room.

"That's my guess, but even after living in a similar room for two months, I still haven't figured out how to get them to work." Kirk searches the wall.

"You lived in one of these?"

"Yeah, both Ellie and I did." He stops his search and turns to me. "Did you find the city like this one to the north of the Portal Mountains?"

"You mean the one in the valley just below the portal?"

"No, that's a village compared to the one north of the Portal Mountain range."

"Really? There's another city like this?" My heart stirs. If only I could explore it too.

"Not just like this—it's bigger and newer. I wasn't afraid those skyscrapers would fall down on me like these."

"And you lived in one?" How could I miss such a big city? I loved living on Fort Jake, but maybe if I'd traveled north and lived in the city, the ocean current wouldn't have whisked me away.

"Ellie and I decided living in a creepy tomb-like structure was safer than risking it with all the wrinklefaces. Especially after Tia died. I discovered these buildings aren't watertight. And as the ocean rose, we couldn't make the elevators work, so we found some floating scrap metal and tried to paddle back to the mountains." Kirk looks down for a moment. "The current caught us and swept us away. We haven't set foot on those mountains since."

Kirk sweeps some dust off the wall and coughs. "Ah, here we go." He slides his fingers into four holes in the wall as he did outside.

A giant four-legged tentacle-bearded creature materializes.

I yell and dash back to the hallway. I'm halfway to the exit when Kirk laughs behind me.

I step back toward the large opening. A strange voice drifts through the air. No, the sound isn't in the air; it's in my head. The words are foreign and rhythmic.

"It's not real. Just a mental projection."

I step back into the large room. The four-legged creature now stands on its thick hind legs. It's at least twelve feet above the ground. Some sort of glistening armor covers its chest, waist, and legs. More tentacles grow out of the top of its head.

"A mental projection?"

"Correct. It's not a hologram, as I've never found any projectors. My best guess is that it's some sort of mental projection. I think these snake beards are native to this world and also have a connecting sense. But they must've figured out how to mechanize this ability to project an image into our heads so it looks like we see it, even though it's not there. Just like the words."

The words are guttural and have hiss-like undertones. The

snake beard's tentacles flick and twist in rhythm with the words. It stares at Kirk, as if waiting for an answer.

"I never learned how to speak to it. Maybe one day you can help me crack the code."

It's incredible. "So, all this mental projection does is talk to you?"

"Yup. It's creepy. It'll stand around and wait for me to answer and then disappear after a few minutes; until I activate it again."

Suddenly, the whole building starts humming. Bright lines race through the walls and pulse like veins.

"Oh, kankle chompers! We're missing it!" Kirk turns to me. "Quick, outside!"

Kirk races out of the building and I follow. We both slide to a stop at the exit.

The city is alive. On every building, the lines that cover the metallic walls like giant fingerprints glow every color. The colors dance and weave.

On some buildings, the colors create images. The whole city is bright and alive. Is this really the same place I saw moments before?

Kirk beams a wide smile. "They do this every day at about the same time, unless the moon blocks the sun."

"It must be like the portals."

"Huh?" Kirk cocks his head.

"They get their power from the sun through a lens of some sort. If the sun isn't in the right spot in the sky, they lose power."

"Interesting." Kirk faces me. "Since you are obviously good at figuring out puzzles, I have a question for you."

I look away from the dazzling colors. A warmth spreads inside me. Am I good at puzzles? "Yes?"

"I don't want to be limited to this island, but the thing that keeps me from journeying with the ocean is the problem of gathering food and water while on the ocean. How did you find food and water in the open sea?"

"I didn't need to. I packed my own."

Kirk raises an eyebrow. "How long did the ocean current carry you?"

"Only one night."

Kirk's expression lightens. But something in his eyes doesn't appear surprised. "How many islands did you pass before you reached this one?"

"None."

"Jake!" Kirk puts his firm hands on my shoulders and shakes me as if to wake me up to his excitement. "You said you lost the portal and that you'd never find it again, yet you landed on the first island you passed?"

I glance down and back up. Am I missing something?

Kirk lets go of me but can't stand still. "Do you understand what this means?"

"No."

"It means we can finally go home!"

A spark ignites in my chest, but I won't let myself believe the impossible news so easily. "How?"

"Jake, when Ellie and I got sucked out to sea, we floated for days. We tried to land on several islands as the water carried us west, but the current was too strong. I've spent years trying to make my way back to the Portal Mountains, but I never knew if I was going in the right direction. I always hoped I was heading the correct way, but I was afraid I missed it and had gone too far to the north or south. But"—his volume increases—"if you only floated for one night, then we must not be far west."

The butterflies in my stomach are frantic, but I'm afraid to hope. "But how are we going to find them? I lost them in the horizon."

"But you lost them *to the east*. And we are talking about finding mountains in an endless ocean of plains. Even if you drifted a hundred miles north or south of them, we would still see them on the horizon. All we need to know is they are the next closest mountains to the east!"

The corners of my lips fight to make a smile. "Are you sure we'll find them? What if the ocean rises again while we are out on the plains and carries us farther away?"

"I know we'll find them, and don't worry about the ocean. I've made it this far, after all."

"But what about Jip? I can't leave him."

"We'll find him, Jake," Kirk says in a fatherly tone. "I promise. With the prairie so wet after the tide, we won't be able to leave for a few weeks. We can search for him until then. The real question is, once we get to the mountains, can you lead us to the portal? There's a lot of mountains in that range."

My legs feel antsy to move. I'm going home? Once we get there, we will still need to wait until the end of the year for the portal to open, but knowing it's possible to go home almost sounds too good to be true. "Definitely! The portal is right next to a volcano that recently erupted and burned a lot of trees. The volcano still smokes every now and then. That should be easy to find."

"Perfect!" Kirk laughs. Again, the laughter draws on a little too long. Mixed in with his apparent eagerness, there's a hint of something else. Something darker and unnerving.

The lights on the buildings fade as the sun must've journeyed too high into the sky. The city falls back into the ominous mystery once more.

Kirk smiles again, but something's off about it. "Thank you, Jake. You have no idea how much I wished you'd say that."

CHAPTER 32
THE RAKKEN

DAY 97

I hang my head as we head back to Kirk's cabin. The afternoon eclipse is still a good forty minutes away, but darkness hangs over me.

"I'm sorry, Jake. We'll find Jip tomorrow." Kirk pats my shoulder. He sounds genuinely sad.

I nod, but I don't believe him. We've widened our search each day and have covered almost the entire valley. Though my legs, back, and shoulders are no longer sore, I don't know if my heart is strong enough to search tomorrow.

But Jip must be alive. God wouldn't let him die, would he? Then again, I also didn't think God would force me to stay here on a crumbling planet.

"Be strong and courageous. Do not be afraid; do not be discouraged, for the LORD your God will be with you wherever you go."

Why does believing Joshua 1:9 have to be so hard? Why can't I trust God and never fear again?

Kirk clears his throat. "My secret to defeating predators is to figure out what senses they are strong and weak in."

I look at him. That came out of nowhere. "What made you think of this topic?"

Kirk appears troubled. "It's been on my mind recently," he

says dismissively. "For the wrinklefaces, they use sound, which is why I made my horn. For the pterodactyls—as you call them—they connect by feeling your fear. That's how they found me at least. And once I made a practice of not fearing, they had a much harder time finding me."

"Really?" Did Kirk just read my thoughts? "But then—"

"For the Rakken," Kirk interrupts as if he didn't care what my response was, "they seem to be weak in sight and sound but are strong in their sense of smell and feeling vibrations in the ground. Which means your bear spray may work well against them." Kirk glances at the can clipped to my belt loop. "I doubt it will work much on their eyes because their eyes are different, but I bet it would throw off their sense of smell. You'd need to aim for their nostrils, which are located on both sides of their neck, I believe."

"How do you know so much about them?"

Kirk shrugs. "Just make sure you remember all of that."

I stop and face him. "What's going on?"

"Nothing," Kirk says, a little too defensively. "Your grief for Jip is making me think of my girls. I don't want to lose you as I lost them. If they knew all that you now know, I wonder if they'd still be alive."

I look him over. Kirk has always been strange, but this... this is a new type of strange.

"Come on, we don't have long before the eclipse." Kirk puts a gentle hand on my back and nudges me down the trail. His eyes are red, and he seems to be on the brink of tears.

We continue in silence.

I remain on high alert. Something is going on. It can't be that Kirk cares this much for me. Maybe he knows I'm his ticket home, and if something happens to me, he'll be stuck here. But why worry right at this moment?

I scan the shadows in the trees on both sides of the forest.

Kirk wouldn't hurt me, right? If he wants to go home, he

needs me, doesn't he? Even if he didn't need me, I'd be able to help.

Something is wrong.

Even the birds and animals are still. Or are they preparing for the eclipse?

We step into the small clearing that Kirk built his home in. The disgustingly familiar scent of the poo-rimiter assaults my nose.

Kirk grabs my wrist.

My pulse spikes. I pull away from him, but his grip is iron. His eyes are still red, but now a shiny tear trail leads down to his beard. "I'm so sorry, Jake," he whispers.

"What are you doing?"

Kirk doesn't look at me. Instead, he scans his home and the forest. His gaze betrays a flicker of fear.

"Let me go!" I pull again, but Kirk's grip holds tight.

My mouth opens but—as reality sinks in—my words dry up.

Kirk was never my friend. He was only being nice so I'd stay.

But why?

I don't want to find out.

I go to knee him in the crotch, but he dodges. I punch him in the stomach only to meet firm abs. I go for his face.

He ducks.

Why is he sorry? Why hold me? The unknown threat fuels me.

I knew there was something more to Kirk. Why didn't I listen to that voice? Why didn't God warn me?

I reach for my bear spray. My hand fumbles on the clip.

He grabs my other wrist and wrenches both my hands behind my back. I kick backward and buck my head forward.

As I do so, he pins me to the ground.

Oof! I wheeze. "Kirk, please!" I croak.

A clacking comes from my right where a disgusting

spidery creature emerges from the trees. It has six long, skinny legs and a long body like a large praying mantis. Sparse hair grows all over its body, but each follicle is thick and several inches long like that of a spider under a microscope.

I shudder.

Two large black eyes take up half of its face. It doesn't have pupils or eyelids. Below its eyes are two mandibles with sharp teeth that clack together threateningly.

The Rakken.

As Kirk said, they resemble a mammal version of an ant.

It walks toward us.

My breathing grows erratic, my vision darkens.

No, not now!

I focus on my bed at home. The warm covers, my video games… Pax.

It doesn't calm me; my world turns to darkness.

———

I wake a few seconds later. Cold sweat covers my body.

The Rakken stands before me. Its large empty eyes staring at me like I'm trapped in some horror movie.

Kirk dives back on top of me. Knocking the air out of me.

"I have the boy just as I promised," Kirk says between gritted teeth as he holds me down.

The Rakken stamps its feet.

"We see," comes a slow voice from a tan orb that hangs around the Rakken's neck. "This is the one you told us about? The one who knows the way to your home portal?" The voice doesn't sound mechanical or human but garbled and oddly smooth. It stretches out the *E* sounds and pronounces every *S* with a shh sound.

"Yes, he told me himself."

I glare at Kirk. "What are you doing?"

Kirk ignores me.

The Rakken lifts its front two legs to stand on its hind four. Standing like this, the Rakken is about six feet tall. It reaches into a pack on its back and pulls out some sort of eel. It points it at me. Half a second later, the eel's tongue launches out and pierces me in the side.

I wince in anticipation, but it pricks me like a small needle. I put my knees under me and try to buck Kirk off, but my strength fails me. My legs and arms fall limp. I try to thrash again, but my arms and legs don't respond.

The creature retracts its tongue, and the Rakken puts it back into its pack. More Rakken step out from the forest.

Kirk stands up and positions my limp body to sit against a stump. I glare at him, but he avoids my gaze.

Six Rakken surround us now.

"I promise, O mighty Rakken, that my home planet's resources will make your empire stronger than it has ever been before."

Several of the Rakken stamp on the ground in quick patterns.

"Kirk, what are you doing?"

He ignores me again.

The first Rakken stomps some sort of response. "We are intrigued, human," speaks the blob around its neck a half second later.

"You will not be disappointed." Kirk steps between me and the Rakken. "But before I give you the boy…"

A chill runs through me. "Kirk, please," I whisper.

Kirk turns a fraction back to me before he stops himself and clears his throat. "What guarantee do I have that you'll uphold your side of the bargain?"

The first Rakken steps closer. A moment after the creature stomps its feet, words sound from the orb. "Do not insult us, human. The Rakken do not lie as your kind does. We are a noble race. Only after the child leads us to the portal and we have smelt and seen the riches of your world, will we uphold our promise."

"I will never cooperate!" I spit out.

The Rakken's large unblinking eyes focus on me. It stamps its feet, and the orb translates: "The human child is stubborn. How can we trust him?"

"O mighty Rakken, I know your empire is vast, powerful, and seeking new land. I would not dare to waste your precious time. Please permit me a moment to retrieve a method of securing his trust."

"You may retrieve it," the orb says, drawing out each *E*.

Kirk turns and walks behind me. A Rakken follows closely behind him.

I try to stand and run, but my body doesn't listen.

I want to scream.

Why are you letting this happen, God?

I fight to keep my breathing regulated.

The five remaining Rakken stare at me. Their eyes don't move, but they bob their heads and stamp on the ground in intricate rhythms. They approach me one at a time and sway their heads back and forth.

God, help me!

Each time they wave their heads in front of me, holes on both sides of their necks open and suck in air. They stamp out more rhythms.

A few moments later, a rustling sounds from behind.

Kirk appears with a three-foot-wide wooden cube and a grass-woven bag. He sets both down and opens the box's lid. A blue blur rushes out of the box.

I gasp. "Jip!"

RAKKEN

STRONG SENSE OF
SMELL THROUGH
NECK
NOSTRIL
WEAK
EYESITE
TWO LARGE
FLY-LIKE EYES,
NO PUPILS
OR
EYELIDS
LONG BODY
LIKE
PRAYING
MATIS
MANDIBLES
WITH SHARP
TEETH
HAIRY THREE-FINGERED
HANDS

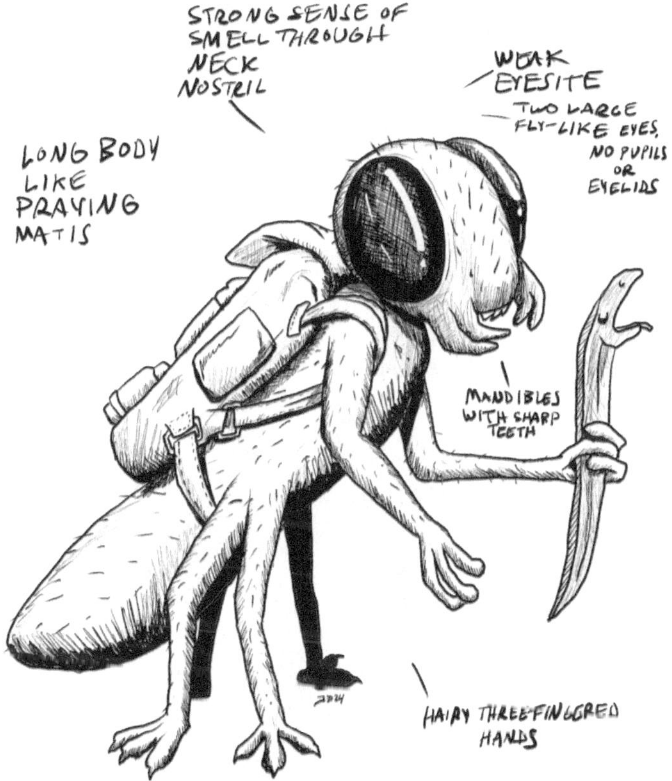

CHAPTER 33
THE INHALER

DAY 97

Jip's feet fly out from under him as a rope pulls him back.

Jip's alive? Kirk found him?

The poor little guy is muzzled, and a leather harness is tight around his chest. Jip's eyes widen as he notices the Rakken. He stumbles back and flattens his catlike ears. A muffled cry escapes his mouth.

My terrified little friend's eyes lock on me as if to say, *"Will you help me now?"* He gives a soft *kee* through the muffle.

My heart melts. I try to crawl to him, but I still can't feel my arms or legs. "I'm sorry, Jip." Tears well up in my eyes.

Jip doesn't run to me. He's uncertain. Confused. Bound.

Kirk holds the rope that entraps him.

Kirk.

I glare at the despicable man.

I go to lunge at him, but my body doesn't move. My chin quivers. I clench my teeth. "I never should've trusted you!" I spit out.

Kirk intentionally turns his back to me. "The child may not be willing to comply, but he can be coerced. He can't live without his animal friend." His movements seem sluggish.

"So long as you hold his pet hostage, he will do exactly as you say."

The Rakken angles its head to focus on me with its empty, unmoving eyes. "Are you certain, human?"

"Absolutely. I'm willing to risk our entire agreement on it."

The other Rakken stamp something in the ground. "What else have you brought us?" says the first Rakken as he steps up to the bag.

"This is the creature's food. But be careful or else it will float away." Kirk slowly opens the bag, and a balloon fruit escapes and rises into the air. Kirk catches it, holds it out to the Rakken, then slides it back into the bag.

The other Rakken stamp out several thoughts. The leader continues to face us even as it stamps a response to the others. Are they blind?

"Thank you, human, for your cooperation. The Rakken empire always treats with kindness those who are loyal to us." The Rakken steps around Kirk and moves toward me.

Kirk follows the Rakken to me. "If the animal isn't enough to make him listen, you can also use his bag."

"His bag?" the Rakken asks without turning away from me.

"Yes, he can't survive here without his supplies."

"Bring us his supplies," mumbles the blob hanging from the Rakken's neck.

Kirk hands Jip's leash to another Rakken and runs to the house. Jip glances up at the terrifying creature, then back to me. His body trembles and he flattens himself against the ground.

If only I could hold and comfort him.

The other Rakken gather around me. They tower over me as they decide what to do to me. Their large mouth pinchers clack inches from my face.

I clench my mouth shut to keep from yelling. Who's going to hear me? Who's going to care?

I'm alone.

I can't run or fight.

They pull at my worn shirt. Their hairy three-fingered hands grab me all over, but I can't feel it. The thick hairs on their hands and arms occasionally brush my face as the disturbing creatures turn me over.

I hate this!

One of them discovers it can pull my tattered shirt over my head. It slides off and my limp body slumps back against the log.

God, save me!

"Do not be afraid." The words come too quick after my prayer for them to originate from me.

The Rakken pull off my dad's compass and then unclip my bear spray.

Two of them lift me onto the back of another and tie me in place with leather cords.

Where are you God?

One of them rises high on its back two feet, then falls and pounds the ground with its hands. It does this twice. Immediately after, a rumble shakes the ground.

An enormous fishlike bird leaps into the air beyond the forest and glides toward us. It's nearly the size of an airplane and much bigger than the small aircraft I saw at Fort Jake. Its wingspan is over a hundred feet long. It flaps to slow itself and then makes a delicate landing in the clearing with its four small legs that seem very out of place. Wind blasts us. It folds its gray wings into its back and lies down. It doesn't have a neck or a beak, only a gaping mouth and large fishlike eyes that stare at nothing.

The Rakken approach the bird without concern.

Jip fights against the Rakken who pulls him. He squeals and *kees* through the muzzle.

"Jip!"

He glances up at me. His body trembles.

But what do I say? I can't lie again and say it will all be okay. I can't go to him, nor will he understand why I'm not fighting to rescue him.

"Jip, I'm here with you."

Jip focuses on the Rakken and fights against the harness to no avail. The Rakken carry us to the fish-bird.

"Focus on me, Jip. Not them." As I say the words, the truth hits me. These aren't my words to Jip; they are God's words to me.

"Be strong and courageous. Do not be afraid; do not be discouraged, for the Lord *your God will be with you wherever you go."*

The promise isn't that there won't be any difficulty, but that God will be with me in the difficulty. He is here. He isn't powerless like I am.

"Help me to see you," I whisper.

"Wait!" Kirk yells.

All but the Rakken leader and the one I ride on turn and face Kirk. They each reach back and grab a small orange creature out of their packs and point them at him.

Kirk lifts his hands in surrender. In one of his hands is my pack. "I have his supplies."

The leader stamps his feet a few times and another Rakken takes the bag from Kirk.

"Where is the boy's shirt?" Kirk asks.

"You have no authority to question us, human."

"I apologize, mighty Rakken. I desire only to help. Why did you remove his shirt? It poses no threat to you."

I glare at Kirk. What is he doing?

"We removed his weapons," mutters the leader's blob.

"O warriors of the Rakken, that's a shirt, not a weapon." Kirk steps up to the Rakken leader. He glances in my direction, then averts his gaze.

"Yes, but underneath the shirt was a weapon." The Rakken leader pulls the compass out of his pack.

"That's a compass. It tells the direction. It isn't dangerous."

"A compass?"

A few of the Rakken stomp something.

"And what about this? A weapon?" The leader holds out my bear spray.

"No." Kirk laughs. "That's his inhaler."

I narrow my eyes.

Kirk ignores me and continues with a smile. "He has a condition called asthma."

"Ashma?" the orb says, once again slurring the S.

"Yes, he sometimes needs the inhaler to breathe. Without it, he will die."

"Not a weapon?" the Rakken's blob says.

"No, not a weapon." Kirk flashes me a quick wink.

My mouth parts. Who is this man? What does he want?

"Then we keep it with his supplies so he cooperates."

"Mighty Rakken, I request that you allow me to give him back the compass, shirt, and inhaler."

Several Rakken stomp their feet, but the leader silences them with a few stomps of his own. "Why?"

"His condition is critical. If he does not have immediate access to it when he needs it, he may die before he finishes leading you to the portal."

The Rakken stomp their feet all at once. The leader stomps back occasionally. Then he gives a firm stomp, and they all settle down.

"You may return only these three to the child."

Kirk nods. "Yes, O mighty Rakken." Kirk grabs my shirt, compass, and bear spray and faces me. His eyes dart fearfully between the Rakken.

The other Rakken approach the neckless bird. The bird

opens its mouth, and they walk inside like they're walking into the back hatch of a cargo plane.

I throw all the hatred I can at Kirk through my eyes. As he clips my bear spray to my belt loop, he avoids my eyes.

I know I can't trust him. But why—after all the lies—is he now lying for me?

As he slides my shirt and compass around my neck, he presses his sweaty hand over my mouth. "I'm sorry, Jake," he whispers into my ear. "I wish things could be different, but a father will do anything for his children, and three years away from my little Ellie is far too long."

I scowl at him.

"The least I can do is offer you a fighting chance." He gives a sorrowful expression. "Aim for the nostrils."

He backs away and mouths, *Good luck,* before the Rakken turns me away from him and heads for the fish-bird.

"I hate you!" I scream. "I trusted you!" I throw every ounce of strength I can't use in my arms and legs into my verbal assault.

Kirk pushed me and Jip into a pit of lions and then tossed me a pocketknife like he's some sort of compassionate hero?

Words, insults, absurdities. I don't care. I throw them all at him and hold nothing back until the Rakken carries me into the fish-bird.

N
NW
NE
W
E
SW
SE
S
(Magnectic North)
ABANDONED
ALIEN CITY
(BETTY)
KIRK'S HOME

CHAPTER 34
GUIDANCE

DAY 97

I want to punch something. I want to run. I want to do anything, but I still can't feel my arms or legs. So I scream out all my anger and frustration.

Muggy air fills my lungs as I inhale. Inside, the fish-bird smells musky and foul, like an animal burrow.

Just as frustrating as not being able to move, my yelling doesn't bother the Rakken. The creature I'm tied to carries me up a small tunnel that leads to an odd control room. Two circular screens as big as the fish-bird's eyes display the outside world.

Weird blobs stick out of the floor and walls like upside down and sideways uvulae. One of the Rakken pulls a uvula on the wall, and the floor shakes as the mouth-door closes on the floor below.

What kind of animal is this fish-bird?

"Tell us where we must fly, child," the leader says as it walks into the control room behind the Rakken I'm tied to.

I glare at the leader. "Why would I tell a big, hairy insect how to find my home?"

The leader stomps something, and another Rakken unbinds me and carries me to the back of the control room.

He ties my hands behind my back and through a loop in the wall.

The wall, floor, and loop are all firm and soft, like flesh-covered bone.

A Rakken drags Jip in. Jip fights against the restraints. His claws scrape along the fleshy floor, but the fish-bird doesn't seem to mind.

"Child, neither you nor your pet matter to us. We will kill you both if we have to. But it will not be a short or pleasant death."

Jip lets out a soft murmur. His ears are flat against his head, and he crouches low. Does he know I can't move? Does he still believe I don't care for him even though I spent the last week searching for him?

I try to convey my thoughts to him, hoping Kirk is right about Jip's ability to connect, but he appears just as terrified.

A bright orange ball of plasma launches toward Jip. It strikes the floor two feet in front of him.

Jip screeches and jumps away from the explosion and me. A black spot smokes where the orange ball struck. The fish-bird doesn't grunt or groan. Is it an animal at all?

The leader holds an orange chameleonlike animal and points it toward Jip.

"Stop!" I yell.

"Where must we fly, child? Tell us or we will kill it."

I can't. But I must. But then they'll invade Earth. But Jip.

I clench my eyes shut. I don't have time for this!

God, speak to me!

"Fly east." The words spill out of me.

The Rakken lowers the orange chameleon.

I slump my head against the wall behind me and stare at the ceiling.

What have I done?

My home. My family. Billions of lives. Will I be the cause of all their deaths?

I shake my head. *Did I do the right thing, God?*

Do not be afraid.

I cling to the words, even as my soul splits within me.

"How far east?"

I close my eyes and shake my head. "Until you find another range of mountains."

The Rakken stamp a few things, then the fish-bird lifts a few feet. The whole body of the creature shakes as the wings start flapping. A Rakken pushes one of the three control sticks at the front of the room and the fish-bird starts running.

According to the two eye-screens, we move toward the trees on the other side of Kirk's clearing. Thirty feet from the end of the clearing, the fish-bird jumps and flies. We bash through the top third of the nearest trees, which throws me, Jip, and all the Rakken forward. Then we are clear of the trees and continue rising in the sky.

Another Rakken steps up to the two control rods in the center of the room and slides the left one to the left and forward. Immediately, the angle of the left screen shifts left and downward. The Rakken pushes the rod down into the floor a little as the view on the screen zooms in on Kirk standing outside his house. He rubs his eyes. His shoulders are hunched.

The image darkens as the eclipse begins. The fish-bird flies over a saddle between two peaks. As we pass the peaks, a flat expanse stretches as far as I can see. Ponds and lakes are all that remain of the ocean tide Garfield brought, then pulled away. Then the world goes dark.

The screens shift from color to black and white to compensate for the darkening eclipse.

"Thank you for your cooperation, child."

I stare down the Rakken leader. "I'm not a child."

The Rakken cocks its head as if genuinely curious. "But adult humans are larger and stronger than you."

I clench my fists but keep my mouth shut. Getting upset won't help me. "Everyone is different."

"Fascinating." The Rakken steps closer to me. "We are eager to learn more about your kind."

I fight against the restraints, but they hold tight.

Wait. I can feel my arms and legs again.

The leader stamps its feet. Three other Rakken approach me. One unbinds me, another points an eel at me, and the third holds a fire chameleon to Jip.

"It's time we take you to your cell. If you resist, your animal will die."

Jip watches me, a hopeful will-you-save-me-now expression flickering in his eyes.

"I'm so sorry, Jip. Please trust me," I whisper as I let them lead me away. My legs feel like Jell-O.

The Rakken lead me to a small room. The moment I stumble inside, the doorway shuts behind me like a drawstring bag being pulled shut.

A yellow gland in the ceiling lights the small cell.

I lean against the fleshy wall and slide down until I'm sitting.

The rhythmic flapping of the fish-bird thrums through the fleshy walls.

"God, what are you doing? I trusted you and now look where I am."

I drop my head into my hands. "Is this the decision you were talking about? That I'd have to make the choice to sacrifice myself and Jip to save Earth?"

Even as the words come out, I know I can't. That's exactly what my dad would do. He'd say Jip's life isn't valuable. That he's just a small animal and other people's lives are more important.

My dad is wrong.

If Jip isn't important because he's small, weak, and different, then what about me? Am I also insignificant? Besides, it's because of me he's here in the first place, and I promised him I'd take care of him.

But to lead them to the portal…

My heart pounds.

There has to be a better option.

I picture my mom finally sitting down to eat after a long day. She screams and jumps to her feet as a hairy Rakken breaks through the back sliding-glass door. Hundreds of other Rakken invade the neighbors' homes as the creatures sweep through and destroy Earth.

I can't lead them to the portal. But what other choice do I have? If I don't show them the way, Kirk will help them find the portal. But even if he doesn't, they'll find it eventually, won't they?

"'Be strong and courageous. Do not be afraid; do not be discouraged, for the LORD your God will be with you wherever you go.'" I sigh.

If God can use a man and a wooden staff to part the Red Sea for his people to escape and defeat the Egyptian army, can't he use me and my bear spray to fight off six Rakken to save Earth?

"God, I need you. I can't fix this on my own."

CHAPTER 35
THE PORTAL TOWER
DAY 97

"Where is the portal?" the orb around the leader's neck mumbles two feet from me. The leader holds the fire chameleon to my head.

Another Rakken holds me in place, gripping the coarse rope that rubs my wrists raw.

Through the two eye-screens of the fish-bird, mountains and puffy clouds slide under us.

Between the clouds, a small plume of smoke rises from a volcano. To the east of it is Portal Mountain.

It's unmistakable.

I'm back.

My stomach lurches. I clamp my lips shut and swallow the bile in my throat.

I thought I'd be happy to see this mountain again. I thought seeing it would be an answer to prayer.

I shake my head.

I'm leading the Rakken to Earth.

I'm betraying my kind.

Kee! Jip glances at me, then up at the fire chameleon another Rakken points at him. At least they took off his muzzle.

Tears fill my eyes.

Why, God?

"Tell us, or else we kill it."

I clench my eyes shut. Tears roll down my cheeks. "It's on the mountain east of the smoke."

"Thank you, child."

My strength evaporates. I fall, but the Rakken holds me up.

The fish-bird speeds up, heading straight for the portal.

What am I doing? I know they'll find the portal even if I don't help, but how can I assist them in invading my home? Will I ever forgive myself?

This makes totaling the 1966 Ford Thunderbird my dad and brothers restored seem like forgetting to shut the fridge door.

One of the Rakken angles the right eye-screen and zooms in on the top of the portal structure by pressing the control rod into the floor.

"Thank you for your cooperation, child."

I convulse and vomit what little remained in my stomach.

The Rakken back up. They make clacking noises with their jaw pinchers and stamp their feet.

In a matter of minutes, the Rakken land the fish-bird next to the portal. One Rakken holds my bindings and escorts me outside. Another drags Jip by the leash in one hand and points a fire chameleon at him with the other.

The portal tripod towers over us. One of the tripod legs has a big dent in it. A small crack in the metal crosses under the leg and up out of sight on the other side. Did a rock from the volcano hit it?

The pink crystal in the top of the tower glows in the evening light, but the angle is significantly off. The entire dish-like base of the portal is shaded by the crest of the mountain.

What's their plan? It will still be months before the sun shines perfectly through the crystal to open the portal.

Two Rakken scurry over to one of the tripod's three legs. They open a panel and work at the control panel. A minute later, lines of light race across the entire structure like they did in the abandoned city when Kirk and I explored it.

Kirk. Did he purposefully use that expedition to drop my guard so he could find the location of the portal? I force my anger away. I have a much bigger problem on hand.

The structure's cylindrical foundation lifts out of the ground as the tripod top angles toward the sun.

My jaw drops.

The structure creaks and groans until it lifts ten feet out of the ground. One side of the cylindrical foundation opens and a ramp leading up to the tripod base slides out. Then the tripod twists until the pink sunlight shining through the crystal perfectly aligns with the black center of the base. The center circle lights up pink.

I hold my breath.

Suddenly, all but the rim turns transparent. Evergreens appear through the rippling surface. Sunlight touches the tops of the trees and lights the edges of the wispy clouds on the other side of the portal.

The Grand Tetons. My home! The portal is active!

I step toward my home.

The Rakken pulls me by my bindings, snapping me back into my cruel reality. My hope is as false as a reflection.

I'm not here to go home; I'm here to betray it.

I hang my head as a Rakken scales the ramp that extends up to the portal base.

God, if you care, if you love me, do something now. Stop the Rakken!

Nothing happens. The Rakken marches through the portal like an ant eager to discover a new world to ravage.

"There's no use in fighting now, child," the orb says as the

Rakken leader steps near me and stamps out his next words for the orb to translate. "We've sent this location to our base. Our whole empire knows how to find your portal."

What would Dad think of me now? Even my mom would be disappointed in me.

Moments later, the Rakken returns through the portal, dragging a small tree in its mouth pinchers. It drops the tree and lets it tumble off the tower to the rocks below.

It stamps some sort of sentence on the ramp, and all the other Rakken clack their jaws excitedly. They stamp so hard and so energetically, they remind me of children throwing a temper tantrum.

"Your friend was right," the leader says. "Your home world is abundant with life. Our scout reports trees for miles in every direction."

I inhale. "I may be powerless to stop you, but my people are strong. They will destroy you."

The Rakken clacks his jaws in what must be a laugh. "We have conquered hundreds of worlds, most of which held civilizations far more advanced than yours. You humans are too dependent on your electricity." The orb around the leader's neck draws out each *E* sound. "We have weapons stronger than what your kind calls EMP. After we destroy your kind, we will feast on your world. The Rakken Empire will grow stronger than ever." Its jaws clack with enthusiasm.

I shake my head.

God, what are you doing? Did I fail again?

I fall to the ground, and this time, the Rakken lets me. The jagged rocks embrace me like a cactus. I welcome the jarring pain. I deserve it. It doesn't matter that I saved Jip. I'm the one who led the Rakken to Earth.

My family will die for my mistake.

My world will die.

Overhead looms Garfield who stares down on me.

"You were right about me, Dad. You were right."

SNAKE BEARDS
(THE ANCIENTS)

CHAPTER 36
KNOTS

DAY 97

As the sun sets, cold mountain air blows past me. It smells fresh and crisp. The portal powers down.

From inside the fish-bird, the Rakken lead out several animals about the size of a dog. They follow the Rakken like robots, never observing their surroundings and often stumbling over the uneven shale.

Do these creatures have a will of their own?

Once the dog creatures are in place, a Rakken taps each one on its nose, and they suddenly inflate into tents.

Another Rakken carries a yellow rod, which must've been some sort of wild animal long ago. Now any sign of an animal is bred out of It. It has four long legs, the back two of which are tied together. Judging by how they carry it, it must be light.

They stand the eight-foot-long creature vertically in the ground. They pile a few rocks over its feet to anchor it in place, then tap its nose. The creature's long front legs swing out to the side like a cross, revealing two long, fleshy wings connecting between its front and hind legs. The wings illuminate and gradually grow brighter until the whole camp is lit by this crosslight creature.

Once their camp is unpacked, two Rakken lead me back to my cell inside the fish-bird. This time, they drag Jip along and leave us both in the same cell. One Rakken unties me while the other points a fire chameleon at me. The cell door locks us in and the yellow gland illuminates.

The warm air and musky smell is a sharp contrast to the cold mountain breeze.

"I'm so sorry, Jip."

For the first time since I lost him, I can finally pet and hold him. I bend down to pick him up, but he gives a threatening *kee* and leaps away. He glares at me with his ears flat against his head and claws extended into the floor.

Ice creeps into my heart. "Jip, please."

He claws at the harness, but it doesn't budge.

I step toward him. He stops attacking the harness and prepares to scurry away.

"I did all of this to save you."

Can't he sense my intentions toward him?

"It's okay, Jip. I only want to help you."

He watches me carefully as I slowly step closer. I hold my hand out with my palm up. "It's okay, buddy. It's me."

His body is tense.

"Please, God, don't let him do this to me. I can't handle another heartbreak." I slowly drop to my knees and inch closer.

With my hand just before him, he reaches out and sniffs it. All the while, his eyes are round and pleading like he's begging me to care once more.

"I love you, buddy. I will never abandon you again." I make this promise to Jip as much as I do myself. I can't live with myself if I abandon him again. Nothing will ever separate us again.

My fingers brush the soft fur on top of his head.

Jip lowers his head a tad. He doesn't press his head into my hand as he used to, but he also doesn't run away. I want to race in and hold him close to my chest, but I resist. One step at a time.

"I love you, Jip. Everything's going to be—" I cut myself short. I can't lie to him as I did Pax.

I move my hand down to the leather cords tied around his chest and stomach. I start with the knot around his chest. The knot is tight, so I lie on the ground and use both hands.

Jip flinches when I bring my second hand near him, but he stays put. When the knot gives way, I move to the three knots under him.

Jip *kees* and jumps away.

I climb back to my knees. "Trust me, buddy. I'm trying to help. You can't free yourself."

Jip looks at me uncertainly. And in that look, I see myself.

I see myself yelling at God when I first fell through the portal. I see myself wanting to die the next day when I realized the portal wouldn't open for a year. I see myself rejecting God's direction and jumping on my raft.

A cool sensation spreads through me. I crawl backward until I'm sitting up against the wall. A familiar electric sensation fills the air.

God is here.

A strange tingling sensation tickles inside my chest.

The knots. Not the knots that bind Jip, but the ones that bind me. My fears. My insecurities. As much as I've hated tying knots, I've tied them around my own heart without knowing. God's been reaching out to help me, and I've fought him. He's been trying to free me, and I've run away.

Trust me.

"I want to. But I can't just will my fear away. How do I trust you?"

Let go.

"Of what?" The moment the words slide out of me, I know the answer. My dreams. My goals. My fears. Returning home. Proving myself to my dad. Discovering who I am. Controlling my life and future.

My chest aches. Each hope, each desire, wraps around my heart like a warm blanket. I can't let these go.

But as I hold on to them, I realize their comfort is confining. They aren't blankets. They're ropes binding me like Jip's harness.

You worry because you fear what you may lose.

The soft words fill me.

You can't trust me because you lean on your own understanding of what is good.

The simple truth hits me.

Let go of your understanding. Let go of your plans and dreams and trust me. Cling to me and I will give you rest.

"Let go." How can such a simple idea be so impossible?

I pull the compass out from under my shirt and lift it over my head.

"I gave a compass like this to your brothers as a reward for becoming Freedom Rangers and for entering manhood. I'm torn now whether I should give it to you." Dad's words echo in my mind like they have every time I've held this compass. Even though he didn't mean to drop it through the portal, it was the last gift he gave me.

A gold medal hanging around my neck like a noose. A trophy I never won from a dad who never saw me for who I am. Yet I still cling to it with the fleeting hope that I may one day change that.

Even in this world, I've longed to make it back and show my dad the man I've become. To show him I'm worthy so he can see me and be proud. Because what was the purpose of being here and overcoming all these challenges if I can't show him my growth?

To enjoy, Jake. The soft words come with a warmth that builds inside me. *To explore and wonder. And yes, to grow, but not for others. For me. I see you. The true you that not even you see.*

I take a deep breath. My hands grow sweaty as I cling to the compass. Why is it so hard to give this up?

Didn't I quit Trail Life to surgically remove the desire to make my dad proud? Wasn't choosing to save Jip by revealing the portal's location to the Rakken evidence I had overcome this binding dream?

My unwillingness to part with this compass is proof I have yet to fully give up this hope.

But if I give up this desire, who will I be?

Find your identity in me, Jake. I know you, and I'm proud of you. Lean on what I say of you.

The revelation pierces me like a spear to my stomach.

I close my eyes and focus on the warmth of God's words. I exhale and let go.

As the compass falls from my fingers, the pressure on my chest releases like a knot being unbound.

I lean back against the fleshy wall of my cell. The room seems brighter and bigger than before. Life feels full of possibility.

I don't need to become someone I'm not. I'm loved by God.

I smile and glance up.

Freedom.

It doesn't make any sense as I'm still trapped in this cell, but for the first time in years, I'm finally free.

Jip cautiously steps up to me. His eyes betray a hint of fear. He lifts his front left leg to reveal the three remaining knots.

"It's okay, buddy. I won't hurt you."

Jip flinches but doesn't run away. He rests his lifted paw on my hand for balance as I work. When the last of the knots slide apart, he gives me a look of thanks and steps away. I move toward him, and he glares back at me.

"All right. One step at a time, buddy."

He plods to the other side of the cell and curls up against the wall.

His old harness is soft in my hand. The untied leather cords dangle. The symbol of his freedom. Of our freedom.

"We're unchained."

I hang his harness—my new freedom necklace—around my neck and tuck it under my shirt. It feels strange, but it's different and new, just like me.

"So what do I do now God?"

Do you trust me?

I let the warm sensation comfort me. "Yes, I think so."

Good.

Suddenly an idea strikes me.

My mouth falls open. Hot and cold waves course through my body.

"N-no, God," I stammer, but I know without a doubt this idea is God's will.

It's the only answer.

A cold sweat breaks out across my body.

The Rakken will destroy my home if I sit by and do nothing. The same is true if I run away with Jip or escape into the portal and go home. I only have one option. To save myself, Jip, and my home, I have to…

The weight of this decision is too much to verbalize, but there's no avoiding it.

I drop my head into my hands. Tears well up in my eyes. My chest throbs with what this would mean.

The more I roll the terrible idea around in my head, the more I know God is right.

It's the only way.

I have to destroy the portal.

CHAPTER 37
THE PLAN

DAY 98

According to my watch, the sun's about to rise.

I didn't sleep at all. My mind feels foggy.

I can't believe myself… or God.

After spending ninety-eight days on this planet dreaming and planning how to get home, I'm now going to destroy my only way back?

I'll confine myself to this planet for the rest of my life.

Alone.

With no hope of ever returning.

No more Christmas or family dinners. No more evening Scrabble games with my mom. No more laughing with Matt and Oliver while playing video games. My nephew will forget me. I'll never get to ask Sophie out on a date. All I will be to anyone is "the guy who disappeared."

But I'll save all of planet Earth from the Rakken.

"Be strong and courageous," I remind myself again.

I know God is calling me to this. Despite my hesitation, I don't dare disobey. I learned that lesson when I ended up on a raft and almost lost Jip forever.

As I lean against the wall, I pull my knees to my chest and drop my head into my hands. "Is there any other way, God?"

Why do I still question what God is saying? I've thought through this dilemma all night. I know the answer. It's not only God's answer; it's mine too.

I have to do this.

I touch my freedom necklace under my shirt. Last night, I etched a farewell note to my dad into the leather harness using the corner of the compass. There's no going back now.

"Well, God." I slowly climb to my feet. My head feels light, and I stagger a little. My stomach growls. I last ate yesterday morning. Judging by Jip's rumbling stomach, it's probably been just as long for him too.

"I'm weak, tired, and hungry. This task is impossible, and I doubt either of us will make it out alive." I shake my head at the sheer impossibility of my plan. "I know this is your will, so I trust you will at least strengthen us until the task is accomplished. But—if it's not too much to ask—please help us survive. Or at least Jip."

Jip stares at me with unblinking eyes.

I reach down and pet his head. He doesn't run away, but he doesn't lean into my hand as he did before.

I crouch and face him. His big eyes watch me.

"When they open this door, I need you to run for the exit, Jip. Don't worry about me."

My chest feels heavy.

I may never see him again.

If the Rakken put the yellow crosslight creature on board, there's a chance I could use it to survive my insane plan. Even if I do make it out alive, there's no guarantee Jip will ever choose to be with me again.

It doesn't matter if I survive or if he chooses to stay with me, I will keep my promise to him. If I die, I will do so holding to my convictions.

Jip winces as I touch the top of his head. I swallow past the lump in my throat as I see all our shared moments: all the days we spent together at Fort Jake, his relentless begging for food, snuggling in my dad's sleeping bag at night, and throwing him into the air on our way to Canyon Lake so he could glide.

"Whatever goes down out there, I want you to know that I'm sorry for forcing you onto the raft. I'm sorry for diving after my backpack before rescuing you. I was wrong, little buddy. And if we both survive this, I'll never do that again. I love you, Dr. Jip.

"If I do survive and you choose to part ways with me, I want you to know that I'll understand. I'll miss you, though. Whatever you decide, I hope you have a great life."

Kee!

I give a nervous laugh and wipe away a tear before reaching to scratch his head again.

Soft thuds sound on the other side of the door.

I jump to my feet. My breathing quickens, like it always did during the few silent moments before the starter fired the gun at a cross-country race.

My dad's compass lies on the floor. I gulp and touch my new freedom necklace with trembling hands.

I detach the bear spray from my pants as the door slides open. Two Rakken stand at the door. One holds an eel and the other a fire chameleon.

"Now, Jip!"

Whether he recognized the command or not, Jip bolts through the door.

The two Rakken aim their creatures at him. As they turn, they expose the sides of their necks.

I take one last gulp of air and fire my bear spray at their nostrils. I clamp my eyes shut and tuck my face into my elbow to protect myself from the fumes. The can vibrates in my grip as fumes spew out.

Panicked stomping and stumbling fills the hallway.

I release the nozzle and careen out the door. With my face

still tucked into my elbow, I feel my way up the tunnel toward the control room.

Fifteen steps later, I open my eyes and risk a glance back.

The two Rakken race into wall after wall. Their legs scrambling as if the ground were rolling under them. In their agony, they clack their jaws violently.

Kirk was right.

I scowl and force his name out of my mind.

Ten feet up the ramp, I sneeze as a burning grows in my nose. I sneeze again and press on.

One of the two Rakken crashes into something far behind me.

I dash through the doorway at the top of the ramp. The control room is empty. I sigh and slap the skin panel on the side of the door to shut it. Next, I pull the lever that shuts the mouth-door. I'm sure Jip made it out in time.

My heart lurches at the thought. Am I really going to do this?

I push the fear away.

For my family, friends, Sophie, and for all of humanity, I must carry out this plan.

I stop at the three levers in front of the control room and picture what the Rakken did to control this fish-bird. I pull the left lever toward the right.

The massive fish-bird lifts up onto its feet and turns right.

Good!

Through the eye-screens, I see four Rakken outside. They abandon packing up their camp and charge the fish-bird. If four are outside, only the two I sprayed are on board with me. Even better, I don't see the crosslight creature in their camp.

I smile. I may just survive.

I jam the leftmost of the three rods forward, and the fish-bird starts running downhill. We pick up speed fast. But we don't take flight.

My pulse spikes.

The wings!

I grab the right control stick and slam it forward.

Nothing.

I try the middle lever. The whole creature starts bouncing slightly as it flaps its wings.

"Whew," I exhale.

The fish-bird lifts off the ground, but we continue downward. We fly straight for the trees at the bottom of the rock field.

I grit my teeth and pull back the left lever.

Nothing.

Our speed increases. My feet lift off the floor as we fall. I grab the right lever again and pull myself back down to the floor before pulling the lever toward me. The motion flings my weightless self toward the eye-screens. I fall on the other side of the controls as the fish-bird climbs in the sky.

I feel twice as heavy and have to push off my knee to stand. Why doesn't this thing have a seat or some sort of harness?

I hobble back to the correct side of the controls. With each step, my feet feel so heavy it's as if they're glued to the floor.

With a slight push to the right lever, the fish-bird evens out, and I feel normal once more.

I'm alive! And I'm flying a fish-bird!

With everything balanced out, I pull the right lever. The fish-bird begins a steady climb in the sky. I also push the middle lever. Since it made the bird flap, maybe pushing it forward will speed it up. I'm right.

So the left lever controls the legs; the middle lever, the wings; and the right lever, the altitude?

I test my theory and pull the middle lever to the right. The bird tilts and we slowly turn to the right.

Yes! I'm getting it!

Soon the portal comes back into view. We are at about the

same altitude, so I let the fish-bird continue spiraling higher into the sky. The center of the portal tower base glows pink.

The portal's open?

Through the pink portal the familiar evergreen trees near the Grand Tetons are bathed in sunlight.

My chest aches. Am I strong enough to destroy my only way home?

"Let go," I remind myself.

But it's so much to let go of. My future. My past. Even the little things hurt. I'll never play the piano again. I'll never get to plop a buttery piece of popcorn in my mouth while watching a movie in the theaters.

As the portal slides out of view, I exhale.

The Portal Mountains sprawl out before me.

I imagine my future seventy-year-old self staring out at these same mountains, alone, talking to Jip's weathered pelt as Kirk talked with his creepy recreation of Duke.

Is that who I'll become? Is that what I'm choosing?

One more full rotation, and I level out the fish-bird. We are now hundreds of feet above the portal tower and a half mile away. I push the right lever so the fish-bird angles down toward the portal. Our speed picks up.

Will it be enough?

Sure, the fish-bird broke through the trees near Kirk's home with no problem, but can it break the damaged leg of the portal tripod?

I turn the fish-bird to the right slightly to recenter it on the portal.

Even more importantly, will I have enough time to find the crosslight creature? I didn't see it at the Rakken camp, but that doesn't mean it's on board.

The fish-bird vibrates as it tears through the air.

I have about forty seconds to find the crosslight creature and jump out before the fish-bird crashes into the portal and kills me and everything else onboard. This is all assuming the crosslight is big enough for me to use as a glider.

The control room door opens.

My stomach drops.

The two Rakken stand in the doorway. One of them carries a fire chameleon and the other an eel, both of which are pointed at me. They twitch in pain from the lingering effects of the bear spray.

They stamp something on the floor, but they don't have the orb to translate their words.

I don't need a translation.

"God, help me," I whisper.

CHAPTER 38
LET GO

DAY 98

The Rakken stamp a few more times with their feet and clack their jaws for added emphasis.

I glance back at the eye-screens and the portal tower directly before us.

About thirty-five seconds until impact.

I can't fight two Rakken, find the yellow crosslight, and jump out of this fish-bird in time. But I can't leave them here or they'll redirect the fish-bird and save the portal.

God, I'm doing this for you. Give me the wisdom I need to follow your plan.

An idea crosses my mind.

Who said I need to fight these Rakken?

I grin and slam the right lever forward.

The fish-bird tilts downward.

The Rakken slide down the control room toward me before we all become weightless. As I float away, I grab the right lever again and pull it back. We all drop to the floor, but —having expected the fall—I land on my feet.

The Rakken land hard, their legs splaying out to the sides. The green eel slides away from the Rakken's hand, and I jump on it.

Before either of them find their footing, I squeeze the eel. Nothing happens.

My body tenses. How do I fire?

I tap its nose, but it doesn't shoot.

The Rakken are climbing back to their feet.

I flip the creature upside down. There's a blue spot on the eel's underside that's slightly indented. I press it and jump back as its tongue launches out and sticks into the Rakken's side. The Rakken turns to me, jaws clacking furiously.

It takes a step toward me, but one of its other legs gives out. Then it falls to the floor.

A bolt of orange fire sizzles as it flies over my head.

The other Rakken is on its feet, but it's still unsteady from the bear spray.

I press the blue button to retract the tongue and aim at the other Rakken before pressing it again. Nothing. I press it again and again, but the stupid eel is dormant in my hands.

Thankfully, the Rakken doesn't fire again either. Instead, it reaches for its own eel in its back pouch.

Do they take time to recharge?

I dive for the paralyzed Rakken's back pouch, grab its fire chameleon, and roll to the side.

The remaining Rakken spins to face me.

My finger finds the indentation on the chameleon, and I fire.

The bolt of fire strikes the Rakken in the face and explodes. It falls on the two center control rods and flails. The view on the screens swirls as the Rakken's spasming legs move the control levers.

In the dizzying display, I spot the portal. It's close, maybe twenty seconds away.

As the twitching Rakken stills, the view on the screens comes to a stop. The four Rakken on the mountain aim and fire orange balls of flame at the fish-bird. The fish-bird rattles as the fireballs hit their mark. Black smoke billows over the display, blinding my view.

Another fireball strikes the fish-bird and the whole creature shudders. But judging by the rhythmic motion of our flight, it's still flapping and we are still careening toward the portal.

I push the lever to open the fish-bird's mouth-door and race for the exit.

Wind howls through the main corridor. I'm only fifteen seconds from impact.

"Jesus, help!" I yell.

I race toward the back of the bird.

The crosslight creature sticks out of a pile of bags, crates, and creatures.

Jip is sitting next to it, claws extended deep into a wooden crate.

"Jip? I thought you escaped!" There's so much I want to say, but I don't have time.

He *kees* and jumps toward me.

"One sec, Jip."

I dash past him and pull out the crosslight.

The whites of Jip's eyes show as he waits for me.

As I race for the exit, he digs his claws into the floor and leaps toward the fish-bird's mouth-door just two strides ahead of me.

The portal tower looms seconds away.

I hit the crosslight's nose as we both launch out of the fish bird.

Wind crashes into us.

The crosslight opens under me into a perfect glider and catches the turbulent wind. It throws me to the side.

I grip the front of the wings, find my balance, and lie on the crosslight. The invisible wind tears at my uncut hair. My eyes water, and I can't hear anything other than the screaming air as it whips past me.

But I'm flying like a bird!

I lean slightly to the left, which causes the crosslight to tilt and veer our trajectory leftward.

Jip appears, gliding above me. He extends his claws and expertly lands on my back. His claws pierce my skin, but I don't care. He came to me!

He *kees* into my ear.

The portal is right before us. The sunlit evergreens on the other side ripple like a reflection.

The fish-bird is right behind us, but we somehow stay ahead of it. Black smoke billows over its top. It isn't flapping, likely due to the new black burn spots under its wings.

Jip is with me, the fish-bird behind us and the portal tower before us.

And the portal is open.

My spirit soars.

Everything slows at the realization.

I can do it. I can save Jip, go home, and destroy the portal if we fly through the portal before the fish-bird hits it!

But only if I can expertly steer us through it.

"God, guide me."

Ten seconds to either impact or freedom.

I lean slightly forward and to the right. The crosslight dips downward and steers to the right.

No, too far.

I lean to the left but overcorrect.

A tingling grows in my fingers. My heart drops into my stomach.

No! Not now!

The sides of my vision darken.

I picture my warm bed. The bed I'm so close to seeing again—if I can just hold on a few seconds longer. The soft pillow that enabled me to escape my dad and enter a life of my own. My video games, with all the digital fun and endless worlds to explore.

The darkness creeps inward.

I grit my teeth. Why doesn't picturing my bed work anymore?

Jip *kees* again and lets go of my shirt.

"Jip?" I call after him.

He spreads his legs so the skin between catches the wind. He glides to the left and toward several pink dots on the ground.

Balloon fruit?

I gasp.

A tent creature is set up behind the balloon fruit, likely with a Rakken inside. Waiting.

They know he's hungry.

"No," I whisper.

I glance between Jip and the evergreen trees of Wyoming beyond the portal as I remember my promise: *"I'll never abandon you again."*

N
NW
NE
W
E
SW
SE
S
(Magneetic North)
HIGH-OCEAN PLAINS
ABANDONED ALIEN CITY
(BETTY) KIRK'S HOME
JAKE ROGER'S PLANET

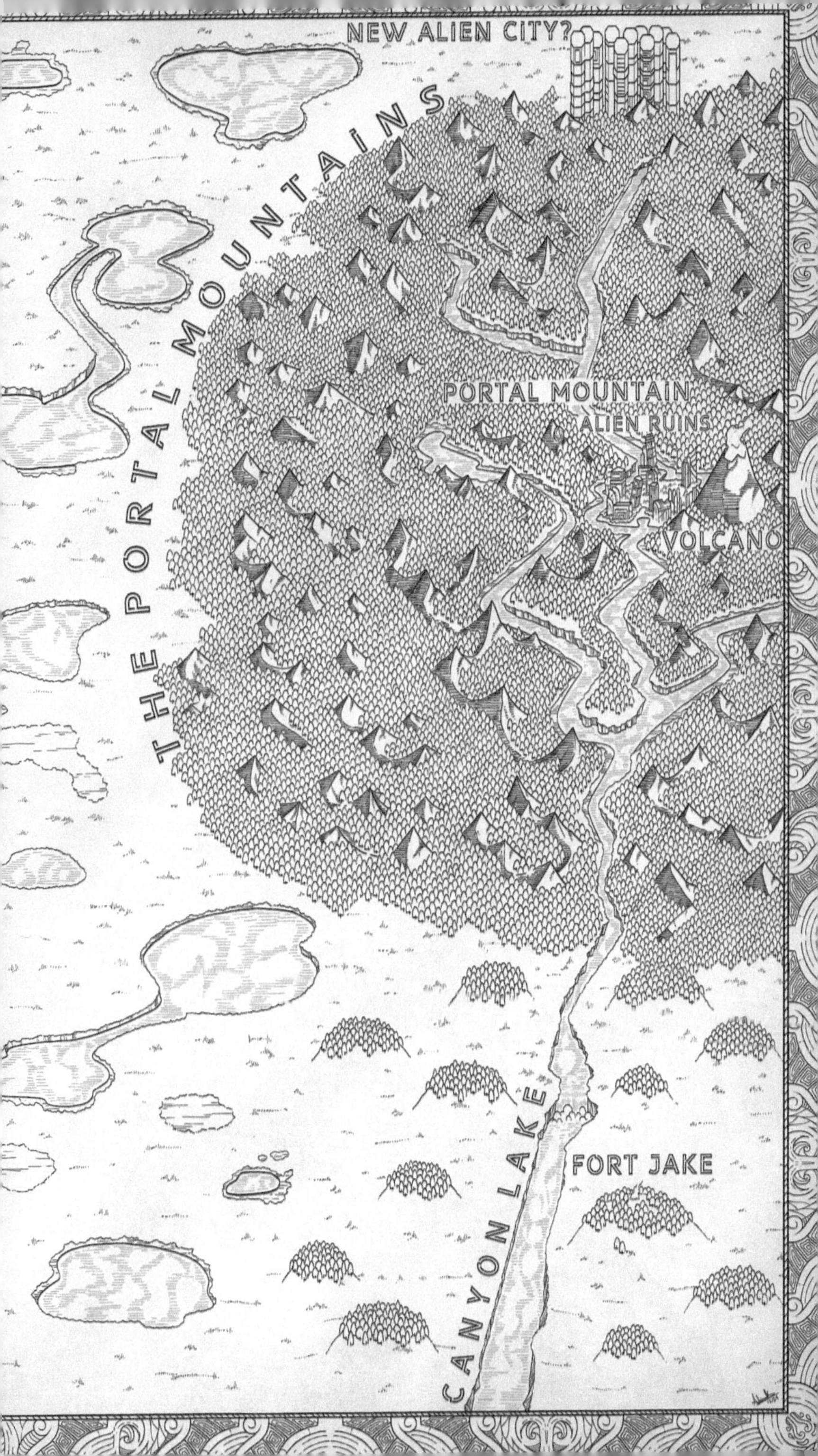

NEW ALIEN CITY?
THE PORTAL MOUNTAINS
PORTAL MOUNTAIN ALIEN RUINS
VOLCANO
CANYON LAKE
FORT JAKE

CHAPTER 39
THE DECISION

The whistling wind becomes a gentle breeze. My hammering pulse decreases to a slow tempo as the decision faces me.

Either my home and my old life or Jip. I cannot choose both.

A tingling in my chest grows as a cold sweat breaks out across my body.

I angle the crosslight more to the left, centering my trajectory on the portal.

My vision darkens.

I picture my bed again, but it only makes the darkness creep in faster.

A lump forms in my throat.

My bed no longer brings me peace. Its comforts don't appeal to me. But the thought of Jip and Fort Jake does.

Deep down, I've known all along: My comfy bed on Earth is no longer my home.

And I promised Jip.

I slowly exhale and focus on the life Jip and I had back at Fort Jake. Our early morning walks to Canyon Lake. The stupid reed raptors. And all those slow evenings when Jip and I watched the stars come out from atop Crow's Nest Tree.

The tingling in my fingers fades at the thought. The darkness recedes.

Just before I reach the portal, I lean back and pull up on the front of the crosslight. The crosslight angles upward.

I quickly pull Jip's harness over my head. My freedom necklace with my farewell message etched into it. As the open portal zips under me, I drop it behind.

My only way back. The sunlit evergreens. Earth. Humanity. It all whisks below me and forever out of my life.

"Goodbye, Dad," I whisper. But now they'll be safe. Tyler and Jennifer can raise my nephew, Blake, in peace. I'll never have to worry about a Rakken attacking my mom. They can have a future. Even though I won't be there, at least they can continue being a family.

I'll never get the chance to ask Sophie out, but now she can live a life without fearing the Rakken.

Tears sting my eyes as I pull back on the wings and fly over the top of the dish-like base. I turn left and toward Jip.

Kaboom!

The fish-bird crashes into the portal tower, destroying the weak tripod leg. The fish-bird smashes into a second leg, which buckles with a loud *crack!*

As the pink circle vanishes, the evergreen trees in the portal fade.

The pink crystal at the top of the structure shatters. Each fragment sparkles in the sunlight like falling snow.

The second leg creaks and groans as it teeters, but it doesn't fall.

I lean back on the crosslight to slow myself as I steer toward a patch of grass and soil near the crest of the mountain. Before I touch down on the mountain ridge, I hit the crosslight's nose and drop it to the side as I tumble through the grass and dirt.

I slide to a stop. My hands and back burn with scrapes. The back of my shirt is likely shredded, but I'm unharmed.

Thanks to Garfield, my impact was much lighter than it would've been on Earth.

As I stand, I find the four remaining Rakken marching toward me. The leader holds Jip, an uneaten balloon fruit in his claws. I smile. Not even when his life is in danger does he drop his food. That little stinker.

The Rakken march up the mountain toward me like the football jocks in high school. Thanks to my endurance, I outran them most times.

But this time there's no running. Not when these Rakken have my friend.

I pick up the crosslight and plant my feet.

The Rakken aim their eels at me.

How long until their fire chameleons recharge?

"What do you want with me? The portal is destroyed. What more can I give you?" I yell into the wind.

The Rakken come to a stop about forty feet downslope. "By decree of the Rakken Empire, you are under arrest and must face your punishment," the Rakken leader's orb mumbles.

"For what?"

"For inhibiting the Rakken Empire's progress. For destroying our aircraft. And for killing two of our kind."

I feel bad about killing a Rakken and leaving the other to die on the fish-bird, but I don't regret my decision. They attacked me, and they were planning to kill everyone I know.

I give a half smile.

That's right, I did do what they are accusing me of. Jake Rogers is a threat to the *mighty* Rakken Empire.

This time, I'll make my stand against the bullies.

"If you surrender, we will let your critter go free."

Or what? Their fire chameleons need to recharge. All they can do is temporarily immobilize him. Besides, if they capture me, Jip will likely follow me back with them.

Creeeeaaak!

The second tripod leg falls toward us, but it's too far to cause any harm. The Rakken are also distracted by the tripod leg.

I take two quick steps downhill and jump into the wind. I tap the crosslight's nose and swing it under me.

The wind catches the wings, sending the crosslight right into me. My chin bashes against the top of the creature's head as the wind rips me skyward. I grip the front as I lie on top of the wings.

I steady myself and scoot forward to peer over at the ground. I'm forty feet above the top of the mountain crest and climbing.

The Rakken glance about nervously, but none of them search the sky. They stamp their feet. The wind carries the faint sound of their clacking jaws. They turn their line into a tight circle with their heads facing outward.

They must not be able to see much more than a hundred feet away.

"You guys scared?" I laugh to myself. "I guess your incredible sense of smell and vibrations don't work too well against a winged attacker, now do they?"

More than a hundred feet above the mountain crest, I lean forward.

I narrow my eyes and hold back a laugh. My dad and brothers would be way too heavy to fly like this. Nor have they ever kicked an alien's butt.

Thank you, God, for making me the way I am.

I slice through the air and redirect myself to attack them from the side.

"It's time to ruin your sense of smell too then." I laugh.

I zoom over them, crop-dusting them with my wonderful friend named Bear Spray until the can is empty. I hope I don't hit Jip with the spray, but even if I do, I know its effects will only be temporary. I use my momentum to steer back to the peak and catch the wind once more. My speed drops rapidly.

I aim for a soft patch of dirt. After slowing as much as possible, I toss aside the crosslight and land on my feet. I stumble forward and fall, but the impact is mild.

I dust off my hands and jump to my feet.

The Rakken's orderly circle has broken into a panicked frenzy. Each Rakken hobbles around, thrashing its head as if an angry swarm of bees is attacking them.

Except for the leader, who still grips behind Jip's neck and doesn't appear at all fazed. It charges me with a coordination that tells me the bear spray didn't reach it. Jip also seems unscathed.

Halfway to me, the Rakken leader drops Jip, who still carries the full balloon fruit. It reaches into its pack and pulls out an eel.

I search for a weapon; all I find are rocks and the crosslight. But…

I smirk, grab the crosslight, and tap the nose so it closes its wings and becomes a funky-shaped staff. I hold it before me as the Rakken charges closer.

I'm no longer the victim. The prisoner. The weakling.

I'm strong. I'm capable.

And. It. Feels. Awesome.

No more will I be called Fake Rogers by the bullies at school. That past is a billion light-years away.

I'm a new man.

The Rakken aims his eel, and I jump to the side. The tongue whips forward. It corrects its course toward me, but not enough.

Before the eel recoils its tongue, I leap forward and whack the eel out of the Rakken's hand with my rod.

The Rakken clacks its mandibles.

I swing the crosslight at its head. The Rakken catches it in its hand before twisting and wrenching the crosslight out of my grip.

So it's hand-to-hand combat then.

But what should I aim for? Its eyes are well protected, and its neck is too thick.

The Rakken rushes at me. I dive forward and under it. I slide through the dirt and stop myself before the jagged rocks start. The gritty dirt shreds my already-tattered shirt. I climb to my feet and face the Rakken.

It spins around as it searches for me with jaws clacking.

Right. The Rakken's strengths are smell and vibrations, but it can't see or hear well.

I grab a rock and throw it to the right. The Rakken turns to the rock. It takes a moment before it recognizes the movement isn't me. Then it spots me.

The Rakken lashes out as quick as lightning and grabs my arm. I try to twist free, but the creature's grip is like iron. Its other hand latches on to my other arm and pulls me toward its mouth. Sharp teeth line the bottom of its mouth and the top of its mandibles like the Covenant aliens in *Halo*.

It opens its mouth wide and draws me in.

My pulse pounds in my ears as I imagine those teeth slicing through my neck.

I twist in its grip and kick its left mandible.

The Rakken drops me and reels backward. I stumble a few steps away and catch my breath.

A tan blur launches over the crest of the mountain.

What is—

A pterodactyl swoops in and grabs one of the scrambling Rakken and flies away.

My heart rate triples. I forgot.

There are more threats than the Rakken here.

My opponent sniffs the air as if to figure out what happened to its ally.

Another pterodactyl appears out of nowhere and swoops down at another bear-sprayed Rakken.

To the south, another pterodactyl glides in to join the

party. They focus on the Rakken, who fight the air like terrified ants with no hole to crawl into.

I gasp.

They sense the Rakkens' fear. Just as Kirk said.

Which means I may be next.

My mouth goes dry.

Do not fear.

God, you knew all along I'd reach this moment where I'd have to stop fearing to survive. Is this why you've kept bringing this verse to mind?

God doesn't answer, nor does he need to.

I tear my focus from the pterodactyls and force away all my panicked thoughts.

I stop fearing by letting go. Letting go of my plan. My expectations. My future. My dreams. And focusing on God.

Please give me the peace I need, God. I trust you. You have good plans for me. Even if that plan is simply an eternity with you starting today.

The Rakken leader watches me as if waiting for me to make the first move.

I saved my home. I kept my promise to Jip. I have heaven promised to me through Jesus. If I die now, I still win.

A deep peace settles over me. I need to make this Rakken fear.

I crouch and ready myself for the Rakken to attack.

Jip watches anxiously from the side with the balloon fruit in hand.

A fourth pterodactyl arrives and carries away the last bear-sprayed Rakken.

"You surprise me, human," the orb mutters as the Rakken stomps its feet. "The other human is bigger and stronger than you, but he wasn't strong enough to resist us. He told us everything we needed to know about your kind and your planet. But you"—the Rakken clacks its mandibles—"you are a trickster. We let the other human live because he cooperated, but the Rakken Empire will understand if I don't show you the same mercy."

"You've lost your ship, your portal, and all of your crew. I'm not—"

The Rakken lunges at me and I duck. I grab a rock and chuck it at the giant creature's head. The Rakken reels back. I throw another rock, but it blocks it.

It charges me and pins my shoulders to the ground.

Jip gives a panicked *kee* and hops to my left side.

As the Rakken comes in for the kill, I find a rock with my right hand and strike it on the side of its head. It pulls back and shakes its head before adjusting its grip on my shoulder to pin my right arm to the ground.

Jip drops the still-inflated balloon fruit and launches at the Rakken's face with his claws extended.

While the Rakken clacks its jaws and thrashes and tries to throw off Jip, I grab the balloon fruit. I bite a hole in it and press it into the Rakken's left nostril as it inhales, breathing in all the balloon-fruit gas.

The Rakken's attention snaps to me, but with only one leg pinning me down, I kick it and roll away before scrambling back up to my feet. Jip leaps off its face and glides to my shoulder.

The Rakken faces us.

I hold my ground and wait.

The Rakken stumbles, then catches itself and staggers again. The Rakken falls into a drunken dance until even standing is too much. The creature crashes to the ground. Its head turns back and forth, totally disoriented. Its spindly legs flail desperately above it.

"You should've fled when you had the chance." I search the sky for a pterodactyl.

As if on cue, one flashes over the top of the mountain.

I yank the orb from around the Rakken's neck and back toward the crosslight. "Let's get out of here, Jip."

I tap the crosslight on the nose right as the wind blasts us. Jip takes to the air and I follow.

I twist around in the air and land on top of the last-standing tripod leg. Jip alights skillfully on my shoulder.

We watch as the pterodactyl swoops down and grabs the Rakken leader in one fluid movement. It carries the Rakken downhill and drops it hundreds of feet above the ground. It falls out of sight, and the pterodactyl swoops in to finish it off.

I gulp down air, intuitively searching for the next threat, but we are alone. Black smoke rises from chunks of broken fish-bird. The wind quickly whisks it away.

I take a deep breath. "We did it, Jip."

He rubs his face against my cheek, and I stroke his soft fur. A warm sensation spreads through me.

"I missed you, buddy."

Kee!

I rub my face into his side.

Below us, the portal creaks and groans as the wreckage continues to settle. Which reminds me.

"There's one more thing we need to do before we go, Professor."

CHAPTER 40
HOME

DAY 98

As my adrenaline fades in the calm aftermath of battle, one thought rises in my mind: Did I make the right decision?

I will never go home. I'm stuck here. Forced into a life of isolation.

After searching the wreckage, I find my backpack with my depleting supplies. My bear spray is gone. The fluid in my lighter is nearly empty, and all my clothes are one step away from tearing. But now I have a crosslight to fly with and an eel and fire chameleon for hunting and self-defense.

I stand and hoist my backpack's straps over my shoulders. Time to go. I take in the sight of the destroyed portal tower one last time. The wind carries the smoke from the fish-bird over the crest of the mountain. Two of the three tripod legs are bent and broken on the ground. There's no reason to come back anymore.

There's no hope of ever seeing my family or friends again.

But I did follow God, and I upheld my promise to my only friend on this planet.

Jip jumps and glides up to my shoulder. He rubs his forehead into my neck.

My chest feels heavy and hollow.

"We can trust God, Jip. He knows our situation and our future. If he hadn't equipped us over the past ninety-plus days, we wouldn't have survived that battle. If he led us here, this must be what's best."

Saying the words out loud doesn't remove the heaviness on my shoulders. I will spend the rest of my life on this planet. The thought is crushing.

"One day at a time, Jip. Let's not focus on years or decades. We will worry about tomorrow when tomorrow comes. And he will be with us through it all."

The fear recedes.

I'm not alone. I may not have Jip forever, but I will have God.

"'Even though I walk through the darkest valley, I will fear no evil, for you are with me; your rod and your staff, they comfort me,'" I quote the verse from somewhere in the book of Psalms. "He will lead us, Jip," I say more to comfort myself than him.

Kee! Jip says in agreement.

"He brought us back together. He's kept us alive all this time. We can survive and live a good life here." And for the first time, I believe it.

As the fear evaporates, I recognize the nudging within me that's been there for days.

Something draws me to the crumbling skyscrapers Kirk told me about to the north. The pull is stronger than just my own desire. And whenever I think about it, a deep peace fills me.

God has a new mission for me: I need to find out what happened to that lost civilization.

I take the leader's orb and hang it over my neck. Maybe it can also translate what the snake-beard mind projection says.

Living here won't be easy. I won't just have to survive the

predators. Winter is coming. And Kirk is still out there. Once he discovers what I did, who knows what he'll do to get his daughter back. On top of all that, I might've defeated this Rakken group, but the Rakken Empire will send more patrols. I'm now their enemy, and they won't rest until I'm captured or dead.

"Our odds have never been worse, God, but I've learned not to doubt you. You must have a plan for all of this."

The crisp air buffets my face. Storm clouds grow to the west. The sun blips out behind a puffy cloud.

Last time I left the portal I went south. I know the way back to the plains. I know the threats there and how to overcome them, but this time I turn north. Toward the unknown and the crumbling city.

With everything in hand, I head up to the crest of the mountain. Jip hops beside me, glancing up at me eagerly with every step.

"Thank you, God, for giving me back my friend." I look up and smile. "I never should've doubted you."

As I navigate through the random chunks of metal and fish-bird, a flash catches my eye.

My dad's compass.

I pick it up and check it for scratches. There are a few on its front and back but—

I stagger. The crosslight slips out of my grasp.

Words.

Carved by a machine into the back of the compass are words… from my dad.

I stumble and catch myself on a chunk of metal. How did I not notice this before? Did I never examine the back? The letters are small, and they aren't carved deep, so it would've been easy to miss.

Without taking my focus off the compass, I slowly sit on the debris.

To my son, Jake.

My eyes sting, and I choke back tears. My jaw trembles.

Manhood is never earned or rewarded; it's stepped into. It's a position you take on when you start carving your own path. It's a journey only you can walk. Follow God, Jake, and he will do amazing things through you.

I shake my head and wipe tears from my eyes.

I am always rooting for you. Love, Dad

"Dad," I choke out. "I love you."

And he loves me too.

I see it now.

His terrified expression as the portal started to close between us. The pain on his face before I stormed away from the fire. After all the insults I threw at him and all the times I shut him down, he still came back. He still tried.

And I know that if he were here today, he'd pull me into a hug and say, *"I knew you had it in you."*

I clutch the compass and look up.

"God, I know I let this compass and my desire to please my dad go, but please let me keep it."

The tingle in my heart returns.

"Jake," the words rumble through the mountain, "some dreams I'll ask you to give up just so I can hand them back, refined and perfected in a way you never could've imagined."

Jip jumps onto the wreckage and presses his nose into my hand with a soft *kee*. I stroke him and pull him close to my side.

I'm proud of you for stepping out to become exactly who I made you to be. God's words fill my soul with life.

Then it hits. Like a blast of thunder, it jolts every fiber in my body.

Dad's last question before I fell through the portal echoes in my mind: *"What do you want to be, Jake?"*

I know my answer now.

I want to be me. I want to be Jake Rogers.

I stand and stare out at the mountains that stretch for miles in every direction.

And this… is my home.

This is my planet.

EPILOGUE
DECEMBER 13

Brian Rogers hobbled up the small hill to the campsite. The low sun cast a long shadow before him.

The hike was easy. He'd grown used to it after all his trips back to the spot where the ground opened and pulled his son away. But it wasn't only the backpack that weighed on him.

Jake was gone. Was he okay? Would he come back? And where did that hole take him?

Brian tried asking the police and several federal agencies to put out a missing persons alert in other countries, but no one believed him.

Why should they? He wouldn't believe it himself if he hadn't seen the hole open.

He hung his head. "God, please. Give me something. Anything."

He, his family, and entire search parties had scoured the whole area for any evidence of Jake or the portal, if that's what it was. Nothing turned up, as Brian feared.

The hole had opened and closed without a trace, leaving him under investigation for his own son's murder. They had no evidence, but that didn't keep people from wondering.

The ways they eyed him. Strangers who saw his face on

TV. Neighbors—who never said hi before—watched him, fearing they may be his next target.

None of that mattered, except that it all reminded him that he could've made it through the portal with Jake if he'd run faster.

But how was he supposed to know it would close so quickly? If he'd known, he would've jumped in right away. But reminding himself of this didn't take away his regret or give back his lost son.

Family gatherings changed. They laughed less. Talked less. The emptiness of Jake's room filled their hearts. The questions surrounding his disappearance hung over them.

He'd give anything to have Jake back. Even just to hear him point out and identify a bird. Or hear the video games playing in his now-silent room.

Brian crested the small hill. He scanned the ground until he found the small depression: a perfectly round patch of dirt. Grass grew everywhere else, but not there. Not where Jake had fallen through.

As he stepped closer, something seemed different. Normally, tracks or pinecones were scattered across the circle of dirt. Not this time. He couldn't even find small pockmarks left by the rain. The circle was perfectly smooth, as it had been only after Jake first vanished.

Brian straightened.

It couldn't be.

"Jake?" His voice echoed back to him in the still evening. "Jake, are you here?"

Silence.

Brian rushed up to the perfect circle of dirt as he unclipped his backpack. He set his pack on the ground and ran his fingers through the soft soil. The portal must've reopened only a day or two ago.

He scanned the clearing, the trees, the forest beyond.

"Jake, it's me—Dad."

A gentle breeze swooshed through the evergreen needles.

Something tan flapped in a tree to his left.

Brian cocked his head and walked over to it.

Leather? Several cords hung off the piece. It didn't have any fur on it and seemed well cured. Did it come from the portal?

Brian's heart fluttered.

If it did, and it was indeed leather, a DNA test could identify which animal it came from and where on Earth he could continue his search.

It could prove his unbelievable story.

With a small jump, he grabbed the branch and pulled it down.

It was leather all right, but what was it doing in the tree?

Brian untangled the cords. His jaw dropped. He stumbled backward and steadied himself on a tree.

Someone had etched words into both sides of the leather.

Dad, I'm sorry. The leather read.

I wanted to go home, but I can't. The aliens here seek to conquer Earth. Destroying the portal is the only way to stop them. I tried to live up to your expectations, but I couldn't.

Brian clenched his eyes shut as tears spilled over. Deep sobs rocked his body.

I'll never be like you and my brothers, and I'm okay with that. I like who I've become. I like this planet too. God's taught me a lot, and I have a feeling there's much more he has in store for me. But to follow him, I need to let go of my desire to make you proud. I need to let go of my hopes of returning to Earth, of seeing mom, the others, and you. This is my decision. There's a life of unknown adventure for me here like I've always dreamed of. I hope you understand.

I love you, Dad.
Jake

Brian clutched the leather close to his chest and crumbled forward onto the ground.

His boy. His little boy was gone. Never to return.

But amid the tears, he smiled.

"Thank you, God," Brian muttered between tears of joy and sorrow. "Thank you for helping Jake find his way even when I did so much wrong."

He'd miss Jake every day. They all would. But how could he want anything less for his son? He was carving his own path and making his own decisions.

The Jake he'd known was gone. Replaced now by this bold and brave man. A man Brian always knew Jake could become.

He couldn't be prouder.

THE END

The Epic Adventure Continues November, 2026.

The portal to Earth is destroyed.

Now stranded on the alien planet, Jake feels God leading him to a new mission: uncover the truth behind the mysterious disappearance of the ancient alien civilization. What happened to them? Why did they build hundreds of portals to other worlds? And why is it so important that Jake finds these answers?

Time is short. Jake must uncover these mysteries while evading the Rakken Empire and continuing to fight for survival amid hostile predators in this bizarre world. Then there's Kirk—will he hunt Jake down to free his daughter?

In a world where anything can happen, each step is uncertain, and every path seems doomed to fail, God calls Jake to "just start walking."

Don't miss Jake's next adventure. To follow the Kickstarter or be notified when this book releases, sign up for Philip's email list or go to philipwilder.com/jake-rogers-mission.

AUTHOR'S NOTE

I hope you enjoyed this novel. It was a blast to write. Journeying through this story helped me sort through many of my own insecurities, and I pray it did the same for you. God is so good, and following him will always lead to wonderful things, even if they might be scary and unknown.

God has a plan for you. A plan that will bring him glory and make your heart sing. He wired you the way he did for a reason, because he wants to do something unique through you. You may doubt this, just as Jake doubted it in the story, but God never makes mistakes. He has an important role for you in his magnificent plan.

Part of God's plan for me is to help readers like you wake up to this stunning truth. You can join God on your own adventure. There is a cosmic battle over lost souls, and God wants to use you to make an eternal impact.

If you want to step out and join this battle, I'd love to help. You can find me at www.PhilipWilder.com or on Facebook and Instagram @Philip_wilder_author.

If you enjoyed this novel, please consider signing up for my newsletter by visiting my website so you can be updated when new books are released. I'd also love to connect with you and hear how God used this story in your life.

God bless and live wilder,

Philip

ALSO BY PHILIP WILDER

What if God wanted to take you on an amazing adventure like he did Moses, King David, Peter, and Paul? Is it possible God has a specific calling for your life that will satisfy your deepest desires and fill your life with meaning?

It's true. Without question.

You are irreplaceable. You are essential to the kingdom. God designed a massive rescue plan for the lost, and the King of the universe has equipped and hand-picked you to play a critical role.

Will you join Him?

Life is too short to live in the mundane, and the stakes are too high to not play your crucial part. So let's start this exciting journey together.

Through this book, I'll map out what God has taught me on my crazy adventures around the world and help you discover your unique superpowers (yeah, you've got 'em). By the time you finish this book, you'll have a battle plan to grab hold of the wondrous life to which God has called you.

Sometimes it feels impossible to believe that "it is good to remain single" (1 Corinthians 7:8).

In a society that glorifies romance, many of us have fallen for the lie that singleness is second-best…or that maybe even *we* are second-best compared to our married and dating friends.

This book and its companion video series, *Navigating Christian Singleness* (access information provided in book), provide biblical truths and practical steps to help dispel that "grass-is-greener" syndrome, tackling questions like:

How can we learn to believe singleness is good and truly experience its blessings?

How do we handle loneliness, temptation, societal pressure, the desire for kids, and the heartache of breakups?

How do we find our place in a world set up for couples?

How do we embrace what we have instead of wishing for the things we don't?

It's not about being single forever; it's about being content now. Singleness can be just as good as marriage—and sometimes better.

If you're wrestling with learning how to be content in your singleness, this book and its companion video series will provide empathy, encouragement, and experience from those who have gone before. You don't need to wait for marriage to live the abundant life Christ offers all believers.

GROUP DISCUSSION QUESTIONS

1. (Chapter 1) Jake lists several things he's proud of accomplishing that his dad doesn't find much value in. Is there anything in your life that you are proud of but that others might not see as significant?

2. (Chapter 13) Jake doesn't know how or if God will save him from freezing to death, yet he steps out in faith (albeit hesitantly) to follow God when he says, "Just start walking." Is there some area in your life where you believe God might be calling you to "just start walking"? You might not know how he will make the path clear or make the end goal possible, but what's one step you can take now?

3. (Chapter 16) Jake reflects and recognizes how much he's accomplished and grown. What's one way you've seen God work through you and one way God has grown your character?

4. (Chapter 19) Jake realizes his problem is not his circumstances but his fear, and God is using his circumstances to help him overcome that fear. In what area of your spiritual walk do you struggle,

and what circumstances is God giving you to help you grow in that area?

5. (Chapter 23) God asks Jake to give up his dream of going home. Though Jake doesn't listen to God, he learns the importance of trusting God. What is one thing you might be struggling to give up to God? Would you give it up if he asked you to? Why or why not?

6. (Chapter 36) Jake sets aside his idols and leans on God to find his identity and value. What are some things you might be tempted to find your identity and value in?

7. (Chapter 39) Jake discovers that his unique qualities —which he used to consider weaknesses—are actually his biggest strengths. What's something about yourself you used to be embarrassed of but now see God using in mighty ways?

8. (Chapter 40) Jake learns not to fear the distant and uncertain future, but to take each day as it comes and trust God with the rest. In what way do you fear the future, and how might you trust God with that?

9. Throughout the story, Jake gradually learns to overcome his fear and trust God. What's one thing about Jake's journey to overcome fear that stuck out to you?

10. What core truth about following God impacted you most from this novel?

A SPECIAL THANKS TO:

My God and Savior, whose ever-present companionship and guidance have brought me where I am and given me the inspiration I needed to create this wonderful novel. Without the comfort of his love and my security in the salvation he purchased for me on the cross, who knows where I'd be today.

My wife, for all her love and support when I hit the inevitable discouragements every author experiences.

My mom, for being my first and biggest fan through all those books that will never see the light of day.

Joshua Chadd, for just being awesome and always finding the time to help me when I had no clue what to do.

Jeanne Leach, for being an awesome editor and helping me develop my writing into what it is now.

Julee Schwarzburg, for her incredible work editing and helping me refine the direction of this book.

To my critique group for all their amazing insight: S. L. Dooley, Jenn Lees, and P. S. Patton.

To all my wonderful beta readers who helped me test and refine my writing: Judah Ashley, Brent Baker, Russell Baker, Andy Duke, Elisha Hoey, Annalin Kettler, Evan Kitto, Karl Kitto, Joseph Morrison, Meghan Renfro, Jarrett Slusher, Madeline Smith, Micah Thompson, and Simeon White.

KICKSTARTER BACKERS

I can't thank my Kickstarter backers enough for making this book possible and for being the first people to ever buy a fiction book from me.

Aaron DeMott
Adam Budris
Adare Elyse
AJ
Andra Marquardt
Andres
Andy Duke
Becky Minor
Ben
Ben Mulhern
Brady Cone
Brandon
Brent R. Baker
Bryan Timothy Mitchell
C. Jonah Abbott
C.E. White
Celeste Richardson

Chad Abbs
Charles H. Diediker
Christy S
Cynthia Morales
D. T. Powell
Dane Hershberger
Danielle Jo
Dave
David Garlick
Dawn Carter
Debbie
Debs DiGiorgio
EL
Elaine
Emily L Brantley
Eric P
Erin Dydek
Eugene
Evan Kitto
Ezra Alonso
Forrest McCleary
Gruffy McDangerbaby
Heather Griffin
Henry T
Hoey Family
Jacob Mozeika
Jaime Rodriguez
James R. Hannibal
Jared Bridge
Jarrett Slusher
Javier Vega
Jen Booth
Jenna Hendricks
Jenneth Leed
Jeremiah Friedli

Jeroen
Jessica A. Tanner
Jessica Bertrand
Jill Fromer
JJ Johnson
Johnny
Jon Dewey
Jonathan Hults
Jordan Cox
Josh G
Josh, Jessica, Claire, Collin, Tucker
Joshua C. Chadd
Josiah DeGraaf
Julia Border
Kaden J. Kitto
Kathie Wilken
Kimmie
Kingsley K. Charles 'Kase'
Kristin, McKynlee, and Harkynn McIntyre
Krzysamm
Laura White
Laurie Nave
Lindsey Funtik
Luke
Luke Arledge
Luke Ganger
Luke W
Lynn P
MadiJoy
Merrie Destefano
Michael and Christy Wuest
Michelle Kachuriak
Morgun Family
Mr. West
Nancy Franks

Nathaniel Herbst
Nick Carico
Noah G.
Parker Porter
Peter Garlick
Philip and Laura Stephens
Randon Squier
Rocco Levitas
Sam Garlick
Sam Sleep
Samantha Rae Ortiz
Sean Johnson
SL Dooley
Sofia Corey
Sofia Simpson
Stephen Charles Curro
Taylor S Newport
The Slade's
Troy and Stacy Hooker
Vaporous Realms Publishing
Vin Lee
Virginia Pohlman
Walter Willis
Wyatt King
Z.R. McCormick
Zach Burnham
Zack Esgar
Zackary Russell